THE BEASTLY
ISLAND MURDER

THE BEASTLY ISLAND MURDER

CAROL W. HAZELWOOD

Aventine Press

Published by Aventine Press
55 East Emerson St.
Chula Vista CA, 91911
www.aventinepress.com

ISBN: 1-59330-799-3

Cover by Arthur A. Hazelwood
Arthazelwood.com

Also by Carol W. Hazelwood

Fiction
Assume Nothing
Coyoacan Hill
Dark Legacy
Rising Mist
Twilight in the Garden

Non Fiction
A View from the Jury Box
Co-author of
Tiger in a Cage, The Memoir of Wu Tek Ying

Acknowledgements

Many thanks to my writing critique group:
Janice Clark, Jim Harder, Nancy Poss-Hatchl, Adele Kopecky,
Tom McCranie, Dorran Nadeau,
and to my sister, Joan Blue, and Valerie Newman.

Dedication

In memory of George,
Dan and Blaise's Newfoundland

Chapter 1

Jennifer paddled her sea kayak past the naked cliff into the quiet waters of Beastly Island's cove. The moored sloop surprised her. The fog bank looming to starboard seemed more ominous now. Although the sun had burned off the morning mist, by nightfall dense clouds would again swallow the island. She let her boat drift in a sea that lay flat as cooled pudding. Her Newfoundland, perched in the front cockpit of the tandem kayak, barked. "Hush, Lydia, I see it."

Jennifer stroked through the icy waters toward the sloop's stern to read the name stenciled in glossy-gold script: *The High Life,* out of Seattle. Water lapped against its black hull as she circled the unwelcome visitor. The cockpit was white, the rigging tidy; her brass sparkled, her teak rub rail shined. No one was aboard. She scanned the beach—empty. With a nervous flutter in her stomach, she paddled toward shore, passing the buoy that marked shallow water.

The Newfoundland jumped into the sea, sending the kayak skittering sideways. Jennifer braced with her paddle, leaned into the wash, then stroked for land. She nudged the boat's nose into the pebbly shore and snapped the spray skirt off the coaming. Stabilizing the craft with her paddle across the hull behind her, she swung her legs to one side, and stood. Even with her feet protected by wetsuit booties, the chill of the seawater elicited a shiver. Stowing her paddle in the cockpit, she picked up the bow and dragged the kayak farther out of the water.

She glanced around and spotted a small dinghy hidden behind a large driftwood log. Lydia bounded out of the surf and shook, then raised her muzzle. A deep growl rumbled from her throat.

Jennifer shielded her eyes from the sun as she watched a man stroll toward them. She fingered the knife strapped to the outside of her thigh but concealed under the spray skirt that hung from her waist to her knees.

"Stay," she commanded Lydia.

The man waved. She did not. Even his saunter irked her. Acts as if he owns the place, she thought. As he drew near, his khaki slacks and white T-shirt showed off a tall, wiry build. His short black hair with traces of gray at the temple offset a tan face without the deep wrinkles of sailors.

When he was about ten feet away, he stopped. "Hello. I've been sightseeing. There's a cabin on stilts high on the slope and an eagle's nest atop a hemlock just down the beach."

"I know." She pointed to the large sign that read *Private* nailed to a pine at the edge of the forest where reed-like grass grew.

He shrugged. "I called out, but no one answered. The island seemed deserted. Lovely spot."

He smiled. She did not.

"Are you having trouble with your boat? Are you in need of medical help?" she asked.

He frowned, stood straighter and hooked a thumb in his belt. "No. I didn't know the island was private until I landed. Hey, islanders and seamen share camaraderie. You live here?"

"I'm the owner who is not in need of camaraderie. Now, I'd appreciate it if you'd leave my island."

"Your island?" He raised an eyebrow. "The whole island?"

"Yes." She did not intend to elaborate.

He hesitated and looked at Lydia. "Nice dog. Big. Powerful." Again he paused as if waiting for her to say something.

She didn't.

"Well, I guess I'll set sail." His clean-shaven jaw jutted forward as if he was about to vent his displeasure, but then he lifted his hand in a halfhearted salute. "Thanks for your hospitality."

She ignored his sarcasm.

He walked to his dinghy, got in, and pushed off.

Jennifer didn't move until he'd rowed halfway to his sloop. Only then did she lean down, pat Lydia, and whisper, "Good thing he doesn't know you're a one hundred and twenty-five pound lapdog."

When she released Lydia from her 'stay,' the dog scampered toward the forest to investigate smells and chase chattering squirrels, while Jennifer pulled her homemade sled down to the shore. Sometimes she used Lydia's pulling power for the sled, but the stranger's unexpected appearance had jangled her nerves and work would help her regain her composure.

She pushed the kayak onto the padded two-by-four planks, lashed together by canvas and rope, and uncoiled the reins fastened to the sled. Fitting the sling around her broad shoulders, she trudged up the slope, hauling the ninety pound kayak to a small clearing below the path leading up to her cabin. She stopped and tossed the sling aside, then picked up a bucket, scooped fresh water from a large barrel and wiped down the yellow fiberglass hull with a rag. Satisfied, she popped open the bow hatch, extracted her gear, then drew a tarpaulin over the boat. As she walked up the winding trail, she ran her hand over the carved wooden sign that read: *Beastly Manor*.

Suspicious that the stranger may have gone up to the cabin, she inspected the thin wire she'd buried under the sand by the gate. It had not been disturbed and her tension eased. Releasing the spring, she folded the wire behind the gate post. She took this precaution whenever she left the island for long kayak trips or departed for the mainland. Her grandmother had taught her that trick, as well as other ways of keeping herself safe on the island, and it was her grandmother who had given her Lydia after Carla's murder.

She unlatched the gate with its dangling cowbell, whistled for Lydia who dashed ahead as Jennifer snapped the redwood gate shut behind them. The cowbell's deep clang echoed above the island's lush foliage and sent a raven cawing skyward. The wire mesh fencing around the site was laden with elderberry bushes that her great grandfather had planted as a windbreak. Every autumn, these needed hard pruning. She'd already hacked back much of the dense growth but had yet to haul the branches down to the beach to burn.

Under the cabin in an outdoor shower, Jennifer wiggled out of her spray skirt. After unstrapping her sheathed knife from her thigh, she shed her booties and wetsuit. She pulled the rope connected to a small storage tank above. As the cold water pummeled her long slim body, Lydia pushed forward to share the shower. "Okay," Jennifer said. "Let's get the salt and sand off you." After letting water soak through the dog's thick fur, Jennifer shoved her out.

What would her grandfather think of a Newfoundland enjoying the flow from the water tower he'd installed? He'd also constructed the septic tank, but it was her grandmother who'd developed the filtered water system. Water from a small well plus rainfall were the sole sources of fresh water, a precious commodity on the two mile long island. Grabbing a towel from a nearby hook, she dried off, and slung her wetsuit over her arm. Wearing only a bikini, she ran up the stairs to the porch where Lydia sprawled.

She placed her booties and the knife on a bench. After laying her wetsuit and spray skirt over the railing to dry, she fed Lydia a biscuit from the large covered tin by the front door. "You're happy, wet, and very grungy," she told Lydia, who eyed her mistress as if waiting for another biscuit. "Quite enough for you."

Once inside the expansive room that served as the living, dining, and kitchen area, she climbed the spiral staircase to the loft and changed into jeans, a long sleeved flannel shirt, and sneakers. There was another bedroom downstairs, but the loft is where she and Carla had slept, and the warm memories of late night chats with her younger sister remained embedded in her psyche. A toilet and basin were off the downstairs bedroom. Tucked under the spiral stairs was a cedar closet with extra warm clothing for foul weather. It was the only place Jennifer hadn't cleaned out since she'd inherited the island from her grandmother.

After running a comb through her cinnamon-colored hair, she pulled it into a ponytail and slipped on a green hair band. She glanced into the small mirror hung on the roughhewn wall. Her tan emphasized the freckles that laced across her nose and cheeks. She rubbed on lotion that had a nondescript fresh smell, unlike the perfume Alex had given her. She hesitated, unable to recall the name. "Oh yes, L'air du Temps," she mumbled. The perfume went down the drain shortly after he'd left.

Back downstairs she heated clam chowder on the propane burner. Through the window, she saw the sloop still moored in the cove. She mulled over how snippy she'd been. In fact, she'd been rude and normally she was friendly and outgoing. How much she'd changed.

Since her grandmother's death four months earlier, she'd only been to the island a few times. The last time Joe had come with her. He seemed to understand that the island was her sanctuary where she could grieve and remember the good as well as the bad that had occurred on Beastly.

Her parents were furious that the island had been left to her and not to them, but her grandmother knew they would sell it. After Carla's murder, they never returned to the island. Her grandmother understood that Jennifer would maintain Beastly Manor and the land as long as she lived.

The loss of her grandmother made her more appreciative of her surroundings. The cabin's homey interior contained so many memories. Her mother had sewn the cranberry red canvas curtains; her grandmother had made the olive green denim slipcovers on the couch and the two over-stuffed chairs; Carla contributed the flowery cushions to the décor, and Jennifer, not prone to sewing, had made the coffee table from the island's pine trees. Her father and grandfather had worked on the outside and surrounding area. "Decorating is women's work," they'd declared as they'd gone off together. When her grandfather died ten years ago, her dad continued his outdoor chores, accepting Jennifer's help now and then. When Jennifer's fiancé, Alex, came to the island, her father had accepted his help grudgingly.

After her sister's murder, Jennifer and her parents had fallen into a state of confused alienation. A psychologist friend told her this was a phase that would pass, but the chasm remained. They blamed Alex for Carla's murder; the police blamed Jennifer and Alex. She blamed her parents for her breakup with Alex. The circle of unhappiness continued.

She paused as she was about to cut a slab of Havarti cheese, thinking how the past haunted her and froze the present into an all-consuming drive to find the murderer. Sighing, she put the cheese and a slice of rye bread onto her plate with the bowl of hot soup. She took her lunch out to the porch and sat in her grandmother's wicker rocking chair. Lydia's snoring throbbed in counterpoint to the pine needles brushing against the cabin walls. A golden-eyed oystercatcher, black as a crow, darted overhead. She heard the sloop's engine and watched the man weigh anchor. The sloop glided out of the cove like a sleek black swan.

"So much for that interloper," she said, rubbing the nape of her neck. She could have been more diplomatic. Until the murder and the media attention, her family had welcomed strangers. Afterward, everything changed. Like poked sea anemones, her family had pulled into themselves. Was it time for her to stop being so defensive toward every stranger who approached the island? If Joe had been with her, it would have been different, but he couldn't get off duty, so she'd come alone.

After finishing lunch, she set her dishes on the porch's cedar planks and rocked. She had four more days on the island before she returned to Books & Tea. Aunt Emma Mae had been the sole owner of the bookstore until Jennifer bought in a year and half ago. Jennifer's research to locate and appraise rare and old books for clients was not only an endeavor essential to the store's dwindling bottom line, but also allowed her to learn about vintage books circa 1900s. The book, *The Big Sleep* by Raymond Chandler, taken from Carla was the only clue to the murderer. It was all Jennifer had to go on.

"Enough dawdling," she said out loud. "Time for chores." Jennifer picked up her empty bowl and went back inside. The cabin's windows needed caulking, the hewn dead brush waited to be dragged to the beach and burned, and a few roof shingles had to be installed where a raccoon had clawed through to the plywood.

As she washed her dishes, she thought of how she and her grandmother had worked side-by-side making repairs to the cabin. The work had been filled with fun. Once, her grandmother had accidentally nailed her shirt to the side of the house. When she'd quickly descended the ladder, she ended up topless. Or the time the two of them caulked the bathroom window only to find that they'd sealed off the vent. Jennifer smiled, remembering the shared work and laughter.

The afternoon spun by as Jennifer tackled one chore after another. Toward early evening, she dragged the last elderberry branch to the beach. Tomorrow she'd burn them. The air had cooled as the sun dipped behind the island's tree line. It was then she heard the muffled sound of an engine. The same black-hulled sloop entered the cove, its sails furled.

"Damn!" She shoved the last branches into the large pit she'd dug and wiped her forehead with the back of her gloved hand.

The man dropped anchor and put his dinghy over the side. Lydia bolted toward the water, barking and splashing in the shallows. Shrugging off her irritation, Jennifer resumed breaking branches into smaller pieces, while out of the corner of her eye she kept track of the man's approach. As he neared shore, Lydia's barking became frenzied so Jennifer went to quiet her.

When the man was a few feet from shore, he called out. "Ahoy." He lifted a salmon. "I've brought a peace offering."

She hesitated, then waved him in. "Let's give the guy a chance, but stay close." She stroked Lydia's massive head.

The small craft bumped the gravelly bottom, but he didn't get out. "I'm Rick Carlson. We got off to a bad start. I thought I'd try again. Okay if I land? I don't want your dog to attack me."

She nodded, stepped back, ordering Lydia: "Sit. Stay."

He got out of his boat, dragged it up above the tide line, then turned toward her, holding the fish out in front of him. "I thought you might like this for dinner."

"Nice." She stood a short distance away, not sure what to make of him or how hospitable she should be. "You went out to sea, caught a fish, and came back to offer me dinner? You're certainly industrious and persistent."

He grinned; his gray eyes danced with mischief. "Actually, I didn't catch it. I met a fisherman moored off another island. After I explained I needed to make amends to a woman, he sold it to me."

In spite of herself, she laughed and put her hands on her hips. "An honest man. Are you going to cook it as well?"

"No. I gutted and scaled it. I thought you'd cook it." He turned back to the dinghy and pulled out a sack. "I brought charcoal in case you didn't have dry wood."

She hesitated, wondering if she should trust him. "You make it hard for me to turn you away."

"That's the idea."

She bit her lower lip, realizing that at some point trust had to return. "I've got a brazier at the cabin." She pointed up the hill. "By the way, I'm Jennifer Frost."

"Hmm. The name suits you," he said.

She bristled, but knew she'd been "frosty," so she let his barb pass. "And this is my guardian, Lydia," she said, making sure he understood her dog would protect her.

He nodded. "Does she eat fish?"

"She would if I let her." Jennifer released Lydia from her stay, and the dog moved forward to sniff Rick and the fish. "We could make a fire down here on the beach." She tossed out the suggestion, although this idea would still entail her going up and down to the cabin.

"Or you could come out to the boat and I could cook dinner." He stood still, the fish in one hand, the sack of coal in the other.

Silence fell between them as they took the measure of one another. "Let's go up to the cabin," she finally said, pointing toward the path. After a few steps, she stopped. "Lydia's my bodyguard."

"I promise not to get you or your dog mad at me." He raised his free hand in a Boy Scout salute that made her smile.

With Lydia between her and Rick, she continued, fighting off her instinctive reaction to not turn her back to him. Although trust was no longer in her DNA, having Lydia nearby inspired some of her old confidence.

When they came to the Beastly Manor sign, he asked, "Is there significance to the name?"

"Yes," she said, but added no details. They passed through the gate she'd left unlatched and continued up the stairs. After they'd gained the porch, she explained, "My great grandmother was English." She dragged out the grill. "She hated the island and the cabin. In those days it was more primitive than it is today. Thanks to my grandparents there's running water and a flush toilet."

She put a handful of dried wood chips in the bottom of the brazier, and he placed charcoal on top. After he'd lit the fire with his lighter, Jennifer finished her story. "According to my grandmother, her mother kept saying, 'The place is absolutely beastly, just beastly.' So...when my grandmother inherited the island, she named it *Beastly* and put up the sign. I've always liked the name."

"I thought perhaps it had another meaning, more dramatic, perhaps even ghostly." He produced a fresh tomato and a head of lettuce out of the bag he'd carried. "Thought you might not have had your greens lately."

Her eyes widened. "That'll be a treat. I have some Marsala vinegar and olive oil for a salad dressing. I'll add pine nuts for crunch." She grinned as she took his salad offerings. "I picked elderberries this morning. We can have them for dessert. How does that sound?"

"My mouth is watering already. Do you have any rice?"

"Yes. Good idea." She went into the kitchen and made the rest of dinner while he kept an eye on the fish grilling, and Lydia kept an eye on him. With the rice cooking, Jennifer returned to the porch and relaxed in the rocker, while he sat in the cane chair.

She puzzled over his coming to her island. "Are you vacationing or do you just sail around looking for islands to explore?"

He gazed toward the sea where wisps of mist began to swirl above his sloop's mast. The beacon light glowed from the masthead. "Most of the time I live on board," he nodded in the sloop's direction, "and do a little of this and that to keep my head above water. I have no intention of settling in one place."

"I noticed it was registered out of Seattle. Mooring her there must cost you."

"I manage."

"She has classic lines."

"You've got a good eye. She's about fifteen years old, a Morris 36. I refitted her from top to bottom." He stood and went over and tested the fish with a long fork. "It's ready. How about the rice?"

"It should be done." She went inside, put the salad and the rice on individual plates and took them out, handing one to Rick.

After they helped themselves to pieces of salmon, they sat and ate quietly until she said, "I've been living on dried food, canned goods, and some fish catches for the past week. This is a pleasant treat. Thanks."

He bowed his head. "My pleasure." After another mouthful, he asked, "What do you do when you're not on the island playing Robinson Crusoe?"

"I'm not playing. This island has been in my family for generations. It's my rock when the world goes topsy-turvy."

"Is your world topsy-turvy now?" He smiled in an odd way. "How do you feel about that?"

"You sound like a psychologist.""Oops. Didn't I tell you I'm a psychiatrist at a mental health clinic?"

For a moment she thought he was serious, then realized he wasn't. "You've got a weird sense of humor."

"You're not the first to notice." He put down his plate and sipped the tea she'd served. "So what do you do for a living? Or maybe you don't have to since you own an island."

"I'm part owner of Books & Tea, a bookstore in Brandon, a small town north of Seattle. Ever been there?"

"Sorry, can't say I have."

"Not surprised. The town is small and so is our store. Brandon's very quaint; the locals like their privacy. Not many newbies, despite the influx from California, but the store does well enough."

"There must be a lot of readers in Brandon to make a go of a privately owned bookstore these days."

"We manage," she said, thinking she could be just as evasive as he'd been. "What about you? Retrofitting your sloop must have taken a bundle."

"I came into some money. I put in a 42-horsepower Westerbeke and a 130-amp alternator because of the new refrigeration compressor. It took a long time to refit her. The teak had to be matched, sanded and repaired." He must have seen her blank stare. "Sorry, I do go on about *The High Life*."

She nodded. "There's nothing wrong with taking pride in doing something well." She finished the last bite of salmon on her plate. "There's a lot of fish left. Do you want to take it back to your boat?"

"I'm not into taking a gift back. Don't you have a fridge?"

"A small one, runs on propane." She took their empty plates inside and dished up the elderberries with a tad of honey on top. When she came outside, he was scratching Lydia behind the ears as the dog drooled on his pants.

"I thought Newfies were water rescue dogs," he said. "She's not really ferocious is she?"

Jennifer raised her chin. "Do you want to test her?"

He shook his head.

"She'll take care of anyone who gives me a bad time." Jennifer handed Rick a bowl of berries and sat down. "She's well trained."

"A good thing since you're out here alone." He began to eat the berries with a relished sigh.

"My grandmother taught me to be vigilant."

He looked up between mouthfuls. "She must be quite a woman."

"She was. She died four months ago." She turned her head away.

"Sorry."

She shrugged. "You couldn't know." After a time, she said, "Fog's getting thicker. The light on your ship's mast is barely visible."

"Yeah, I noticed. I'd better head back." He stood. "I've wanted to ask, how did you get out here? I didn't see a skiff. Don't tell me you kayaked out."

"Hardly, although it's possible. We're about twelve miles off the coast. Sometimes I rent a boat and moor it in the cove, but this time I used Clarence's ferry service. He'll pick me up, and I'll haul out trash when I leave. My cell phone keeps me in touch."

"Good arrangement." He glanced at his empty bowl and glass. "Can I help you clean up?"

She shook her head. "Not necessary."

"What are you doing tomorrow? Looks like the fog will keep me moored here at least through tomorrow." He must have noticed her tensing, for he added, "I won't bother you, but if you need help with chores, I'm handy with a hammer or shovel."

She swallowed, thinking of Carla's bashed skull, but she regained her poise and replied, "Everything's taken care of, thanks."

After the fog swallowed his retreating figure, she walked down, checked the gate and secured the cowbell. Her trust went only so far.

A fish dinner didn't warrant letting down her guard.

Chapter 2

Unnerved by the man's visit, she put in a call to Joe. He'd be off his shift by now and talking to him always cheered her.

He answered immediately. "Hi, Jen. Miss me?"

"You bet."

"Miss you too. How's it going in Beastly paradise?"

"It would be paradise if you were here. The peregrines are back, but the eagles seem to have abandoned their nest."

"How's the kayaking? I...."

"What did you say? Couldn't hear you. Static."

"It's your cell phone," he said. "When are you going to get rid of that ancient thing? The new ones will give you better reception."

"Nag." She grinned as she said it.

"Yeah, well I care."

"I know and I'll get a new cell soon."

"That's what you always say... I...."

"What? Lost you again."

"Hang up and save the battery."

"I love you," she said, then added, "Nag."

"Ha, ha. See you in a few.... Weekend after you return we can go for a hike or something."

"Or something sounds delightful."

"Oh, yeah, I'll be thinking about it. Give your mutt a pat. Bye."

After she hung up, she put on Emma Mae's Dionne Warwick CD and swayed to the rhythm, thinking of Joe. He kidded her that her taste in music was dictated by her elders. He was right, but she noticed that he enjoyed some of the oldies too. She passed the rest of the evening reading an Agatha Christie novel and sipping red wine.

In the loft that night she awoke from a parade of haunting images: Carla's head oozing blood; a shovel protruding from the sand; a sailboat bobbing in shallow water; Alex holding books; pages fluttering in the wind. Sweating, she rolled over and stared out the window at the gray wisps of fog hovering at the pane.

"Lydia," she called out and was rewarded with the sound of a healthy bark. Jennifer fumbled for the large flashlight at her bedside and flipped it on. Rising, she pulled on a fleece robe over her pajamas, then slipped into mukluks before descending the circular staircase. Dampness had crept into the cabin. Downstairs she opened the damper on the wood-burning stove and put a match to the kindling. As the wood flamed, Lydia came to her side and jabbed at her mistress's thigh with her front paw.

"It's not playtime. You won't be happy with the heat, but it's too cold for me." She unlocked the door and let Lydia out. At first Jennifer roamed the room, then stretched out on the sofa and pulled a wool throw over her. Normally, the fog didn't bother her, although it reminded her of the night she'd found Carla's bludgeoned body on the beach. Perhaps the appearance of the stranger and his anchorage in the bay prompted her dreams.

She castigated herself for giving in to memories of that other sodden September, and yet she understood that until her sister's murderer was caught, she would have no peace. Like her parents, she was a victim of Carla's demise. In the past two years since then, Jennifer's life had spiraled out of control.

She rubbed her forehead as the image of her sister's body sprawled in the sand, blood covering her face remained imprinted on her mind. According to the coroner, death was due to blunt force trauma to the head with an unknown wood object. No weapon had been found, no footprints, no clues. There were no leads, except the book Carla carried with her was gone. Why she took a signed first edition of Chandler's *The Big Sleep* with her that night the family couldn't say.

Jennifer and Alex had been the last to see her alive, so suspicion had fallen on them. First the police accused Jennifer—her motives: desire for Carla's inheritance and jealousy over Carla's secret affair with Alex, which he vigorously denied. When they couldn't substantiate Jennifer's guilt, they turned to Alex, noting his obsession with collectable antique books. The police were unable to find enough evidence against him to charge him with the crime. Nevertheless, the accusations, publicity and family recriminations led to her split with Alex.

When he left, he'd said, "Find the book and you'll find the murderer." That idea had spurred her investment in her aunt's bookstore, since it might help her find the rare book that might solve her sister's murder. Jennifer attended Antiquity Book Fairs, talked with book dealers and collectors and learned the business. She had traced Carla's edition to a donation to the Friends of the Library by the estate of Helen Jacobi. Mr. Arnett, the estate's executor, had explained that the sole heir was a distant cousin living in Israel. Arnett had little information concerning the rest of the Jacobi family. No record of the books donated was available. A dead end.

To Jennifer the only plausible reason for Carla's murder was that someone had coveted the Chandler book. There were jackals who took risks to secure and own rare books or to sell them for a heady price. Despite the intrigue surrounding book collectors and their foibles, killing for a book with a value of eighteen to twenty thousand dollars seemed out of character for even the most ardent book thief. Besides, she always ran into the same barrier. Who would have known that Carla would be on the island with the book? The police had checked on Carla's old boyfriends; all had airtight alibis.

As she huddled under the wool throw, she tried to take her mind off the past by turning her thoughts to her upcoming assignment to catalog and appraise Clifford Wedgeworth's new book acquisitions while he and his bride were on their honeymoon. His book collection was legendary and this was a huge opportunity for Jennifer.

She'd been informed that his personal secretary, Warren Peabody, would let her into the house. All the arrangements seemed peculiar. The initial contact had been a letter, and at his request, subsequent correspondence had been sent to a post office box. Her report was to be put on a CD and mailed to the same box. Even more peculiar was that the payment for her services would be made in cash and delivered to her home address. It was as if Wedgeworth didn't want their dealings traced. Why? Despite the irregularities, the money was too good to pass up, and she'd accepted the conditions. Had she been foolish to do so? She'd sloughed off her misgivings, convincing herself that the rich felt they had a right to be eccentric.

Jennifer turned off the flashlight and sat in murky darkness. On nights like this, she often took out her tape recorder and verbalized her ideas, but not tonight. The heat from the stove dispelled the dampness, but not her thoughts. She went to the door and checked on Lydia, but left her outside knowing she'd prefer the cooler air. She'd still be able to hear Lydia's warning bark if Rick or anyone else approached. After locking the door, she retreated to the loft to try to gain the reprieve of sleep.

Chapter 3

Morning crept to life. Determined to take the day in hand despite the brooding fog, she strode to the beach after breakfast intent on burning the dried branches she'd placed in the pit she'd dug earlier. With a shovel, a pail of crumpled scraps of paper, and a small can of lighter fluid, she walked down to the beach. Lydia trotted ahead sniffing the brush. A muffled bell tolled from the sloop, reminding Jennifer that she was not alone.

She stuffed the paper trash in amongst the branches, sprayed them with lighter fluid and set it afire, then paced the pit's perimeter to see that no wayward sparks drifted into the forest. Although the foliage lining the shore was damp, she never took chances with fire, something she'd learned from her grandfather's experience. Years ago a boat of party goers had come ashore on the island's northern tip and their camp fire ignited the nearby shrubbery. Only a heavy downpour prevented the flames from spreading across the two mile wide island.

Lydia barked and trotted to the water's edge. Startled, Jennifer looked up.

"Ahoy. May I come ashore?" Rick's voice rolled through the drab grayness.

Although still uneasy about his presence, she called for him to land and quieted Lydia. Like an image stepping through a curtain, he strode forward dressed in jeans and a raglan navy-blue sweater.

When he was near, he said, "I smelled smoke, then caught sight of flames. Are you all right?"

"Just doing a bramble burn before I leave." She moved back toward the pit, but kept a wary eye on Rick and maintained a grip on the shovel. "I let it burn completely, then toss water on the ashes and cover the pit."

"Very thorough." He sat in the sand at the edge of the pit with his arms on his knees, gazing at the burn.

Jennifer knelt a few yards from him, passing grains of sand from one hand to the next, enjoying the soothing soft trickle. For a time they were silent, observing the fire.

Over the crackling flames, he said, "I began to think about your sign, 'Beastly Manor,' and recalled a story in the newspapers dubbed, *The Beastly Island Murder*. Did that happen here?"

She nodded and a lump rose in her throat.

"Sorry to bring up bad memories. Was it anyone you knew?"

She gripped the end of the shovel tighter. "My younger sister."

"That had to be rough. Did they catch him?"

She could feel him watching her as she shook her head, cleared her throat and said, "No. The case is still open." Unable to look his way, she stared straight ahead. A soft breeze shifted the heavy mist into wandering wisps. The sun broke through and sparkled in a hit and miss pattern upon the water. Slowly the shrub dwindled to embers, then orange glows. Ash fluttered like butterflies above the pit. "Fire's done its work." She stood, picked up her bucket and walked to the water's edge. As she stooped to fill it, Rick moved to her side, taking the heavy pail from her. He strode back to the pit and sloshed the water over the sputtering fire. Before she had a chance to pick up the shovel, he grabbed it, too.

Lydia growled; Jennifer quieted her. Rick pulled out a pair of work gloves from his back pocket and began shoveling sand into the hole.

"You don't have to do that." Her annoyance at his usurping her duties made her voice strident. Over the last few years, the trait Alex had called pig-headed independence, had become more prominent.

Ignoring her, Rick continued shoveling until the pit disappeared. When he was finished, he handed the shovel back to her. "Wanted to make amends for bringing up bad memories." He took off his gloves and jammed them back in his pocket.

She studied him for a moment. "How good are you with repairing roofs?"

"I've never tried. It can't be too difficult."

"It can be dangerous."

"Ah, danger. Sounds like an adventure."

"Adventures I like. Foolish risks, no." She paused, not wanting to expose her vulnerability. Picking up the bucket, she started toward the cabin with Lydia at her heels. "Come on," she said over her shoulder. "I'm going to take advantage of your guilt."

After they got to the area under the cabin, she took out a ladder and handed it to him to carry to the water tower. On the way she grabbed an armful of shingles, nails and a hammer and stuffed them into a pack. At the bottom of the tower, they stopped to gaze upward. The fog had lifted enough to see the top of the structure.

"I'm surprised you don't have a permanent ladder leading to the one located on the tank." He moved the ladder into place and again put on his gloves.

"Dad thought it made it too easy for animals to get up top. I never understood why he thought animals could climb ladders." She shrugged. "I re-tacked a few shingles on the cabin roof yesterday. When I was up there, I noticed shingles missing from the top of the tank, too." She appraised him. "Do you think you can handle the job?"

"Now that's a challenge I have to take." He looked at her. "I need both hands to climb. How am I supposed to carry the shingles? You coming up?"

She grinned and patted the pack. "Everything you need is in here."

"Okay, boss." He shrugged into the pack and began to ascend the ladder. When he was almost to the top, he looked down, waved, then scrambled onto the roof. As she waited below, she felt pleased with herself. The pounding of the hammer was rhythmic assurance that he was tackling the problem. About twenty minutes later he backed off the roof and descended the ladder.

When he reached the ground, he bowed. "Job accomplished."

"I thank you, Sir Knight," she said and laughed.

"Well, don't thank me too much. I'd say you're due for a re-roofing job on the tank."

"I kind of thought so." They walked back to the cabin and stowed the ladder and gear. "I was hoping the roof would last one more year. Getting a crew out here isn't easy."

"It might last a while yet, but I'd have a roofer check it out." He yanked off his gloves and wiped his sweaty brow with the back of his hand.

"Would you like some lemonade?" she asked. "I don't have ice, but it's cold."

"Thanks. That would be great."

After stowing the ladder and the tools, he followed her up to the porch. "You've been very hospitable today. Would you come on board my sloop for lunch? I can offer you ice, white wine or beer, smoked salmon, Brie cheese."

"Thank you for asking me, but when I'm on the island, Lydia and I are Siamese twins. I've seen how your ship glints with spit and polish, and her paws would do damage."

"Don't you ever leave her behind?"

"Not while I'm on the island. When we're here, she's like velcro." He started to follow her into the cabin, but she pointed to the chair. "Why don't you stay out here and relax."

He raised an eyebrow, but nodded. "Sure. I like to be waited on."

Having him on the porch was one thing, in the cabin quite another. She went to the kitchen where she took out the pitcher of lemonade from the small fridge. When she returned and handed him a tall glass, Lydia was leaning against his leg.

"She does drool, doesn't she?" He raised the glass to his lips.

Jennifer laughed. "That's an understatement." She smiled at her Newfie. Her loyalty to her dog seemed outrageous to some. Leaving Lydia behind wasn't the only reason she refused his invitation. While on the island, caution continued to be her mantra. Her grandmother had taught her well.

She sat on the porch rail and looked over her domain. Other than Joe Baker and her Aunt Emma Mae, most didn't understand her attachment to the island and her dog. They were her anchors in a world that had turned bleak.

"How do you stand it out here alone?" he asked, pacing the porch. "No news, no way to contact anyone if you need help."

"You sound like my parents. I'm not that isolated." She swung her legs back and forth. She didn't want him to think she had no means of communication, even though his concern seemed genuine. "I have a short wave radio, and of course, a cell phone. The coverage is good." Jennifer felt a breeze wash over her face. "The fog's lifting just like the weatherman reported this morning."

"Touché." He leaned against the rail next to her. "Guess I sounded a little condescending."

"A tad."

He shook his head and grinned. You don't give an inch do you?" He held up his hand. "Don't answer that. You're up on the weather conditions. Fog's lifting sooner than I thought. Guess I'll head out to sea after I've had a hearty lunch." He nudged her arm. "Come on. You have to accept my invitation."

"Thanks, but no."

"High living doesn't entice you, does it? I admit this island is lovely, but I don't think I'd like to live here for long. Too primitive. I had enough of that growing up."

"Tough childhood?"

"Let's just say my dad believed in roughing up his son while my mom stood by and watched." His voice grew gruff. "She wasn't much of a woman."

"I'm sorry."

He shrugged. "I left that behind long ago and eventually got a taste of the good life. I enjoy the bright lights and the atmosphere of the big city."

"But you live on your boat, hardly a palace, even though it's trim."

He finished off his lemonade. "I've got a condo, but with my sloop I can visit any port and find almost any lifestyle."

"Like the name of your boat, *The High Life.*"

"Exactly!" He placed his glass on the porch rail and studied her. "I've never met a woman with your sense of duty to a piece of land. Most of the women I've met want money, malls, and a mansion."

"I have a manor." She laughed, then added, "I enjoy nice things and good food, but my island is more precious to me. I could sell it, but what would I have then? This island is my treasure. It's a no-brainer for me."

"It's good to like what you have, but I figure there's always more excitement at the next port. Life's too short to be dull and stuck in a rut."

His lifestyle reminded her of Carla's view of the world. Carla had partied hard and lived fast. Is that why she came to such a terrible end?He held out his hand. "Nice to meet you, Jennifer Frost. Perhaps we'll meet again, maybe in Brandon or another port."

She shook his hand and was surprised when he held hers longer than was warranted. His palm was smooth, his fingernails well-manicured, not like a sailor's at all. He released her hand, reached down to give Lydia a pat, then went down the stairs and through the gate, whistling. The cowbell's bass voice echoed through the forest.

His departure was as abrupt as his arrival. She had an odd sense of foreboding. She watched as he rowed back to his sloop, then sat in the rocker and waited. After an hour, he weighed anchor. As he departed the cove, he turned and waved. He must have known she was watching, and this made her feel small and embarrassed. He'd been pleasant and helpful. Yet…why had he come to the island? She'd learned very little about him.

Some might believe his arrival on the island was happenstance. Jennifer wasn't so sure.

Chapter 4

When the day arrived to leave the island, Clarence, an old salt who ran a ferry and fishing guide service, picked up Jennifer in his sturdy trawler, the *Bertie Blue.* As usual he dropped anchor beyond the buoy marker. Although his hull had a shallow draft, he didn't take chances. Sudden wind storms at low tide had grounded many boats around Beastly.

Clarence's gray-whiskered face was always a welcome sight. He was a bear of a man, with a belly that protruded over his belt. His wife, Bertie, a jolly woman and a long time friend of Jennifer's family, was as wide and as tall as Clarence. It had been Clarence and Bertie who had convinced Jennifer's grandmother that, despite the breed's size, a Newfoundland would suit a sea kayaker.

"How's the cabin?" Clarence asked after she and Lydia were on board with her kayak, duffle bag, and other gear.

"I think I need a new roof on the water tower, maybe the cabin too," Jennifer said. "Know anyone?"

"I'll ask around." He chucked Lydia under the chin. "She looks like she had a good time."

"Are you referring to her tangled fur?"

"Yep." He grinned, then motioned to the open water beyond the cove. "Ocean's stirred up. Coming over was rough and it's getting worse. Going to make for a nasty crossing back to the mainland. I'll winch up the anchor while you secure your kayak," he said over his shoulder as he walked to the bow.

Lydia stayed out on deck sniffing the sea air, while Jennifer joined Clarence inside the wheelhouse and stood next to him, swaying with the trawler's motion as it cut through the cold sea. "I had a visitor. A guy named Rick Carlson. Do you know him?"

Clarence scratched the bristle on his cheek. "Nope."

"He owns a 36 foot Morris sloop called *The High Life.*"

"There was an old Morris docked up in Grotto Place a long while back. Wood, old, a real relic."

She shook her head. "This one was pristine, totally refurbished."

"The one I'm talking about would have cost a pretty penny to overhaul. I think it was sold for salvage." He motioned to a tin on a shelf behind him. "Help yourself to some of Bertie's chocolate chip cookies."

"Thanks." Jennifer pried open the lid and handed a cookie to Clarence before taking one herself. They munched as they watched the spray wash over the prow of the boat.

After a while, Clarence said, "Now tell me how you're really doing. I've been thinking of you out on the island all alone."

"I wasn't alone; I had Lydia and the unannounced visitor."

"Damn it, Jennifer. You know what I mean. Bertie and I have been getting calls all week from your mom and dad. Said you weren't answering your cell phone."

"Sorry they pestered you. I go to the island for peace, not to keep in touch."

"They blame me for taking you out there."

"They want me to sell the island and I'm not going to."

He nodded. "I know that." He kept his eyes on his course. "You never talk about Alex. He wasn't a bad sort. Where is he?"

"He got married about a year ago."

"Oh. I guess the gossip was too much for him."

"I don't blame him. He said the suspicion thrown on him would ruin our relationship." She shrugged. "He was right."

"Well, he sure passed up the best gal around here. That's for sure."

"You're prejudiced because you've known me forever."

"True." The boat shuddered as a big wave hit, forcing him to spin the helm to take on the next one. "You used to be a lot more chipper. Have you thought of being an outdoor guide again? Seems that made you happy."

She shrugged. "It did, but they fired me. Didn't want the kind of publicity an accused murderer would bring."

He shook his head. "Daft to let you go." He turned the wheel. "What about selling the bookstore, go back to Seattle and take up with your friends there?"

"The store's important to the town, to Emma Mae and to me."

"Emma says you got into appraising and selling books. Says that's kept the store going. Emma says ...."

"Emma says too much."

"She cares about you just like Bertie and I do. Keeping yourself locked up in Brandon isn't the best place for a young gal. You had Joe Baker out to the island awhile back." He gave her a side long glance. "How did that go?"

"Not for you to know, Clarence. You said you'd keep our trip to yourself."

"I have. No sense giving food to the tongue waggers. Did you know he's got a job offer from a company in Bellingham?"

Her heart skipped a beat. Joe hadn't said anything to her about a new job, much less moving.

"Some kind of company security job," Clarence continued. "Wonder if he'll take it."

"Joe's a good friend," she said, covering up her surprise. As another wave washed over the bow, she glanced out the window. "It's getting rougher; I'll bring Lydia inside."

"Good idea."

For the rest of the trip, Clarence remained at the helm telling one sea yarn after another. The boat's rolling motion and Clarence's voice lulled her into a dreamlike state as she rode out the trip seated on the floor next to Lydia. She knew he wouldn't take offense at her dozing nor would he lose his craggy smile.

When she awoke, rain drummed on the roof of the pilot house as they passed the old lighthouse and cruised into the small harbor north of Brandon. In the calmer water Clarence nudged the *Bertie Blue* into a slip. Pulling on her Gore-Tex jacket, she went out on deck, jumped onto the pier with the bowline in hand and secured it to the cleat, then hurried to the stern to do the same. Lydia leaped off the boat and trotted up the ramp to where Bertie stood wearing a yellow rain slicker.

"Storm came in faster than expected," Bertie yelled to Clarence as he stuck his head out of the wheelhouse, waved, and shut down the engine.

"Hey Jen," Bertie called out. "Come up to the house for a hot drink and sit by the fire."

Bertie and Joe were the only ones who called her Jen. "Gotta get home," Jennifer said as she walked up the ramp to get a hug from Bertie. "I need to get Lydia to the groomer before he closes."

Bertie glanced at Lydia. "She does look ratty."

"But she's happy." Jennifer laughed and gave her dog a scratch behind the ears. "I enjoyed your cookies. Delicious as usual. Thanks."

"Take 'em home with you. Clarence doesn't need any more calories and neither do I." She grinned. "Of course, I'll bake him a hearty dinner tonight."

"You're the best cook around. You should open a restaurant."

"No thanks. That would be too much work. I cook for fun." Bertie followed her back to the trawler, and grabbed the duffle bag that Jennifer slung off the boat. The wind kicked up and the rain pounded down as Clarence and Jennifer carried the kayak to the parking lot and tied it to the roof of her old jeep. After she stowed her gear inside the car, Clarence and Bert hugged her good-bye, then waved as she left.

With Lydia in the backseat, Jennifer drove toward Brandon with the car smelling of wet dog. On the outskirts of town, she stopped at Shu Lee's Dog Groomers. Inside the small shop, Shu Lee took one look at Lydia and shook his head. "It take two people three hour to untangle fur. Comb out difficult," he said. "What you do?"

"Romped in the wild, and she loved every minute of it." Jennifer stroked Lydia's head. "Can I pick her up about six or is that too late?"

"We open, but no later." Shu kept shaking his head. "You promise. Brush her every day. You no keep promise. Bad for dog!"

Shu always made her promise to groom Lydia daily, and she'd agree, then fudged the grooming and returned Lydia full of snarls. "I'll try, Shu," she said, handing Lydia's leash over to him. "Be a good girl, Lydia."

She dashed out to her car through the downpour and drove to the post office, dreading the usual litany from skinny old Miss Burns, the postmistress. The heat inside the building felt like a steam bath. She spotted Joe's six foot four frame near the front of the line with a package under his arm. When he turned and saw her, he left his place in line to stand next to her. "Hi, Jen." His ruddy complexion glowed and his deep blue eyes twinkled as he gave her his warm crooked smile. He looked great in his policeman's uniform with his athletic build. Although he'd been three years ahead in school, they'd been friends. Six months ago that friendship had become something more, but both were careful to keep it a secret from Brandon gossip. So far they'd succeeded. "Glad you're back?" he said quietly in his baritone voice.

She nodded, smiled and resisted the impulse to brush back the lock of his sandy hair on his forehead.

"Have fun?"

"It was marvelous and for the most part the weather was good."

He glanced at the folks around them and lowered his voice. "How about a hike Sunday? Storm might pass by then."

"Rain's no problem, but I've got an appraisal to do in Seattle. If it's complicated, I may need to spend the weekend doing research." She wanted to ask him about the job offer in Bellingham that Clarence had mentioned, but this was hardly the place to do that. "I'll let you know, okay?"

His grin made her feel warm. "You go first." She moved behind him. "I know you don't have much time for errands."

"Okay, thanks." He lifted his package. "My sister's kid left his teddy bear behind." After it was his turn at the window, and he'd settled up with Miss Burns, he turned back to her. "I gotta get back to the station. You take care, Jen." He winked at her shielding his face so no one else could see. "Bye." He hurried out the door.

"Bye," she said and faced Miss Burns, who said, "He's such a nice fellow. You two ought to get together. He's not like, well, you know who."

"Yes, Joe's great." Starting a conversation with Miss Burns was a mistake, and she'd learned the hard way that the best defense was to either agree with her or ignore her. "You've got my mail?"

"Well, of course. You know, dearie, we've been worried sick about you out on that island. Fog's been thick as mush and now we got rain. Lordy, but it's enough to make a body depressed. You give your mother such a time," the postmistress rambled on. "Looks like you got a fancy letter from Seattle." Miss Burns hung onto the letter longer than necessary, as if she wanted Jennifer to open it in front of her. Jennifer said nothing as she waited with an open hand.

The woman could gossip the day away if given a chance. Grasping the packet firmly, Jennifer said, "Thanks for holding my mail. And by the way, the island was lovely; so peaceful, not a soul to tell me what to do."

"Humph." Miss Burns breathed out her displeasure, while Jennifer retreated, smiled at the people in line, and made a quick exit. In Brandon everyone knew everyone else's business. At times Jennifer felt she should take Clarence's advice and move to Seattle where no one, except close friends, knew you. But she'd tied herself to Brandon, the bookstore and Joe.

She stuck her mail under her parka and ran for the car. Once inside, she went through the magazines and catalogues, tossing the throw-outs on the floor by the passenger seat. She took a closer look at the letters and bills then eyed the beautifully embossed envelope that had intrigued Miss Burns. She pulled open the flap. It was an invitation to the Wedgeworths' open house three weeks from Saturday. Her appraisal of his collection must have sparked the invitation, because she didn't know either of them personally. Intrigued, she planned to RSVP with a "yes." Placing the rest of the unopened envelopes on the passenger seat, she drove into the center of town.

Books & Tea was located in a one-story building on the main drag across from Tucker's Inn and Restaurant, the best place to eat and stay in the area. She turned left onto a side street, then right into the alley behind the store and parked next to Emma Mae's old green sedan. Her aunt wasn't expecting her until tomorrow, but Jennifer thought she'd check in.

There was little crime in Brandon, and they often left the back door unlocked. Not wanting to surprise Emma Mae, Jennifer called out, announcing her presence as she entered the long hall off the back storeroom. She found her aunt sitting in one of the maroon-colored upholstered chairs by the cash register, reading. Her marmalade-colored longhaired cats, Crabapple and Maxie, lolled on top of the counter. There wasn't a customer in the place.

Emma Mae turned and waved to acknowledge Jennifer's approach. "You're home early. Glad you're back. Your mother's been in a tizzy."

"So I heard from Clarence and Miss Burns." Jennifer stood at the counter and stroked Crabapple, who looked at her momentarily, then laid her head down and purred.

"Well, you know Eleanor can't stand Beastly." Emma Mae's gray hair hung in strands on either side of her pale, handsome face. "I'd suggest you sell just to have some peace with my sister, but I know how you feel about the island."

"You've been a rock, staying out of the fight." Jennifer turned toward the bookcase behind her and scanned the books waiting to be picked up by patrons. "I see Peter still hasn't picked up the three books he ordered."

"I called him. Said he'd come in soon." Emma Mae rolled her eyes. "You know what that means. Time doesn't seem to mean anything to old Pete. At least they're paid for. Except for today, the store's been busy since you've been away. This is the first day I've been able to relax. When it rains people like to burrow in at home and read by a fire." She let out a soft chuckle. "Maybe it's a good thing we're up here in the northwest. Rains all the time, so people are forced to read unless they veg out in front of the TV, a nauseating thought."

"Sometimes I could use a little more sunshine," Jennifer said.

"We got another shipment from Random House." Emma Mae continued to bring Jennifer up to date on the store's business. "David Dowden has been asking about that book on insects you promised you'd find."

"Actually, I did find it on the Internet. Should've come in by now."

"Might have. There's a package on the desk in the office for you."

"If that's it, maybe you'd call him tomorrow for me and let him know," Jennifer said, giving Crabapple an extra rub. "I have to go out to the Wedgeworths for the appraisal."

"I noticed the appointment on the calendar. Should be interesting. Almost wish I could go with you to see the place." Emma Mae shook her head. "Amazing what you do on your computer. I'm too old to learn that new fangled technology."

"No you're not." Jennifer stood at the register glancing over the sales sheet. "You just don't want to bother. You'd rather crawl into a good book instead."

They both knew that the store couldn't survive without Jennifer's commissions as a rare book dealer. Her newly acquired skill had paid off for the store's bottom line, but had not helped in finding Carla's missing book. The Internet was a boon, but she'd learned to be careful. Book thieves and unscrupulous dealers abounded. EBay, although a wonderful source, was sometimes referred to as the largest legalized fence of stolen property.

Emma Mae rose and stretched. "Maybe keeping hours on Sunday afternoon isn't such a good idea. What do you think?"

"You're the one who insisted we open on Sunday afternoon. Have you checked how many Sunday sales we do?"

"I knew you'd ask me that." Emma Mae rose and walked stiffly over to the magazine rack and re-stacked them. "So how was your stay at Beastly?"

"Lovely. Cabin repairs had to be made, but the kayaking was great. Lydia loved it." Jennifer walked back to the office and checked the package and personal mail that Emma Mae had left for her. She and her aunt shared the desire for independence and privacy, which is why they worked so well together and why both had trouble getting along with her mother, Eleanor. Emma Mae and Eleanor were as different as Carla and Jennifer had been. Loving one's sister doesn't mean one thinks or behaves like her.

Looking out the office door to the front of the store, Jennifer saw Maxie jump off the counter, follow Emma Mae toward the bookshelves and swat at her mistress's long wool skirt.

"Where's Lydia?" Emma Mae called out. "The cats miss her. Maxie has nobody to pester but me."

Jennifer came out of the office holding a few letters. "Dropped her off at Shu Lee's. Her fur was a briar patch."

Emma Mae frowned and studied her niece. "Well, have you looked in the mirror lately? You could do with a groomer, too." She swished her skirt away from Maxie. "By the way, a fellow came in asking about you last week. Didn't leave a name, but said he'd be back when you were in town. A good looker, on the thin side, nice manners, smooth talker." She grinned at Jennifer. "Have you been holding out on me?"

"Hardly. What did he want?" Jennifer scanned through the mail.

"Didn't say, just asked a lot of questions."

Jennifer stopped and stared at her aunt. "What kinds of questions?"

"Where you were, when you'd be back. Those kinds of things."

Jennifer stilled, a sense of unease rode her. "Was he soft spoken, wiry, about my height, short hair, graying at the temple?"

"You do know him." Emma Mae grinned and with raised eyebrows walked over to Jennifer. "You're a sly one, keeping a new beau a secret." She poked Jennifer in the side. "Maybe Joe will get jealous and ask you out."

Jennifer ignored the jab about Joe. At least there was one part of her life that her aunt knew nothing about and she liked it that way. "The mystery man is a new acquaintance," she said, but didn't add that he was also someone she needed to learn more about.

Emma Mae pointed to a calendar on the wall. "You won't have much time to spruce up. Your due to do the appraisal at nine in the morning."

"Right. Sorry to leave you to do my shift again. I'll make it up next week."

"Don't be sorry. The income from your outside book activities more than makes up for my doing extra duty in the store." Emma Mae picked up a stack of books to shelve. "Go home. You need to dress like you were in civilization, instead of in the boonies."

"Right. I just wanted to check in." After Jennifer left the store, she picked up groceries, then went home to her cold, damp, rented house nestled in the hills on the outskirts of town. A long gravel driveway led to the one-story bungalow. It wasn't much to look at, but it suited her needs. She entered through the back door, placed her groceries on the kitchen counter, and turned on the heat. Having no garage meant going into the rain each time she retrieved something from her car. She dropped her duffle bag off in the back room by the washing machine, wrestled her kayak off the roof of her Jeep onto a dolly, and stowed it in the backyard shed. Knowing it would be a while before she'd go kayaking, she gave the craft a long wistful look, sighed and shut the door.

After stowing gear and starting a load of laundry, she took a long hot shower and donned a pair of black slacks and a red turtleneck jersey. At her desk in the living room she phoned her mother. It wasn't a call she wanted to make, but knew if she didn't, her mother's wrath would be worse. Better to get it over with. After only two rings, her mother's strident voice snapped into her ear. "Jennifer?"

"Hi, Mom. I'm home. The island was wonderful, and the cabin is in good shape."I'm glad you're back. Going out there alone is foolish." In her usual flow of consciousness speak, her mother continued without listening to anything Jennifer had to say. "I have a real estate agent who can get you a great price for the island. Then you can buy a house here in town. I'm sure you'll be much happier."

Jennifer's body went rigid. "Mother, I am not selling!" It was like talking into a vortex. Her mother rattled on, and finally Jennifer interjected, "I have to pick up Lydia before the groomer closes. I'll be in touch. Give my love to Dad. Bye." She slammed down the receiver.

Jennifer closed her eyes and yelled, "Mother, why must you be so impossible?" Her head began to pound. She slumped onto the couch and stretched out. Her mother's litany of sell, sell, sell had recurred every week since she'd became the sole owner. Her mother also disapproved of her renting this small home. Control was her mother's major flaw.

Jennifer understood why Carla had chafed at their mother's need to dominate. Their father had essentially stayed out of the arguments. Jennifer often wondered how he withstood Eleanor's carping. Perhaps burying himself in his work as a self-employed architectural consultant was his flagship of survival. However, his relationship with his daughters had suffered because of it.

Looking around her living room, she was comforted by the furniture and artifacts she'd inherited from her grandmother. The cherry wood credenza and matching desk, the grandfather clock that no longer chimed, and the coffee table with marks left from children's mischief gave her a sense of her past. A bookcase was piled high with old and well-read books. A Rosenthal vase her grandmother had bought in Germany held dried pussy willows, and an old oil painting of her great-grandparents' home in Wales hung on one wall next to a seascape by a local artist.

Despite moments of loneliness, Jennifer enjoyed her life in her small rental house. It was a far cry from her modern apartment she'd rented in Seattle before Carla's murder. Everything in her life was either pre-Carla or post-Carla.

Renovations had been made to the old house before she'd moved in a few months post-Carla. The wood floors had been sanded and re-stained, the insulation had been improved, and the windows and doors had been replaced with double-paned glass. However, Jennifer rented it not for the house, but for the large backyard and the proximity to the open hills behind the property. She and Lydia spent hours roaming the thick fir forest with its moss-covered ground and tangled shrub where birds and wildlife thrived. It was the next best thing to the island.

The ringing phone burst through her reverie. She hesitated, wondering if her mother might be calling back, but walked to her desk to answer it. When she heard the voice on the other end, she sank into the swivel chair.

"How are you, Jennifer?" The familiar voice came over the line as if from another world.

"Alex?" She frowned and stared at the wall, seeing nothing. "I can't believe it's you. It's been," she was going to say, "eons," but settled for "a long time."

"I hope you don't mind my phoning." There was hesitation in his voice.

"No. It's wonderful to hear from you. Is anything wrong?"

His voice changed slightly as if she'd offended him. "No. I'm gong to be in Seattle in three weeks, and I was hoping we could get together."

Get together after two years. And he's married. "What brings you up this way?"

"Book collecting, naturally." His chortle made it sound as though he were embarrassed. "I'm meeting Clifford Wedgeworth, a bibliophile. He has some interesting new acquisitions in his collection."

Wedgeworth, the same man who'd hired her to appraise his newly acquired books? She sat with the phone in her hand, thinking about the eerie coincidence.

"Hello? It must be a poor connection. Are you there?" he asked.

"Yes. I'm just surprised to hear from you."

"It's been too long. I didn't know if you'd want to see me."

She felt her cheeks get hot. "Of course, why not?"

"I'll be at the Wedgeworths on Saturday afternoon. Could we meet late afternoon, perhaps have an early dinner together? Would you come down to Seattle? Visiting you in Brandon might not be a good idea, or have your parents mellowed toward me?"

"Let's not get into that, Alex." Even after all this time, the anger of her parents and most Brandon residents toward Alex was palpable. They remained convinced he was responsible for Carla's murder.

"Sorry. Didn't mean to bring up the past, but I'd like to see you."

"Yes, that would be nice." *Nice! Such an insipid word for a meeting with her former fiancé.* Should she tell him she'd been invited to the Wedgeworths' open house? No. He shouldn't have all the surprises. "I can meet you in Seattle."

They settled on a time and a restaurant for that Saturday evening.

Before hanging up, Alex said, "Jennifer, I've missed you."

Her breathing fluttered. "I look forward to seeing you."

After she hung up, she reflected on the conversation, her thoughts overriding the quickening pulse of her heart. She had to admit she still cared for Alex, but love was another matter. Too much had gone wrong between them for that. However, there was no reason they couldn't meet as friends.

Since Alex had left, Joe had come into her life. If she'd been interested in dating a variety of eligible men, she'd have allowed her friends in Seattle to set her up. They'd kept after her for a year, but when she hadn't responded to their offers, they gave up on her. She didn't blame them. Her life had taken a different turn: searching for a book and a killer. Joe understood that. Joe was her anchor. But what if he left Brandon?

With Alex's phone call, the past stormed in like a blast of cold wind. Her reaction to his voice made her wonder if she'd been lying to herself about her feelings toward him. When she'd heard he'd married, she'd mourned and then forgotten him. Now she wondered if she had. Damn. She didn't want to complicate her life.

The wood floorboards creaked as she paced and listened to the splatter of rain on the roof.

Chapter 5

Despite the drizzle the following day, Jennifer took Lydia for an early walk in the woods behind the house. Afterward, she showered and had a quick breakfast of a bagel with cream cheese and a cup of black coffee. A damp Lydia jumped into the rear seat of the jeep for the short ride to the store. Jennifer parked and hurried inside to be greeted by the mischievous cats. While Lydia made a halfhearted attempt to chase Crabapple and Maxie, Jennifer wrote a note for Emma Mae.

I fed Lydia an extra ration this morning, so she should be good until I return. I hope to get back before dark. Jennifer taped the note to the fridge, knowing Emma Mae's first task was to give the cats their breakfast. Lydia settled onto her pad in the office with the cats sitting on the bookcase above her, ready to bedevil Lydia. "Don't be mean," Jennifer said to the cats, who ignored her. "Sorry, Lydia. You'll have to fend them off without my help." With those parting words, Jennifer rushed out the back door, locking it behind her

Due to slow traffic on the slick roads, the drive to the Wedgeworth's took longer than she'd expected. To pass the time, she turned on the radio, heard nothing but bad news, and flicked it off in disgust. The weather was depressing enough without adding the world's problems to her mindset. The rain increased and the distant thunderheads hid the pristine beauty of Mount Rainier. When she turned off the main highway, the road wound deeper into the forest. After following the curvy road for twenty minutes, the estate, tucked into the hills, appeared.

At the private gate, she stopped and pressed the intercom button located in the mouth of a large bronze statue of a lion at the side of the entrance. After a few moments, a deep voice said, "Wedgeworth estate."

"I'm Jennifer Frost. I'm expected."

"Park under the porte-cochere and ring the door bell," the disembodied voice said.

The wrought-iron gate swung open and she drove up the long drive. Nearing the house, she passed a copse of spruce before coming to an expanse of manicured emerald-green lawn. "Home" was not a word Jennifer would have used for the French-style stone mansion with its gables and arched stained-glass windows below the mansard roof.

She'd researched the seventy-year-old Clifford Wedgeworth and learned that his money had come from the logging industry. Although now the wealthy owner and president of his own lumber company, he had worked as a mill hand. He'd recently married a young woman in her mid forties, dubbed a *trophy wife* by the local tabloids.

Jennifer parked her car as directed, picked up her laptop, briefcase, purse, and walked up the slate stone steps to the door. When she pressed the doorbell, deep-toned chimes resounded from inside. She shivered from the damp chill despite her wool pantsuit, turtleneck sweater and stylish boots lined with faux fur.

A heavy-set man opened the door. "Mrs. Wedgeworth told me to expect you today, Miss Frost. Please, come in." Wisps of white hair protruded from under a beret placed at a jaunty angle on his head. His brown cords and well-worn leather jacket over a plaid wool shirt were not what she'd expected from an estate manager of the well-heeled.

As they stood in the dimly lit hall, he introduced himself. "I'm Harold McBain, the groundskeeper."

"Oh, I expected a Mr. Peabody to meet me," she said.

"Mr. Wedgeworth's secretary is on vacation. However, Mrs. Wedgeworth gave me detailed instructions concerning your visit."

The temperature was only slightly warmer inside, and she drew her jacket closer about her.

With a hint of a smile playing on his lips, Harold said, "It's chilly inside, but Mr. Wedgeworth wants to conserve energy when he's away. Please follow me."

The large tapestries hanging on the walls did little to muffle the echo of their footsteps as they crossed the pink terrazzo floor. He walked with a slight limp, and Jennifer wondered how he managed the expanse of grounds at his age. Of course, he most likely had help. She gaped at the paintings and the French provincial furniture in the expansive sunken living room. Skylights, high in the domed ceiling, brightened the room despite the cloudy day.

Harold stopped in front of a door and turned to her. "Mr. Wedgeworth keeps this room secured. He's very particular and insists the humidity be at fifty percent and the temperature at sixty-five degrees. I'll lock the door behind me, but there's an intercom on the desk, and you can contact me when you wish to leave." His gnarled hands fumbled with the key he inserted in the lock. When he swung open the door, the lights came on automatically.

She took three steps and stopped, stunned by the floor to ceiling bookcases wrapping the room. Two large tan leather chairs sat on a cream-colored rug, laid on top of dark red Brazilian wood floors. The massive scale of the ornately carved mahogany desk, as well as a table with an old world globe, lent an aura of rich antiquity.

My God, all these books couldn't be part of his collection. She turned to Harold. "He wrote there were twenty-three books to be appraised."

Harold pointed to the desk. "Perhaps those will answer your question."

She walked over and put her laptop, briefcase and purse on a chair upholstered in a jade color. A key, thin white gloves, a sealed letter and a note were on the desk. She picked up the note. In flowing script, it read: "*The books in question are in the locked glass case behind the desk. When you're finished, give the key to Harold. Per our agreement, deliver your report to the post office box and your payment in cash will be delivered to your house. C. W.*"

Harold remained standing by the entrance; his brown eyes curious and alert. Jennifer turned around and studied the bookcase, then reached for the ivory letter opener and slit the sealed envelope. This message was typed on Wedgeworth's letterhead. "My books are sorted according to their acquisition date; do not change their order. Wear gloves. Harold will check your belongings when you leave. Clifford Wedgeworth."

Odd that he left two separate notes in such different styles, she thought.

"How long will you be, Miss?" Harold asked.

Jennifer looked at her watch. "I'm hoping to get all the information transcribed today so I won't have to return, but I'm not sure how long it will take."

"You can call me," he nodded toward the intercom. "There's a bathroom off to your right. Mrs. Wedgeworth suggested you might like hot tea or coffee now and some refreshments later."

"Tea would be lovely. Black, unless you have lemon."

He nodded and walked out, shutting the doors behind him.

The unnerving sound of the lock click made her think of the character imprisoned in a room for years with access only to books in Anton Chekov's, *The Bet.* She shivered and it wasn't just from the cold. There were no windows. Despite having the world of literature at her fingertips, the room felt claustrophobic.

Before investigating the designated bookcase, she wandered around and marveled at the various tomes. Most were leather bound collections of authors like Dumas, Whittier, Burroughs and Emerson, but she doubted if they were first editions. These seemed to be decorator books meant to impress. Yet there were other titles that intrigued her. One section had post World War II books: *On The Road* by Jack Kerouac, *Hangman's Holiday* by Judith Sayer, *Imaginary Letters* by Ezra Pound. If these were in fine to very fine condition, they were worth a great deal. She remembered an alert from the Antiquarian Booksellers Association that a copy of *On The Road* had been stolen.

Intrigued, she donned the white gloves before pulling out the book even though she realized she wouldn't be able to identify it as the stolen copy. It was a first edition and perhaps valued in the thousands in today's market. She wondered if Wedgeworth ever sold some of his books or merely collected them, or was he one of the few who believed by collecting books he was saving knowledge for future generations? From what she knew about him, money was not an issue. He was a collector, not a dealer. She returned the book to the shelf.

Pacing on farther, she noted a book by Flaubert from a collection titled *A Century of French Romance* with fine leather, well-dressed and supple. Either Wedgeworth, or his secretary, probably used British Museum Leather Dressing to maintain their condition, an unpleasant, but necessary chore.

The room held an astounding array of literature, probably worth millions. He definitely had catholic taste. Many collectors specialized in one area, but Wedgeworth's ran the gamut of children, art, and history from various centuries.

Surely, he must have had all his books appraised for insurance purposes. If so, why hadn't he had this other collection appraised until now? Were they new additions or did their value need updating? As her gloved hand stroked several of the leather bindings, something caught her eye.

Above the entry door, an oil painting of a mournful clown gave her a jolt. It elicited feelings of nostalgic sorrow with its tilted head, down-turned mouth, and a teardrop on one cheek. It was out of place among the antique tomes and classical writings. Clifford Wedgeworth was obviously a man of many interests and most likely a complex individual.

Refocusing her attention on the books, she noted two insets with locked glass doors. She peered into one and gasped. They were incunabula books, written before 1501. She had no expertise in the field, but figured them to be priceless. One was an early bible she had never seen, but the other caused her to stand transfixed. The American Bible, known as the "Natick Bible," had been put up for sale and obviously Wedgeworth had bought it. Printed in 1663 it was an Indian Language translation. She couldn't even estimate its worth in today's market.

Her stomach fluttered. What would she find in the bookcase she was to appraise? She circled the desk, admiring the carvings on its side panels and removed the gloves. As she laid her things out on the desk, the entrance door lock clicked and Harold entered carrying a small tray with a tea pot under a cozy and a china cup and saucer.

"The lack of humidity makes it feel colder," he said, nodding at how she was rubbing her hands together. He was about to set the tray on the desk, but she stopped him.

"Please, no. I'll be working here. Set it over there." She pointed across the room and smiled at his perplexed look. "It's safer in case of a spill."

"I usually have nothing to do with this room," he said and followed her directive. I'm unfamiliar with the proper etiquette." As he set the tray down, a clap of thunder resounded through the house. "Thunder and lightning were forecast, but the storm's moving off to the east. It should let up by late afternoon." He smiled as he exited the room, locking the door behind him. He had a gentleman's demeanor which seemed at odds with his position as groundskeeper.

She poured a small amount of tea into the china cup and held it in both hands to savor the warmth before she took a sip. Setting the cup down, she walked over and unlocked the glass doors to the bookcase. After donning the white gloves, she began her work, starting at the top row to keep them in the order of Wedgeworth's acquisition dates. With meticulous care, she removed the first book, *The Blackboard Jungle* by Evan Hunter. She placed it on the desk, careful not to crack its spine back too far.

Inspecting the copyright page to see if it was a first edition was more difficult than people thought. Different publishers used different numbering systems and stating that the book was a first edition, didn't make it true. In this case Simon & Schuster had printed it as a first with a date of 1954. She checked the numbering system to be sure. Publishers used a set of numbers 1 2 3 4 5 6 7 8 9 0 and the lowest number in the series dictated whether it was a first edition. In this case the number 1 was present and that helped verify the edition as a first. She transcribed the data into her computer before perusing the book to determine it's condition. Checking for foxing or spots showing water damage or age was her first priority. It was a hardback with a pristine dust jacket, which upped its value. When she was finished inspecting it, she typed in VF to F next to the title, meaning the book was in very fine or fine condition. There was no crumpling at the head of the spine, no sign of binding repair; the jacket price had not been clipped off, but it had no other defects that she could determine.

Returning the book to the shelf she continued the same process with each book. Most were in fine condition although two had to be listed as VG, meaning very good. In one the previous owner had signed the back end paper and the other had a small spot in the center page, probably from an insect stuck between the pages. That could be repaired. The hours ticked by and she stopped occasionally to stretch and walk around.

She was transcribing data from *Life of George Washington* by John Corry published in London in 1800, when she heard the lock turn, but continued to log into her computer the long title: *Late President and Commander in chief of the Armies of the United States of America — Interspersed with Biographical Anecdotes of the most Eminent Men who effected the American Revolution.* By the time she'd finished, Harold had put a tray on the table with another pot of tea and a plate of round cheese biscuits with nuts on top.

She looked up, noticed the time on the wall clock, and said, "You came at a good time. I was getting hungry." She leaned back and took off the gloves.

"These biscuits are Mr. Wedgeworth's favorites. They're rather spicy. I'm afraid there isn't much else to eat." He took away the pot of cold tea and replaced it with the hot one. Steam drifted from its spout.

"I only have nine books to go, so it shouldn't be much longer. Do I just hit this button?" She pointed to the one that said intercom, "or pick up the phone?" "Push the button and I'll respond. The rain's letting up, so your drive home should be pleasant."

"Glad of that." She watched him leave, then poured a fresh cup of tea and picked up one of the biscuits. As she bit into it, her eyes watered at the sharp tang of the cayenne-laced cheddar. Clifford Wedgeworth's taste in food was as sharp as his eye for collectable books. Warmed by the hot tea and the spicy food, she returned to her work.

Once again she donned the gloves and studied the book she'd been working on. The cover was new, as it had been rebound. That plus the discoloration and tattered pages devalued its worth. Still, it was a handsome little piece and could bring a good price to the right buyer. She returned the book to its proper place and took out the next one. Swiveling around in the chair to face the desk, she laid the book next to her laptop, then stared at the cover.

The Big Sleep by Raymond Chandler! Carla's book?

Her fingers trembled as she opened the cover. Holding her breath, she turned the page—a first edition published by Alfred A Knopf 1939 with the author's signature. Of course there were many copies, but how many autographed first editions? She squinted as if to bring the book into focus and stroked the signature. Was it authentic?

From research she'd done on Chandler, she knew that if the book was in near fine or fine condition it could bring over eighteen thousand. That wasn't enough to kill for, was it? Jennifer knew there were many book collectors who stole books, but had never heard of anyone committing murder to obtain one.

Alex had notified the American Antiquarian Bookseller's Association that the book was missing and they in turn made book collectors aware if it turned up for sale. Jennifer had no information about any copies of *The Big Sleep* up for sale in the past two years. Some collectors never sold their rare books, but kept them for the pleasure of owning them.

Her gloved fingers hovered over the title page. Could this be Carla's copy? If so, could she prove it? Carla's had come from the Helen Jacobi estate that had donated books to the Friends of the Library. Inspecting the dust cover, she found the initials H. J. clearly written in script on the flyleaf.

"My God. This has to be it. I found it!" Her words bounced off the walls. The initials would devalue the book, but she didn't care. This book was gold to her. Without thinking, she picked up the book and held it to her chest.

How had Wedgeworth acquired it? From whom? When? Questions rolled through her mind. If she knew how to contact him, she'd call him this minute. Her shoulders slumped. She'd have to wait till he returned. She'd waited two years. Two weeks longer shouldn't matter.

But it did.

Slowly she placed the book back on the desk. Her stomach churned. Carla had held this book, valued it, and it had been wrenched from her dead body. Jennifer's heart swelled. She stood and paced around the room unable to contain her feelings and her excitement. Now what? What was so important about this book that someone would kill for it? It's worth alone could not explain murder.

Sitting again at the desk, she caressed the cover. She thought a moment, before removing a soft bristled brush from her briefcase and placed a colored sheet of paper under the book. Anything dislodged would fall onto the paper. With meticulous care, she began to scrutinize every page and brushed the crease near the binding. Three quarters of the way through, her effort yielded a few grains of sand. She closed her eyes and exhaled, then continued page by page. There was a smudge at the bottom of one page—a blood stain? Only a special light could determine that. The stain would devalue the book, but her sole concern was finding anything that would solidify the identify of this book as Carla's.

She continued her meticulous search through to the back cover. At first she thought pen scratches had marred the end page. She brought the desk lamp closer. The markings were faint black letters scrawled backward at an angle. Through her magnifying glass, she studied the smeared ink. The spacing was odd; the script difficult to read. The handwritten entries seemed to be notations on the margins of a piece of paper that had been wedged between the pages. More letters in block print were in the center of the page. These must have been smears from an old typewriter. The carbon from the ribbon allowed some words and letters to leach onto the book's paper. Due to the transfer, all these read backward.

There were a few legible words and in other places there were only imprints of letters with spaces in between. She remained hunched over the book, scrutinizing every line. At the bottom of the page there was an incomplete signature. She took out a mirror and placed it at an angle to the writing, puzzling over it. When she at last made out the signature, her hand flew to her mouth. A. Einstein. "My God, could it be? Albert Einstein."

She leaned back and gave a triumphant smile, and almost yelled, "Yes!"

Her heart pounded. Awed by her discovery, she squinted over the page again with the magnifying glass. On a separate sheet of paper, she wrote the words she could decipher: "Lotti … Presi … en … S … ilar … ucl … ar … chai … r … sorr … writ … future … respo … confe … A … Einstein."

For a time, she sat frowning at this new mystery. A letter or a document must have been set between an end page and the back cover. Was this the actual signature of Albert Einstein? Who was Lotti? What did S … ilar mean? Or any of the rest of it for that matter? She folded her notes and put them in her wallet.

If there'd been a letter or a document of Einstein's in the book, then his words could have been worth a great deal. Enough to kill for? What did the paper with Einstein's signature say and where was it now? Had Carla known about it? Surely, she would have said something if she had.

Alex said he'd gotten a look at the book and the author's signature. Had he seen more than that? Had he known about an inserted document? Had he taken it? Impossible. Carla had stood next to Alex, and knowing her, she never would have allowed him to remove anything.

After Carla had acquired the book, she'd acted aloof, even mysterious. The family had shrugged, believing Carla was in one of her moods, something that seemed to occur every time she became involved with another man.

Now that Jennifer had at last found the book, continuing her task with the remaining books became a grinding task. Her thoughts roamed. Her head ached. She picked up the letter Wedgeworth had left for her and reread it. "My books have been sorted by their acquisition date."

If she could find out the dates of the book in front of *The Big Sleep* and the one behind it, she'd have an approximate date of when he'd acquired it. She turned back to the shelf. A 1925 signed edition of Goethe's *Faust* came before Chandler's book and it was followed by an edition of Arthur Conan Doyle's *The Hounds of the Baskerville*. She noted the order on a sheet of paper. She guessed from the conditions of both that Doyle's book was probably worth more than Goethe's *Faust* in the present market.

Wedgeworth must have a ledger with the data about his acquisitions. She slid the chair back and pulled out the top desk drawer finding the usual office pens, notepads and other paraphernalia. She closed it and tried the other drawers—locked. She sighed. It galled her that she'd have to wait until she could speak to Wedgeworth to find out more information.

Trying to set aside her emotions over her find, she returned to the mundane task of cataloguing the remaining books. She had set aside Chandler's book and was loathe to return it to the shelf, yet she had no choice. The desire to take it was overwhelming, but her things were going to be searched when she left. Maybe she'd be able to come back. She pushed the intercom button and told Harold she was ready to leave.

"I'll be right there," he said. True to his word he came after a few minutes. As he inspected her things and took back the key to the bookcase, she said. "I might have to return for additional information. Shall I call the house number?"

"No, you'll have to call me at my cottage. It's located on the estate." He wrote the number on a card and handed it to her. "I'll have to get authorization to allow you to return. I'm sorry for all the security, but those are Mr. Wedgeworth's orders."

He escorted her down the long hall and waited in the doorway as she got into her car. The rain had abated as Harold had predicted, but heavy clouds blotted out the moon. Her headlights stabbed through the blackness as she drove down the private drive. The gate swung open and she left the estate behind. She turned the heat on high and concentrated on the winding road. After she was on the main highway to Brandon, her thoughts turned toward the Einstein signature.

"I know I'm onto something," she said. "But what?"

She itched to get started on researching Einstein to find out what would connect him to a book owned by Helen Jacobi. She'd already researched Helen Jacobi, knowing that's who donated Carla's book to the library and had found nothing of import. She'd review her notes and inquire anew.

She blinked at oncoming headlights and realized she'd been driving in a trance-like state. She sat up straighter, opened the side window and concentrated on the road. But her thoughts continued to swirl back to the strange afternoon she'd spent at the Wedgeworth house. He must have had the rest of his collection catalogued and appraised for insurance purposes. Those in the small case were recent acquisitions. She thought of the clown painting juxtaposed against the antique setting. What kind of a man was he? More important—when had he purchased this book and from whom? Had he gotten it by some nefarious means?

When she returned to Brandon, she drove into the alley behind Books & Tea and parked. Emma Mae had already closed up, leaving the back room light on. Lydia's bark welcomed her arrival and the cats circled Jennifer, rubbing up against her legs. Although they were used to being left alone at night, they liked company during their night forays through the store. When Jennifer snapped on Lydia's leash, the cats skulked off. Their long-suffering playmate was being taken away.

Upon returning home, despite the late hour, she changed clothes and jogged with Lydia at her heels through the dimly lit streets. The exercise calmed her and she returned with a fresh outlook. She took a hot shower then poured herself a glass of merlot and nibbled on crackers spread with hummus. Excitement dulled her appetite. As Lydia lay by the front door, she put her massive head between her paws and eyed her mistress.

"Different routine tonight," Jennifer told her dog. Bundled in a flannel robe and wool socks, she made a list of possible leads on a yellow pad, then went to her desk and turned on her computer.

On the Internet, she searched for Einstein on Sotheby's web site, thinking a book or papers might have recently come up for auction. Nothing. She googled the name Jacobi and found several. Just as she'd found earlier there was no data on a Helen Jacobi. But she found a Lotti Jacobi, 1896 to 1990, well-known photographer, born in Berlin immigrated to the United States in 1930. She was famous for her casual photos of Robert Frost, Eleanor Roosevelt, and Albert Einstein.

Jennifer leaned back and rubbed her hands together. If Helen Jacobi was related to Lotti Jacobi, a realistic probability, then the impressions left in the book from some documents may have related to Einstein. If so, who had taken it and what did it say? And how much was it worth?

"Carla, I'm getting closer," she said to the quiet room.

Chapter 6

The following day while Emma Mae worked in the front of the store, Jennifer ensconced herself in the office on the pretext of doing paper work. She didn't want to deceive her aunt, but thought it best to keep her recent discovery private, at least for now. Her concentration splintered between appraising Wedgeworth's books, researching Lotti Jacobi, and learning more about Rick Carlson.

Her first call was to Ronald Arnett, the executor of Helen Jacobi's estate. A year and a half ago when she'd discovered her sister's book had come from a donation by the Jacobi estate, she'd questioned him at such length that he'd become exasperated with her. Now when she phoned him, she heard the exasperation in his voice.

"Yes, I remember you, Miss Frost," he said.

"Mr. Arnett, since I last talked to you, I've become a rare book dealer. I have a client who bought a few books that the Jacobi estate had donated to the library, and he's interested in their provenance."

"Miss Frost," he said in a high tenor voice, "the books were donated. The estate has been settled, the heir has no claim on them."

"I should have asked you back then who sent them to the library."

"Miss Abby Gardner, Helen Jacobi's housekeeper gathered all of her mistresses things and meted them out to various charities. I saw no reason to interfere. There was little of value in the estate other than the house. It's been sold and the funds turned over to the only living heir."

"Yes. I remember you said he lived in Israel. Do you happen to know if Helen Jacobi was related, however distantly, to the famous photographer, Lotti Jacobi?"

"There had been some talk of a famous relative, but I have no facts to back up the rumor."

"Could you give me the names of anyone close to Helen Jacobi? Perhaps I could contact the heir."

There was a sigh at the other end of the line. "You are most persistent, Miss Frost, a characteristic that would do you well in the practice of law. However, I'm afraid Miss Jacobi was a recluse."

"Do you have Miss Gardner's phone number and address?"

"I'll transfer you to my secretary for that information. Just a minute."

Jennifer drummed her fingers on her desk while she waited. Soon a woman's voice came on the line and gave her Miss Gardner's information.

Before the woman could hang up, Jennifer asked, "Could you give me the name and contact information of the Jacobi heir in Israel?"

"Oh, I didn't realize Mr. Arnett wanted you to have that as well. I'll have to go to another file. Why don't I fax it to you."

"Of course." Jennifer gave her the fax number and hung up just as Emma Mae came into the office.

"Mrs. Pickering is out front. She wants to know which of A. A Milne's books would be best for her daughter."

Jennifer smiled. "See if you can talk her into buying the complete collection. Dutton is the publisher. Her daughter's the perfect age to appreciate it."

Emma Mae frowned. "It's expensive."

"And beautiful." Jennifer grinned. "If I recall it's her daughter's birthday. I hate to sound mercenary, but Mrs. Pickering can afford it."

"Cheeky today, aren't you," Emma Mae said.

After Emma Mae went back to Mrs. Pickering to discuss her purchase, Jennifer phoned Miss Gardner. A firm voice came on the line. "Hello, who's calling?"

Jennifer raised an eyebrow at the no nonsense attitude of the woman. "Miss Gardner. I'm Jennifer Frost. Mr. Arnett, the executor of Helen Jacobi's estate, gave me your number."

"Yes?"

"Do you remember the books donated to the library from your former employer?"

"Of course, I remember. Is there a problem? Are you with the library?"

"There's no problem and I'm not with the library. I'm a book dealer. I'm trying to determine the provenance of some of the books. Do you happen to know if Helen Jacobi was related to Lotti Jacobi the famous photographer?"

"Well, Miss Jacobi rambled from time to time that she knew someone connected to movie stars and famous people. I never found out if it was true." There was a pause on the line, then the woman added, "Was she related to someone important?"

"I don't know. I'm trying to find out. Since you were her confidante through the years, Mr. Arnett thought you might have information he didn't have."

"Ha. No way. The minute Miss Jacobi died, I called him; those were my orders. He took care of everything. I just bundled stuff up and sent it off to needy places. Thought the library was the best place for the books."

"It certainly was," Jennifer assured her. "You were very smart to have thought of that."

"Miss Jacobi treated me well, but if those books are valuable, maybe I should take them back. I got to keep some of her other things. Nobody else gave a hoot about her."

The woman's comment about the value of the books rattled Jennifer. "You might check with the library if any of the books are still in the *The Friends of the Library's* collection."

"So why are you asking me about them if you don't have them?" The woman was smart and shrewd.

"I have a client who bought some of the books," Jennifer said, "and he's interested in the prior owners."

"Oh, that I wouldn't know. Most of the books seemed old. She read a lot. Nothing else for her to do."

"Let me give you my cell phone number, in case you think of anything that might help."

After a few more niceties to assuage the woman's curiosity, Jennifer hung up.   For a moment she sat back to contemplate her next move.

She flipped on the computer and searched the web for Rick Carlson, but found nothing. He wasn't listed in the phone book, and she couldn't find his boat's registration number even though she'd read on the boat's transom that it was moored in Seattle.

After further futile searches, she returned to her work: shelved books, wrote invoices and paid bills. The day drew to a close with frustration riding her every move. As they closed the store for the night, Emma Mae came over to her and put her arm around Jennifer's shoulder.

"You've been acting like a flea got in your britches. Are you thinking about that man who came asking for you?"

Jennifer almost laughed, since, in a way, she was. She was itching to confide in Emma Mae that she'd found Carla's book. Although Emma

Mae normally kept things to herself, this news might cross the line of her resistance. With Alex's surprise return, she wanted no rumors to revolve around the past and Carla's murder.

Chapter 7

The sun rose resplendent on Saturday and the good weather was supposed to hold through the weekend. Jennifer looked forward to her hike on Sunday with Joe. But today, with Emma Mae covering for her at the store, Jennifer took off to conduct a feet-on-the-ground search for Rick Carlson's sloop, driving south to the harbor area with a list of boat repair yards. If they didn't yield results, she'd head farther down to Fisherman's Terminal.

Lydia hung her head out the window, nose quivering and ears flapping in the breeze. White sails strung across the blue waters just off shore like a garland of white carnations. This windy day in early September brought out every weekend sailor. Rick could be sailing to some distant place, but he had refitted the sloop and someone in the area might know about him. Tilting at windmills seemed to occupy a great deal of her time.

She stopped first at some of the smaller boat repair shops. With Lydia by her side, she ventured among the workmen. One burly guy whistled from atop a cruiser keeled high above the waterline. She waved, hoping a friendly manner would get her further than acting insulted. At dock side she asked several men if they knew Rick Carlson.

"You missing your sweetie?" one fellow with a scruffy beard jeered.

Ignoring him, she turned to some others. "He owns a sloop called *The High Life*. Has a special engine." She took out a small notepad from her jacket pocket. "It's a Morris 36 that's been refitted with a Westerbeke engine."

The men looked at each other then shook their heads. "Sounds great," a younger man said and strolled over to her. "Nice Newfie," he said and put out his hand for Lydia to sniff. "I'll put the word out you're looking." He gave her a big suggestive smile. "How can I reach you?"

"Not a bad pickup line," she countered. "I'm only interested in the sloop and Carlson." She handed him a card with her cell phone number.

"I get your drift, lady." He glanced at the rest of the men behind him. "We'll spread the word for you, no strings attache"Thanks. I appreciate that." She left them and returned to her jeep. She widened her search at the docks and boat repair shops, but came up empty handed. One old guy thought she was an undercover cop and got nasty. For the most part everyone seemed more interested in the boat she described than in the man. Although boat owners generally knew one another, Rick's name drew blanks.

Toward noon she stopped for a hamburger at a fast food stand near the docks. She pulled a dog biscuit from her jacket pocket and Lydia devoured it in one crunch. While she pondered her next move, a middle aged man in a T-shirt and tattoos on both biceps approached her.

"Excuse me, miss," he said. "I heard you were looking for a Morris sloop."

She swallowed her mouthful of burger and sat up straighter. "Yes, that's right. Do you know where it is?"

"No ma'am," the swarthy fellow said. "But I thought of an old-timer who might know. Name's Bjorn. He's got a repair yard south of here. He's known as a first-rate carpenter. I recall him mentioning work he'd done on a Morris sloop. Seemed it needed a total refit."

"That could be it." She shaded her eyes looking up at him. "Can you tell me where his place is?"

"Sure. It's kinda tricky. Let me draw you a map." He took out a stubby pencil and grabbed a napkin.

After taking a look at his sketch, she ran her finger over the lines he'd drawn. "Thanks. I think I see where he's located."

"Glad I could help. Bjorn knows just about everything that goes on in the boat business here about, but he's getting kinda old. Makes people think he can't do the work, but he can and better than most."

"Can I tell him who gave him a glowing recommendation?"

"Sam Grover." He gave her a nod, and left.

There were two small boat docks left on her list, but Bjorn's wasn't one of them. Hopefully, this was the break she needed or else she might have to widen her search toward Tacoma. She tossed the hamburger wrapper in the trash and motioned to Lydia, who eyed the water wistfully. "Sorry girl, not now. We have a few more calls to make before I let you go for a swim."

Back in her car, she studied the map the man had drawn. Afterward she checked her GPS and found the route to Bjorn's. While she drove, she wondered about her compulsive search to find Rick. She could let it go, but it nagged at her. Why had he come to the island, pretending not to know anything about her? His motive was as elusive as Lydia catching a bird.

As she turned off the road onto a gravel lane, the jeep bounced over several bumps and ruts. After about a mile down a frontage road, she came upon a small warehouse and an office building with corrugated siding. A discarded sign entwined with weeds read: *Bjorn Boat Charters.* She parked outside a chain link fence.

With Lydia heeling beside her, she walked through the open gate. The place seemed deserted. As she stepped around a speedboat undergoing hull work, she called out, "Anyone here?" Peeking into the deserted office, she saw an old wooden desk with papers piled in neat stacks. A gunmetal filing cabinet and several wicker chairs furnished the reasonably clean room. She headed toward the dock and at the far end, sitting on a piling, was an old man in well-worn overalls smoking a pipe.

As she drew near, he said, "Nice dog. Don't see many Newfies around here." He stuck his pipe back in his mouth, and puffed, letting the smoke plume out in tight white spirals.

"Her name's Lydia," Jennifer said, taking in her surroundings. "Is the owner about?"

"Yep." He took another pull on his pipe.

She smiled. "Am I looking at him?"

The creases around his mouth grew deeper. "Right you are." He cradled his pipe in his left hand.

"I'm Jennifer Frost." She thrust out her hand.

"Bjorn Halverson. Everyone calls me Bjorn." He took her hand briefly. "What can I do for you?"

"I was given your name by Sam Grover, a dockworker, who gave you high marks as a carpenter and said you might know a fellow I'm trying to find. Rick Carlson. He's the owner of a sloop named *The High Life.*"

The man squinted, thought a moment, then shook his head. "Don't recognize the name or the boat."

Her shoulders slumped, and she stuck her hands in her pockets, but she persisted. "The boat's a refitted Morris 36, black hull, white on the cabin, and white boot top at the waterline, refurbished about a year or so ago."

"Well now, that's more like it." He motioned with his pipe toward a wooden keg across from him. "Have a seat."

"You know the boat?" She took up his invitation and sat on the barrel. Lydia ambled over to the man.

"Maybe." He scratched Lydia behind the ears, and the dog leaned into him. The man chuckled. "You like that, don't you?" His gaze shifted to Jennifer. "Something special about this fella you want to find or do you want to find his boat?"

She decided to be candid. "I met him a while back." Telling him partial truths made it easier. "I own a small island off the coast, and he sailed into my cove a few weeks ago. He might have some information I need."

"About what?"

"Does it matter?"

"It might." The old man kept scratching Lydia, and her tongue lolled out of her mouth in obvious ecstasy.

Jennifer waited and fiddled with the pad in her hand, trying to be patient. Her throat tightened with anxiety. The sun hung low near the ocean's horizon and in another two hours the boatyards would close. Heading back to Brandon with nothing to show for her day would be disheartening.

Bjorn stopped petting Lydia, leaned back, and clasped both hands around his knee, the bowl of his pipe held by forefinger and thumb. "About two years ago, I helped a fella refit his Morris sloop. Closed-mouth and a persnickety son-of-a-gun. Everything had to be ever just so. He paid me in cash, so I didn't complain. Worked with him for about ten months and never learned much about him." He shook his head. "His name wasn't Rick Carlson."

Jennifer felt a tug of uncertainty plied with hope, as the man seemed to ruminate about the past.

"Can't think of what his name was, though."

"Could you describe him?"

"Funny sort of fella. Always wore gloves when he worked. Said women didn't like callused hands."

Jennifer's heart gave an extra thud, remembering how smooth Rick's palm was when they'd shaken hands.

"Is that true?" he asked.

"What?"

"Is it true that women like a man with smooth hands?"

At first she thought he was teasing her, but realized he really wanted to know. "I guess it depends on the woman. To me if a man's hands are clean, but he's hard working, calluses wouldn't bother me."

The old man nodded as if reflecting on her answer.

"Anything else about this man, like height, coloring?" she asked.

He leaned forward. "Well, let me think on that."

While Bjorn thought, Jennifer watched Lydia trot along the pier toward a flock of seagulls. As she bounded at them, they flew upward and circled overhead as if disdainful of those glued to the earth.

"Stand up," Bjorn said, motioning with his hand.

Jennifer almost laughed at his request, but humored him and complied.

"You're kind of tall for a gal. He was about your height, skinny but strong. Had a tough edge to him."

"Do you have an address or phone number for him?"

"You think it's the same guy?"

"The description is similar."

The old man got up, knocked the ashes out of his pipe against the bottom of his boot and stuck it in his shirt pocket. "Come into the office and I'll look up what I've got. Mind you, I'm not the best filer."

She whistled for Lydia who came running from the far end of the dock. Jennifer followed Bjorn back to his office and gave Lydia a stay command, while she ducked in through the doorway and took a seat in one of the wicker chairs.

"I took some old files home. No need to clutter my office, but my sister wasn't any too happy to see me lug home more paper." He took out one file, shook his head, shoved it back in the drawer, pulled out another one and laid it on his desk. She leaned forward, as he stuck a pair of black-rimmed reading glasses on and began to scan the folder.

"I forget names." He poked his finger at a piece of paper. "Ken Sullivan. That was his name."

"Are you sure?"

He looked at her over the top of his glasses. "I might not have a good memory, but I can read."

"Sorry. I didn't mean to imply you couldn't."

He smiled. "Must be some fella for you to go to all this trouble to hunt him down."

"It might be important. I just don't know. What other information do you have about him?"

"I have his phone number. Never needed to use it. No address. Like I said, he paid in cash." He put down the file. "Might not be the same boat. Do you know anything else about the sloop?"

Jennifer pulled out her notepad where she'd written all the things she remembered that Rick had said about his sloop. "A big engine, a German name, Westerbeke, and something about refrigeration."

Bjorn smiled and tapped the file. "That's gotta be it. We installed a 42 -horsepower Westerbeke and a 130-amp alternator and a refrigeration compressor."

"Right! That's what he said." She reached for the file, but he pulled it away.

"Now you tell me the real reason you want his phone number." He leaned back in the chair and smiled. "Give an old guy something to think about other than how bad business is." He wagged his finger. "No big stories. I can smell a lie."

She'd wanted to avoid going into the details. How much should she tell him? Did it matter? She shrugged. "He came to my book store in Brandon when I wasn't there and asked about me. Then he showed up on my island and asked questions as if he didn't know anything about me."

Bjorn bit his lower lip. "Maybe he just wanted to get to know you. Maybe he had a crush on you from afar."

"If that was the case, why did he leave without telling me his real name or how I could get in touch with him?" She sat back in the chair. "Besides there's another reason for me to question his actions." Jennifer studied Bjorn and thought she could tell the man her story. What could it hurt? "My sister was murdered on the island two years ago. The killer was never caught."

Bjorn let out a whistle. "You think this guy had something to do with it?"

"No. Of course not." She hesitated. "Well, I don't know, but I'd like to talk to him and find out what he knows and why he acted so strange."

Bjorn tore off a piece of paper from a note pad and shoved the slip toward Jennifer. "That's his phone number or was. Hope you find him."

Jennifer took her wallet from her jacket pocket and pulled out her business card. As she handed it over to Bjorn, she said, "Please call if you think of anything else to tell me. Can I reach you here?"

"Yep." He pointed at the paper he'd given her. "My number's on the top.

Bjorn opened a canister on top of his file drawers and took out several cookies before walking outside. He held a cookie out to Lydia, but she turned to look at her mistress.

"Doesn't like sweets, huh?" Bjorn said with a frown and stuck the cookie in his own mouth.

"No, that's not it." Jennifer said. "I've trained her not to accept food from strangers."

He nodded as he chewed. "You're a careful one, aren't you? Here." He handed another one to Jennifer. "You give it to her."

She did and Lydia made short work of it.

"Ha. That's like a sample of a taste for you," he said and rubbed the dog behind the ears, then gazed at Jennifer. "I'd like to help you. I'll keep my eyes and ears open. Bars around the port are like sieves. Plenty of odd bits of info float around."

Before she turned to leave, she asked, "I gather from a sign I saw that you once chartered boats."

"Did till last year. Insurance got too high, too much overhead, so I sold 'em." He peered in the direction of the abandoned sign. "Guess I should toss it out."

They shook hands and Jennifer and Lydia walked away. Back in the jeep, her cell phone rang. She saw the number was Emma Mae's and ignored it. Instead, she dialed Ken Sullivan's number. After four rings a recording clicked on. "Sullivan Investigative Agency. Please leave a short message, name and a number where you can be reached, and Mr. Sullivan will get back to you as soon as possible." The voice was unfamiliar.

She hung up. Hugging Lydia's massive head for reassurance, she wondered about Ken pretending to be Rick. "If he's a private investigator, who is he working for, and what does he want from me?" she asked out loud.

Chapter 8

Jennifer remained in her jeep debating whether she should tell Bjorn what she'd just learned about Ken Sullivan. After deciding it didn't concern him, she started the engine and felt a hint of nostalgia as she drove by the battered sign *Bjorn Boat Charters* lying in the weeds. For years her family had chartered boats when they had a large group visit the island. That arrangement had been more cost effective than owning a boat.

In route to Brandon, the similar descriptions of Eric and Ken rolled through her mind. They had to be the same person, but she needed to be certain. But how? The direct approach would be simplest, but perhaps not the best. If the man calling himself Rick was actually Ken, then he'd already lied to her. What both irked and intrigued her was the deception.

With the sun sliding down to the horizon, the ocean's whitecaps had eased. Gold strands shimmered across the graying sea. Lydia hung her head out the window, her nostrils expanding with wondrous smells only she could detect.

"Okay," Jennifer said in a firm voice. Lydia turned to look at her mistress with her big sad eyes. "This is what we'll do. I'll disguise my voice. If he's not in, I'll leave a time for him to call my cell phone." She thought a moment and Lydia again stuck her head out the window. Jennifer ignored her dog's disinterest in her conversation and continued, "I've got to tweak his interest, sound desperate. Once he agrees to see me, I'll suggest a public place, so I can watch unobserved." She smiled and slapped her hand against the steering wheel. "Yes!"

Lydia barked.

"Right you are, girl! We've got a plan."

After returning to her house, she donned sweats and running shoes, and in the purple cast of early evening, she ran through the hills overlooking the ocean. Unleashed, Lydia loped ahead, sniffing at bushes. A startled covey of quail streaked for the sky. Jennifer ran through familiar trails thinking about the new events: finding the book, the imprint of an Einstein paper, Rick's sudden appearance and his deception, Alex's reappearance, and the news of Joe's leaving town for a new job. Sweat poured off her brow, not all caused by physical exertion.

After returning to the house, Jennifer showered, put on a brown pantsuit, fed Lydia, and nuked a stroganoff microwave dinner. She groaned as she glanced at the clock. Walking to the shop was out. In order to relieve Emma Mae for the evening six to nine shift, she'd have to drive. Her aunt had done yeoman duty at the store lately, and Jennifer needed to take her share of hours. Rinsing the few dishes in the sink, she grabbed a jacket and hurried out with Lydia leading the way to the car.

At six fifteen, she parked behind the store and hurried through the back door. She stopped by the office and stashed her purse in the desk drawer. Taking a deep breath, she headed to the front.

"You're all damp and flushed like a wet rose," Emma Mae said, gazing at Jennifer with interest.

Two customers were skimming through magazines, and one was wandering through the mystery section. Lydia nudged her massive head against Emma Mae's thigh in greeting.

"You big galoot. Go say hello to Crabapple and Maxie. They've been pining for you more than I have." Emma Mae brushed at her ankle-length blue skirt, but smiled as Lydia settled into a corner by the front window. The cats immediately turned their attention to the dog. Although both cats were at least seven years old, they acted as if they were kittens around Lydia. Lydia remained stoic, acted bored by the cats playfulness and batted at them with her immense paw when they got too rambunctious.

"Sorry I'm late." Jennifer gave her aunt a light kiss on the cheek.

"Tried to call you this afternoon," Emma Mae said. "Didn't you get my message?"

"Sorry, I was in the Seattle library and had turned it off." She was getting good at lying. They stood at the counter by the cash register speaking softly, so they wouldn't disturb the customers.

"I wanted to ask if you'd take my shift on Saturday, the 15th. I'm going to a party."

Jennifer groaned. "I can't. The Wedgeworths invited me to their open house." After a quick look at her aunt's surprised expression, she said, "Saturday? The Wedgeworths? You, too?"

Her aunt beamed and nodded. "Yes, I'm excited." She took Jennifer's arm and guided her to the back office before confiding, "I haven't seen Clifford in twelve years."

"You know him?"

Emma Mae grinned like the Cheshire cat.

"Why didn't you tell me you knew him when I got the offer to appraise his books?"

"If I had, you'd think I put him up to it, and you'd get defensive. You might even have turned down the assignment," Emma Mae said.

Arms akimbo, Jennifer asked, "Did you put him up to it?"

Emma Mae straightened her narrow shoulders. "I just said I hadn't seen him or talked to him in twelve years." Her voice rose, then lowered. "I worked for him when I lived in Seattle. Clifford's always known where I moved to, but he never contacted me after… well … Let's just leave it at that."

"Leave it at what?" Jennifer leaned forward. "Just how well did you know him?" she whispered.

"None of your business." Emma Mae pulled back and raised her chin. "I wasn't always a sixty-two-year-old lady."

"I know that. Mom always said you were the beauty in the family. And you still are! You've got to tell me about …."

"This is no time to talk about my past." Emma Mae's words snapped like a tortoise's bite. "We'll close the store that day." She paused, then added, "Or bring in extra help like we did last Christmas."

"We could do that," Jennifer said, then turned the conversation back to Wedgeworth. "Does he know I'm your business partner?"

Emma Mae shrugged. "I doubt it. Our last names are different, so how would he know? Don't make a big to-do over a simple invitation."

Jennifer thought she wasn't making a big deal of it, but her aunt was. For a moment she thought of telling Emma Mae about finding Carla's book in Wedgeworth's collection, but cast aside the idea. Some things were better left unsaid. This particular news would only rekindle arguments about Alex and renew pain from the old tragedy.

Emma Mae said, "It will be grand to visit the Wedgeworth house and see Cliff again." She leaned on the desk, tapping her fingers on its top. "I have to leave. I promised my book group I'd meet them at Tucker's for dinner. Oh, I almost forgot. We have to order calendars for next year, and

Mrs. Buffington asked for Patrick Taylor's new book. I said I'd order it, but didn't get to it. Would you be a dear and do it?"

As Emma Mae placed paperwork in an orderly stack, Jennifer wondered about her aunt's past. Just how well had she known Clifford Wedgeworth? It probably didn't have any bearing on Carla's book, but Jennifer had begun to believe that every bit of news connected with Wedgeworth might relate to the murder.

"I fed the cats." Emma Mae hurried on with her explanations. "And I cleaned the litter box, so they're set for the night." She walked to the back office and returned with her large purple purse under her arm. When she neared Jennifer, she whispered, "Call your mother when you get a chance. She's in one of her moods. If you'd listen to your messages, you'd know that's why I called you earlier. Just remember she didn't hear the story from me."

"What story?" Jennifer frowned. "What are you talking about?"

Emma Mae chuckled, waved, and left by the front door.

Chapter 9

The evening hours at the store went smoothly. Lydia lolled on the floor in a corner by the mystery section, ignoring the pestering cats. The front door bell dinged as customers came and went. Jennifer did not call her mother even though she knew she'd pay for her omission eventually. At nine o'clock the store emptied, and she prepared to close for the night. Crabapple jumped onto the counter to establish her place of authority, while Maxie curled up in the chair recently warmed by a corpulent patron.

With Lydia by her side, Jennifer left, locking the backdoor behind her. Her breath fogged from the cold as she gazed at the star-filled sky with its glorious waxing moon. With Lydia in the backseat, Jennifer got in and searched for a rag she kept under the front seat. Unable to find it, she wiped the condensation off the windshield with her sleeve Back home she fussed in the kitchen, changed Lydia's water, and pulled a strawberry yogurt from the fridge, all the while, mulling over the call she planned to make to Ken Sullivan. She dithered, spooning the yogurt out in languid motions, then stared at the empty yogurt carton. "Get to it, wimp," she scolded herself.

In the bathroom she rummaged through a drawer until she found some cotton balls. She stuck them in her lower lip and practiced a high-pitched voice. "Hello. This is Doris Parker." She stared at her image in the mirror and shook her head, then repeated her lines. "Hello. This is Doris Parker." She spit out the cotton and took the rest into the living room.

Lydia padded over and sniffed the cotton, then put her massive head in her mistress's lap. "It's okay, girl. This is just an act." *And it better be a good one.* She stuffed fresh cotton into her mouth and called Ken Sullivan's phone number. Her palms grew moist waiting for him to answer. Eventually, an answering machine came on. Relieved she didn't need to talk to him directly, she left her message.

"This is Doris Parker. I need help finding my brother. I don't want my husband to know I'm calling you, and he's out tonight. So please call me tonight no matter how late." She left her cell phone number, hung up and prayed Ken checked his messages frequently. If he didn't, he might call back when she wasn't prepared.

Jennifer took the cotton out of her mouth and placed her cell phone on the coffee table. Nervous exhaustion enveloped her. She turned on the stereo, filling the room with Mozart's music. Unable to concentrate on the novel she'd been reading, she stretched out on the couch and dozed off.

When her cell phone played *Don't Fence Me In*, she woke with a start and muted the stereo, then jammed the cotton into her mouth before answering. She glanced at the clock. A few minutes before eleven. Steadying her nerves, she grabbed her cell phone and clicked the on button. "Hello."

"This is Ken Sullivan. I'd like to speak to Doris Parker, please," the voice said.

Was this Rick's voice? She couldn't tell.

"Thanks for getting back to me right away," she said in an artificially high voice, muffled by cotton that made it sound like she had a cold. She explained that her husband didn't want her to file a missing person's report on her brother. After giving him more details, they agreed to meet at Sally's Kitchen in Seattle tomorrow at two o'clock. "How will I know you?"

"I'll wear a white cable knit sweater. Describe yourself, so I'll know who to look for."

She caught her breath, and hesitated before saying, "I'll wear a University of California sweatshirt."

He laughed. "That could get you arrested in Seattle. See you then."

After hanging up, she went over the conversation, his intonations, his speech, but she couldn't be sure if the voice was Rick's.

Emotionally drained, she went to bed and slept fitfully. The phone awakened her. With bleary eyes she noted the sun was up and the clock read seven fifteen. For a moment she thought it might be Ken calling again, but realized the ringing came from her home phone. Gingerly, she picked up the receiver and heard her mother's voice.

"Hi, Mom. Kind of early to be calling, isn't it?" She tried to put enthusiasm into her voice, but didn't quite meet the task. "Yes, I got your message, but the store was so busy that I didn't have a chance to call you. When I got home, I just collapsed." She listened as she rose from bed and stuck her feet into warm wooly slippers. "I am not making excuses." Of course, she was making excuses. She always did when she talked to her mother. Jennifer relaxed back on her bed, stretched, and pulled a comforter over herself. This was going to be one of those long calls.

She listened and listened and said, "Um" and "I understand" about ten times. When her mother accused her of neglecting her father and her, Jennifer moved the phone away from her ear.

"We want to know about your new boyfriend," her mother said after she'd exhausted all other small talk.

That stopped Jennifer. Did she mean Joe?

"Remember when Carla had a new beau, and she wouldn't tell us about him? The only thing she told us was that he wasn't from Brandon and was suave. You two are just alike. Well, your father and I think you'd want to tell us about him."

"Excuse me? What you're talking about?"

"Don't lie to me, Jennifer. It's all over town. A young man asked about you. Now, the only reason a man does that is if he's interested in you. You can't deny that."

Of course she could deny it, for it wasn't remotely true in the sense her mother meant. "Mother, I assure you there's no new man in my life. You've been listening to town gossip again." And wishful thinking, Jennifer thought. With her mother, denial was never an end game, but a circle. "I'm sorry you're upset, but there isn't anyone. Alex is visiting next week, and I'm meeting him in Seattle." As soon as she said it, she was sorry.

"How could you meet him? How dare you even speak of him? You know very well he had an affair with Carla while engaged to you."

"That's your assumption." Her bitter reply echoed through her bedroom.

As usual her mother ignored her retort. "You can't possibly have anything to do with him. He killed your sister and dumped you."

"Mother, you're overreacting. You always have."

"What will people think, you taking up with Alex again?"

"I'm not taking up with him again. I'm meeting him for a drink."

"People will talk. You don't care about your father and me. You only think about yourself." Her whine became a shriek.

Jennifer held the phone from her ear, struggling to suppress her anger. There was no easy way to end the conversation, so Jennifer apologized and hung up. Afterward, she groaned and covered her eyes with her forearm.

Mothers were supposed to be a happy part of your life, but hers was like heavy shrink-wrap. She'd always been possessive and excessively critical, but Carla's murder had made her mother more controlling. Even her dad had changed, becoming more of a recluse, and to be honest, her sister's death had changed Jennifer too.

Until Joe came into her life, Jennifer's normal easy-going manner had turned rigid, and suspicion ruled her days and she still had to fight her paranoia of strangers. Hadn't she regarded Rick as an unwelcome intruder when he'd arrived on the island? But in his case, her behavior had been justified.

Her hope for a day in the backcountry with Joe was dashed by her appointment with Rick, or was his name Ken? She called Joe. "Hi," she said when he answered. "I figured you'd be up. I need to go to Seattle today."

"That's rotten. The weather's great for a hike up through Glendale Pass," he said. "Not often we'll get a chance like this, but if you can't, you can't."

"Thanks for understanding. It's an important meeting."

"You taking Lydia?"

"No. I'll leave her in the backyard. I don't want to burden Emma Mae further."

"I can take Lydia. It'd be good for her and I can get my dog fix for the week."

"Hey, that would be great. You're her favorite person."

"Does that go for her mistress too?"

She laughed, then said, "Looking for a compliment, huh?"

"I take them where I can get them."

"You spoil Lydia and me, so naturally we have to feed your ego." She felt the smile on her lips and sighed. "I won't be leaving until noon. When do you want to pick her up?"

"In about an hour. I'll drop her at your place afterward. You know how my apartment manager is about pets."

"Okay. See you soon."

After she hung up, she felt better. Talking to Joe seemed to do that to her.

They'd kept their affair discrete and not even her family had any idea about their relationship. This was no easy task in a town of 15,000. Early on they'd agreed that they'd keep a low profile. Their relationship so far had been uncomplicated, but lately Joe seemed to want a more permanent arrangement. She desperately wanted that too, but before she could commit, she needed to find the killer.

While she waited for Joe, she cleaned the house. Lydia's barking alerted her to his truck pulling into the driveway. Jennifer let Lydia out and watched as her dog slobbered a warm greeting on Joe's well worn jeans. Jennifer walked out and gave him a hug. "New hat," she said, pushing his cap back from his forehead.

His face broke into a warm smile. "Yeah. My brother-in-law sent it. He expects everyone to be a Chicago Bears' fan."

She laughed. "It matches your jacket, but don't let a diehard Seahawk's fan catch you in it."

He shrugged. "If I wear it to a game, I'll put on my armor." He took off his hat and encircled her in his arms. "Are you sure you can't come?"

"Unfortunately, it's important or I wouldn't cancel." After a quick kiss, she gave him a playful push and stepped away. "I have a bone to pick with you."

"Oh, what did I do?"

She leaned against the truck's front fender. "Clarence told me you got a job in Bellingham."

He fiddled with the side mirror. "I was going to tell you."

"Promotion? Better salary? Opportunity for advancement?"

He nodded. "All of those. I'll be in charge of private security for a large telecom company. It's the best offer I've had since I got my Master's." He gazed at her with a puppy dog look that made her heart melt. "You knew I wanted more than be a small town cop."

"I know and I'm happy for you." She grabbed his hand. "but damn it, I'll miss you."

"I was hoping you might consider joining me. A new town, new people, a new start."

"I'd love to, but I need to clear my name. Everywhere I go, I get Carla's murder thrown in my face. People are suspicious. I'd ruin your career."

"We could handle it together." He drew her to him.

"I won't do that to you. You deserve better." She hugged him hard, then pulled back and said what they both knew. "Joe, I can't. God, how I wish I could."

"I thought we might have a chance for something permanent."

"You've got to think of your career. Bellingham's not that far away. We can meet somewhere in between here, there, or the island."

"It won't be the same and you know it."

"We said we'd keep things light between us, no ties until I clear up Carla's murder."

"I know that's what we said, but what about the future? Do we have one together?"

She stepped farther away. What future did she have? At times she wanted to give up and become a hermit and say to hell with everything. But she couldn't. She wasn't made that way. She was a fighter. "I've got to see this through to the end."

"Is there an end? Do you know how many murder cases go unsolved? Hundreds." His blue eyes seemed to penetrate her defensive wall. He pulled her close. "Leaving you behind is going to be tough, but I need to get on with my life."

She leaned back to study his face as if it were the last time she'd see it. "When are you leaving?" Her heart skipped a few beats waiting for his reply.

"A month. I'll leave the force in three weeks."

"So soon?" The loss of Joe would be terrible, but she'd gotten in the habit of blotting out the future. Then she thought of Alex and blurted out, "I need to tell you something." Why did she feel uncomfortable telling him about Alex? "You'll hear about it anyway."

He put his arm around her shoulder. "Okay. Shoot."

She couldn't help but smile at his cavalier attitude. "I love that about you."

"What?" He frowned and a lock of his sandy hair fell across his freckled forehead.

She pushed it back under his cap. "Your attitude about things." She sighed. "Alex is back. In Seattle. I'm going to meet him after a party at the Wedgeworth's estate on the 15th."

"I see."

"Do you?" She searched his face.

"It's not as if you plan to take up with him again, is it?"

"Absolutely not. Besides, he's married."

"Okay. Anything else?"

"So much has happened quickly. I don't know where to start. I think I found Carla's book. It's in Wedgeworth's collection."

He pulled back to study her. "The guy whose collection you're appraising?"

She nodded.

"That's fantastic. Is there anything I can do?"

"Not about that, but I wanted to let you know about a fellow who showed up on the island. I think he's the same one who's been in town asking about me."

"What's he like? Give me his name and I'll run a check on him."

"Not yet. I'll know more today."

He cocked his head and added, "That's your appointment?"

"Good guess, Sherlock."

"Look, Jen, you might be getting in over your head. Don't stick your neck out too far, okay. It's a very lovely neck." He stroked the side of her cheek, then embraced her.

His arms gave her comfort, and she lifted her face to enjoy the passion of his warm, moist lips. She wanted to drown in his kisses.

After a time, he whispered in her ear. "You don't leave till noon, and I can leave anytime." He glanced at Lydia, who sat a few feet away watching them. "I don't think she'd mind some alone time in the yard."

At least he wasn't going to dump her like Alex had. It wasn't in Joe's nature to run from trouble, but she had to make him see that rescuing her was not in his best interest.

He nuzzled her neck, then stroked her cheek. "How about it?"

She gave him an impish grin. "I love you, you big lug." She took his hand, and they walked toward the house.

Chapter 10

On her drive to Seattle, Jennifer thought about the recent events that muddled her once normal life: Joe's imminent departure, Alex's surprise arrival, and the coming meeting with Ken, or was he really Rick?

She gripped the steering wheel tighter and tried to absorb the calm feeling of the ocean and the waves that straggled into shore like reluctant visitors. But her thoughts reverted to her problems. Joining Joe and leaving the past behind would make her feel like a traitor to her sister's memory, yet she longed to do just that. She sighed. Dreams. Nonsense. The impossible.

When she arrived at the restaurant, the lunch crowd had thinned. She carried the University of California sweatshirt and took a table in the corner where she could see the entrance. She ordered a sandwich, but found she couldn't eat. She watched and waited. Minutes ticked toward the appointed time. About ten minutes before the hour, she spotted him. It was Rick. She lowered her head and picked up her sandwich to cover her face. She watched until he was seated several booths away with his back to her. "Okay," she muttered under her breath. "I got him, now reel him in." She laid money on the table to pay her bill and strode to his booth.

"Hello Rick," she said, standing over him. She placed the sweatshirt on the table with the University of California lettering facing him. "Or should I call you Ken?"

His shoulders stiffened, his gray eyes widened, then narrowed, and his lips drew back in a grimace. "Very clever. How did you trace me?"

"I'm the one who has the questions. Why did you come after me on the island?" Her voice was louder than she'd intended. She remained standing, her hands clutching her small purse.

"I didn't come after you, as you say." He glanced around at the people nearby who gawked at them and he motioned to the seat opposite him. "Sit down before you cause a scene. And yes, you can call me Ken."

"Oh?" She arched her eyebrow. "That's your real name, not another alias?" She slipped into the booth, but kept her eyes glued to his face. "You came after me. You went to my store and asked questions. You knew all about me before you came to the island. You knew about my sister's murder. Why come to my island and interrogate me about information you already had?"

He leaned back. "I didn't interrogate you. I thought I was friendly, brought you a fresh caught salmon. I even helped with a few chores. Now you're mad at me?"

"Damn right. Don't treat me like a simpleton. I want to know why you came to my island."

He shrugged. "I have a client who wanted to know what you were like, not just your background. Your personality and your character were important to my client. There was only one way to find out, and that was to visit you."

"You could have done that at my store."

He shook his head. "I would have preferred to meet you somewhere other than your holy island, but the time factor didn't allow that."

"So who's your client?"

He sneered and shook his head. "I never divulge a client's name. I do have professional ethics."

"Oh? They don't show."

He leaned forward, his forearms on the table, his face only a foot from hers. "Don't act so snippy. I run a business. I'm good at what I do and I do it well. I ruffled your pride. For that I'm sorry."

She felt her face flush and she had the urge to slap him. "You stirred up memories of my sister's murder, pretending you knew nothing about it. That was unnecessary and unkind."

"You might think so, but I needed to see how you'd react under pressure." He leaned back again and raised his chin, studying her. "Maybe I should hire you. How did you find me? Did I leave a clue?"

"Your very special boat."

"Ah, I see." He twirled his water glass on the table and gazed at her. "I should have thought of that, but then I doubted you'd care about a stranger visiting your island."

She grasped her hands together on the table. "Questioning my aunt was not a good idea."

He tilted his head to one side and raised an eyebrow. "I had to start somewhere. Tell me, who did you talk to about my sloop?"

"I don't give out my sources."

He laughed—a guttural sound. "Touché!"

Jennifer struggled to remain calm, but her anger seeped out. "You tell me who your client is, and I'll tell you who my source is."

"I don't make bargains when I know the answer."

She realized Ken would know that Bjorn was her source. Who else could have told her? She began to piece together what Ken had told her about how his client had wanted to know about her character. There was only one answer.

"I don't have to bargain either," she said. "I'm quite sure Clifford Wedgeworth is or was your client."

His fingers uncurled from around his glass, and he slipped his hands under the table. Despite his bland gaze, she knew she'd scored.

For a heartbeat they glared at each other, then he said, "I can't imagine how you can jump to such a conclusion."

She smiled, feeling vindicated. "Not a big leap. I'm doing an appraisal of his book collection and naturally he'd want to know about me."

His eyes flickered in annoyance, then his face settled into a bland expression. "Interesting," he said, but his body language spoke more.

That information had surprised him. "Well, I don't mean all of them. Just some of his recently acquired books. He's quite a bibliophile." Ken seemed less cocky. Somehow Jennifer had jarred him, but she wasn't sure why. "Don't you ask your clients why they want information about someone?"

"Not always. That way my clients' secrets remain theirs, not mine."

"Very ethical of you, I'm sure." There didn't seem to be anything left to say. She stood, but he grabbed her wrist before she could leave.

"Be careful, Jennifer. I don't want you to get hurt. Don't wallow in the past. Enjoy your life, your dog, your island, and all the things that make you happy."

Their eyes met. His words felt like a threat. She looked down at his hand and he released his hold. "My sister's murder changed my life," she said and then added in a barely audible voice. "Now, finding her murderer is my life." She turned and left the restaurant, feeling his eyes boring into her back.

On her drive home she thought of Ken's threatening words and his involvement with Wedgeworth. Did he know about the book that Wedgeworth had in his collection? Did any of this relate to Carla's death? So many questions and no answers.

When she drove into her driveway, Joe's truck was parked off to the side and he was hosing Lydia off in the front yard. She called out as she got out of her car, "What happened?"

Lydia barked, wagged her tail and tried to extricate herself from Joe's grip. "I hiked along the beach instead of Glendale pass. She got sandy." He finished hosing the Newfie, toweled her off and released her. Lydia shook vigorously and ran over to Jennifer with Joe right behind with the soddened towel.

"You got more than you bargained for." Jennifer laughed, feeling a release of her pent up emotions from her conversation with Ken. "Come on in." They left Lydia on the porch.

"Do you want a beer?" She asked over her shoulder, as she went into the kitchen.

"Great." He followed her and leaned against the counter. "How did the meeting go?"

She handed him his beer and then poured out kibbles for Lydia. "Tell you in a minute. Let me feed her first."

When she returned, Joe was seated on the couch in the living room. She sat next to him and put her head on his shoulder. "I'm bushed."

Silence folded over them. He took her hand and massaged her fingers. "You have an artist's hands, long fingers."

"Callouses from paddling," she interrupted him. "You know," Jennifer straightened, "that's what bothers me about this guy, Ken."

"Who's Ken?"

"He's the fellow who came out to the island. Only then he called himself Rick." She sat up. "Okay, let me start from the beginning."

After she'd finished, he asked, "How did you find out how to get hold of Sullivan if you didn't know his correct name?"

"Boy, just like a cop. I guess I didn't tell you about Bjorn." After she explained how she'd tracked down Ken, she asked, "What do you think?"

"I think you're a heck of a detective. But I don't like it. Why would this guy Sullivan go to the trouble of sailing to the island and then pretend he didn't know you were there?"

"He explained that."

"Does it make sense to you?" He took a swallow of beer.

"I'm not sure. I'm going to Wedgeworth's party on the fifteenth and I'll ask Wedgeworth why all the mystery about checking up on me."

"I'll run a check on Bjorn and Sullivan and let you know what I find." He turned to look at her. "You seem intrigued by Ken. Is he good looking?"

"Very, in a dark brooding way."

He shook his head. "Whatever that means."

"It means, don't be jealous."

"Yeah." He put the bottle on the table and pulled her to him.

She felt safe and rejoiced in the passion, forgetting Ken, Bjorn, and the muddle of a lost and found book.

Chapter 11

Throughout Thursday, customers dashed in and out of the store, taking refuge from the heavy rain showers. Rivulets streamed down the store's windowpanes. As always, Jennifer and Emma Mae offered tea and a listening ear to their customers while suggesting a good read, but both women were glad to close at five o'clock, their normal Thursday schedule. They used the time to review sales and new orders and nurture one another.

Lydia sprawled in the doorway, while the cats nosed about the store. Normally, Jennifer delighted in the animals antics, but not today. "Go sleep somewhere else," she said, shooing Crabapple off her desk. Lydia glanced at her mistress, then put her head between her paws.

"You've been in a snit all week," Emma Mae said, as she poured herself a cup of tea from the pot steeping on the hot plate in the corner. "Want to tell me what's wrong?"

Jennifer blew on her hands. "Nervous about the Wedgeworths' party this Saturday," she lied.

Emma Mae placed her teacup on the small table next to the overstuffed chair where Maxie had settled. She picked up Maxie, sat, and put the cat on her lap. "Why don't we go to the party together?"

Jennifer bowed her head over the papers in front of her. "Sorry, I've got an engagement afterward."

"Oh? Your mystery man or someone else?"

"Who are you talking about?" Jennifer frowned and put down her pencil.

"You know, the dark handsome young man who came in asking about you."

Jennifer shoved away from the desk. "He's no longer a mystery man. I should have told you. He's Ken Sullivan, a private detective, hired by Clifford Wedgeworth."

"Good heavens. Why would he do that?"

"To be sure I was reliable, I guess." Jennifer fiddled with a pen. "And that means your Mr. Wedgeworth probably knows I'm your niece."

"He's not my Mr. Wedgeworth." Emma Mae picked up the cup and took a sip. "I hope that's not why Clifford invited me to this party. But I must admit that after all these years his invitation did seem odd." She stared into her teacup, then looked at the far end of the room as if brooding. "No matter." She abruptly set her cup down. "I want to see him again."

"Just what was your relationship with him?" Jennifer cupped her chin in her palms, her elbows on the desk top.

Emma Mae shrugged and remained silent for a while, stroking Maxie.

"I don't mean to pry," Jennifer said.

"Yes, you do." She studied her niece, then said, "But I trust you not to tell anyone else." She leaned back, stroking Maxie. "I loved him. But it wouldn't have worked. He was married and had a reputation to uphold. I decided that the best thing for me was to leave town."

Jennifer grinned. "Emma Mae, I knew you must have hidden secrets. Mother always alluded to your scandalous youth. Glad you had more to your life than this bookstore."

"I never did anything scandalous. I just enjoyed living which is more than I can say for your mother. My relationship with Clifford is not something one brags about." Emma Mae continued to caress the purring cat. "Clifford lent me the money to buy this building and start the bookstore." Her lips pursed. "Don't get the wrong idea. I've paid back every penny. But there were other reasons he lent me the money."

"Ethics has always been one of your priorities. I know that." Jennifer reflected for a moment. "But his wife died, didn't she?"

"Yes, but that was five years later. I called him. We spoke, but I could hear it in his voice. For him, our time was passé."

Jennifer thumbed the end of a note pad trying to seem nonchalant, but her curiosity was in high gear. "You must have been furious, frustrated, even vengeful."

"All of those things, but disappointed ranked as my main emotion. Perhaps it had never been true love. If it had, we could have overcome anything. I'm still very fond of him, despite what I know about him."

"Does my mother know about your relationship?"

Emma Mae continued to stroke Maxie. "She might have had a suspicion, but never asked. And if she had, I'd have denied it. You know how Eleanor's tongue wags."

"Do I every," Jennifer said. Her aunt's confession about Wedgeworth forced her to a decision. She took a deep breath. "Since you know Clifford, and you're going to the party, I think I'd better tell you what I've learned. When I appraised Wedgeworth's collection, I found the book Carla had with her the day she was killed."

Emma Mae stopped petting Maxie. "Are you sure?"

"Very. Remember, it was an autographed copy of Raymond Chandler's *The Big Sleep*. It had come from the Helen Jacobi estate. On the dust jacket, I found the initials H.J., and on the end page, I found partial imprints from a letter from Albert Einstein to a Lotti Jacobi. From what I've learned, Helen Jacobi may have been related to Lotti." She hesitated before adding, "It could be that the book is worth more because of Einstein's signature. The other option is that it wasn't the book the killer wanted, but what was in the book."

"But wouldn't Carla have found the letter and said something?"

"That baffles me too, but I'm sure I'm on the right track."

"Wait a minute. You don't think Clifford killed Carla?"

Jennifer shook her head. "No, I don't. With his money he could easily have afforded to buy it or whatever was inside. If I learn the provenance of Wedgeworth's book, then I might have a clue to the killer."

Emma Mae's hand went to her mouth. "Oh my, Jennifer. You might be getting yourself into something dangerous. Maybe you need the services of that private detective."

"No way. He's a liar." Jennifer knew her anger with Ken stemmed from his visit to her island under false pretenses. He was obviously a good detective and must have a good reputation if Wedgeworth hired him. Still?

"Why don't you call Clifford and ask him how he got the book?" Emma Mae said.

"I've tried. He's been back over a week and I've left messages on his answering machine, but he hasn't returned my calls. I even questioned the messenger who brought my payment for the appraisal." She rolled a pencil between her fingers. "And that's another thing. Why did Wedgeworth pay me in cash?"

"I'm sure he had a practical reason." Emma Mae frowned. "He always was very exact about business; competitive, but exact. He was big on record keeping." Again she stroked Maxie. "I hope he hasn't gone senile. He was so virile." She blushed to the roots of her gray hair.

"Wow." Jennifer grinned. "You are full of surprises, aren't you?"

"I've said enough." Emma Mae refused to meet Jennifer's gaze. Instead, she seemed to be very involved with Maxie's paws.

Realizing she shouldn't push further, Jennifer said, "I need to talk with Wedgeworth at the party, so I can ask him about the book. I might need your help to get him alone. If necessary, can I count on you?"

Emma Mae squirmed in her chair, unsettling Maxie. "I suppose, but I'm sure he'll tell you how he got the book. Perhaps, you're upset and too anxious to get information. After all, he did just get back from his honeymoon."

Was Emma Mae right? Was she losing her perspective? Absentmindedly, Jennifer ran her fingers through her hair as she thought of her motives. Alex's words had stuck in her mind these past two years. *Find the book, and you'll find the murderer.* To solve Carla's murder, she needed to learn the provenance of the book. Either the book's value or the value of the letter with Einstein's signature had to be the motive behind the murder. How much money was enough to kill for?

Emma Mae lifted Maxie off her lap and set her on the floor. "I'm glad you told me about the book and all." She stood, looking at Jennifer. "I've been forthcoming about Clifford. What about you? Who are you meeting after the party? Alex?"

Jennifer doodled on the pad in front of her. "Mother told you, right? I shouldn't have told her I was seeing him, but she got me so upset, I just blurted it out. Yes, I agreed to meet him for dinner. But he doesn't know I'm going to be at the Wedgeworths. I wanted to surprise him."

"That's a meeting I want to see," Emma Mae said over her shoulder, as she went to wash out her cup in the restroom. When she returned to the office, she stood next to Jennifer and put her hand on her niece's shoulder. "You be careful around Alex. I know you think he had nothing to do with Carla's death, but he was the last one to see her alive and he had a motive. Don't let your emotions blind you."

Chapter 12

The day before the party, Jennifer drove to a special beauty salon in Seattle to get her hair styled into a shoulder-length bob. Afterward she went shopping and bought a garnet-colored jersey dress with a scoop neck and an A-line skirt. She told herself that her decision to make a good appearance was to fit in with the Seattle crowd. Down deep she knew she wanted to prove to Alex that she hadn't withered away pining for him, that she was attractive, that her life had moved on. She'd changed. Had he? Would they have anything to talk about or would they be strangers?

Of course, Joe had noticed her new hair style and knew of her upcoming meeting with Alex. "It's okay, Jen," he'd said. "Sometimes you have to face the past to see the future, but don't throw away what we have unless you're certain where you're headed." His words had held the distinct flavor of a future together. Was she a fool for refusing to make a commitment?

The Wedgeworths must have had a weather angel, for the day of their party the rain abated with the temperature hovering in the mid-fifties. The drive to the estate was a far cry from the gray day of her first visit. The sun sparkled through the trees, and the fresh scent of wet earth lifted her spirits. Easing off the gas pedal, she drove through the gentle curves, enjoying the scenery. Water droplets clung to pine needles, and vines threading through twigs and limbs glistened like gossamer. The world felt soft, pure, vulnerable.

At the wrought iron entrance gate she stopped, as Harold, looking ill-at-ease in a black suit, greeted her at the open gate. "Nice to see you again, Miss Frost."

"Thank you. You're all dressed up for the occasion," Jennifer said.

Harold glanced down with a sour expression. "Mrs. Wedgeworth's idea." He pointed up the road. "A valet will take your car at the main house."

She drove on and left her jeep with an eager young man in a red vest. Several black vans with gold stenciling, denoting Blakely Catering, were parked at the side entrance. The manicured grass gleamed like an Irish glen, and fall flowers cascaded from large white pots set on either side of the arched main entryway. Flagstone steps led up to the door that was immediately opened by a butler. Talk and laughter from other guests drifted toward her as she handed her long black wool coat to a maid.

An thin, tall man with a sallow complexion and a receding hairline moved to her side and introduced himself as Warren Peabody, Mr. Wedgeworth's secretary. "Miss Frost," he said, checking a list he held. "The Wedgeworths are delighted you could come. You'll find the other guests in the living room. We are serving wine and champagne, but if you wish a special drink, just ask one of the servers." He escorted her down the hall of tapestry-covered walls. A thick oriental rug deadened the sound that in her earlier visit had echoed off the white marble floor. He left her at the entrance to the sunken living room. Momentarily, she stared after him as he returned to his post by the front door. His manner was slightly effeminate, and his gangly frame tilted and hitched as if he were out of step to a musical beat.

At the top of the three steps that led down to the living room, she surveyed the party goers. It didn't take long to spot the Wedgeworths. Newspaper photos hadn't done Clifford Wedgeworth justice. He was tall, tan, and trim with thick white hair. His younger wife was at his side, dressed in a royal blue cocktail dress that clung to her well-endowed body. Her long blonde hair fell over one side of her face like a Veronica Lake imitation and her vibrant deep blue eyes sparkled, enhancing plain facial features. The couple worked the room, greeting their guests with a combination of laughter and cordiality. As if Clifford felt Jennifer's eyes on him, he looked up, but it was obvious he didn't recognize her. Hadn't Ken shown him a picture of her?

Jennifer stepped down into the room and moved to meet the couple. "I'm Jennifer Frost. You hired me to—"

"Ah," Mr. Wedgeworth interrupted and turned to his wife. "Jennifer Frost I believe is a friend of yours, Cynthia."

Cynthia Wedgeworth glanced at her husband with a fleeting look of dismay followed by a frown. "No, I don't believe we've met," she said, extending her hand.

"Oh, of course, just through correspondence then," Mr. Wedgeworth said as he studied his wife.

"I don't know what you're talking about, Cliff." Her smile was stiff. "It's nice of you to come. I enjoy meeting Cliff's friends. Please make yourself at home."

"Best wishes on your marriage," Jennifer said to them.

"Thank you," Wedgeworth said, then gazed around the room. "I hope you'll find the company stimulating. My doctor is here as well as a few city officials. Have you met any of them?"

She shook her head as she looked over the crowd. Then she noticed a man she had meet two years ago, Roger Johns, Assistant Chief of Police. Her dealings with him brought back bad memories. He was holding court over a group of avid listeners.

"And the Mayor is over there," Wedgeworth nodded with his head toward a white-haired gentleman, talking to two distinguished men. "Would you like me to introduce you?"

"That's very kind of you, Mr. Wedgeworth—"

"Clifford, please," he again interrupted her.

She nodded and gripped her purse tighter. "I don't want to intrude on your enjoyment of the party, but could I speak with you privately for a few minutes? It's very important or I wouldn't be so forward. I'll be brief."

"For a lovely lady, I'll make the time."

A stooped elderly server, replete with the standard tuxedo and white gloves, proffered a small plate of crackers to Clifford Wedgeworth. "I was told to bring these to you, sir," he mumbled. "I understand they're a homemade favorite of yours."

"Oh, great," Clifford said, taking the plate from the man, who immediately left. "Darling," he said to his wife. "You made these cheese crackers special. How sweet." He leaned over and gave his wife a kiss on the cheek.

Cynthia frowned. "No. I…." She stopped in mid sentence when he held up his hand to signify nothing more needed to be said.

Clifford turned to Jennifer. "Can I persuade you to try one of my favorite cayenne crackers? They're quite spicy."

"I know. When I was here to appraise your books, Harold brought me some." Jennifer detected a flinty look in her host's eyes, but it passed quickly.

Clifford popped one into his mouth. While he chewed, he tilted his head and his eyes narrowed. After swallowing, he said to his wife, "The taste is different. Did you change the recipe?"

"No. I didn't know there were any left," Cynthia said.

"Maybe they're stale," he said, ignoring his wife's comment. He ate the last two with relish, put the empty plate on a side table and wiped his mouth with a paper cocktail napkin. "Now then, Miss Frost, isn't it? I'll see you in my library in about fifteen minutes." He hailed his secretary, who immediately responded and came to his side. "Would you unlock the library for Miss Frost."

"It's still unlocked from your visitor this afternoon. You said to allow him as much time as he wanted. I have had time to lock it once the guests started to arrive."

"I see. I didn't realize he'd spent that much time there," Clifford said. "Would you like to join Miss Frost and me, Cynthia?"

The woman's hand fluttered to her hair. "One of us has to tend to our guests." She tugged at his sleeve, obviously anxious to move on.

"The library's just down the hall on your right. But then you already know that, don't you?" Wedgeworth gave Jennifer a set smile, then took his wife's arm, and they moved off to speak with other guests.

Jennifer glanced at her watch. The crowd blurred as she mulled over the prospect that in fifteen minutes she'd learn the previous owner of Carla's copy. Another server came by with a tray of red or white wine, and she chose red. When she looked up, she spotted Alex, staring at her from across the room.

He looked tired, frazzled. His brown hair was longer than she'd remembered, and he'd grown a neatly trimmed, luxurious curly brown beard. It accentuated his high cheekbones and sharp nose. He seemed thinner, although still broad-shouldered. His dark eyes behind rimless glasses drowned her in a whirl of emotions. Her throat constricted. She watched, mesmerized, as he made his way through the crowd. When he stood in front of her, his charismatic smile, as usual, charmed her.

"Hello, Alex." Her voice sounded off key.

"Jennifer!" His eyes twinkled. He grasped her shoulders as if he were going to embrace her. She stiffened, and he dropped his hands to his side. "You're as beautiful as ever. You've a new hair style."

"A little different."

"Very chic."

"You've grown a beard."

He smiled. "And?" He stroked it. "What do you think?" He raised an eyebrow. "Be kind."

She tilted her head assessing him. "It fits you."

He straightened his shoulders. "It's so good to see you." He moved closer and raised his head. "You're not wearing L'air du Temps anymore."

She stepped back. "It no longer suited me." She noted his hurt expression.

They stood apart, saying nothing. Suddenly, the room seemed oppressive. She gripped the stem of her wine glass and with her other hand clung to her black purse, feeling its clasp dig into her palm.

Alex's eyes swept over her. "It's been too long. I've missed you, Jennifer. Why didn't you tell me you'd be here?"

"I wasn't sure I'd be coming," she lied and glanced around the room at the other guests deep in conversation.

"I've wanted to call you for some time." He rubbed one hand along the lapel of his blue sport coat. "To be frank, I didn't have the nerve." He glanced down at his shoes, then up into her eyes. "I know little has changed since.... I don't want to bring up the past, but.... Everything went wrong between us."

"It was inevitable. We both understood the barrier between us." She gritted her teeth, trying to forgive him for jilting her. The accusations of guilt that had assailed both of them had severed all hope of their ever remaining together. "Nothing's changed, at least not yet, but soon, things might be different.Again he moved closer as if he would whisper in her ear. "I've prayed the case would be solved."

Jennifer put out her hand, feeling the softness of his cashmere coat. This meeting wasn't going as she'd planned. Part of her wanted to fling her arms around his neck and let the past go, but the other part wanted revenge. Getting hold of herself, she asked, "How's your wife?"

His chin came up. "She divorced me after six months." His mouth twisted into a wry smile. "Said I was too boring. She went off with a stockbroker." He emitted a forced laugh. "Now that's got to be a boring profession." He shrugged. "I couldn't compete with his income."

She thought his being dumped was just retribution, but said, "I'm sorry."

"I'm not. Marrying her was the second worst mistake I ever made. My first was leaving you." He stared into Jennifer's eyes as if he were trying to memorize her image. "I should never have left you. I should have stayed and taken the flack with you. I should have—"

"Stop it!" Jennifer said, clenching the stem of her glass. "It's over. We both agreed. The situation was untenable. I've moved on."

He nodded slowly, never taking his eyes off her face. "Maybe we didn't make the right decision."

"We? It was your decision."

"Don't be this way, Jennifer."

"This is not the time or the place to review the past." Her anger and frustration spilled out, reflecting all the emotions she had suppressed about him over the last two years.

A slight commotion in the hall caught their attention, and they turned to see Emma Mae and Clifford greet one another in a boisterous hello and an embrace.

Alex frowned. "I didn't know they even knew one another. How many more of your family members are coming?"

"Don't worry. Just Emma Mae." Jennifer looked at her watch. "I don't mean to be rude, but I have to meet Mr. Wedgeworth in his library. I'll see you at the restaurant as planned." Before he could say another word, she placed her glass on a side table and made her way through the crowd. As she left the living room, she watched Emma Mae and Clifford chatting like old friends. His arm was tucked under hers as he gestured toward a tapestry. Her aunt's face glowed, and she looked years younger in a lavender wool suit and a superb makeup job. But there was something else. Jennifer smiled. Emma Mae had dyed her gray hair ash blond.

As Jennifer walked by the couple, she heard Clifford say, "You're still a classy lady, Emma Mae. I look at this woodland tapestry and often think of you and the old days."

Not wanting to interfere in Emma Mae's meeting with her old lover, Jennifer continued to the library. The door was ajar. Stepping inside, she went to the glass bookcase behind the desk and bent down, looking for *The Big Sleep*. She didn't see it. Thinking she'd been too hurried, she scanned the books again, using her index finger as a reference. Not possible. No, please, no, she prayed. It wasn't there. Her breathing came in gasps. Had it been moved? She searched through all the shelves behind the glass enclosure. Another book had been added to the bottom of the book case, one she hadn't researched. But the copy of *The Big Sleep* was gone.

"No!" Panic clutched at her. She spread her hands against the glass as if she could will the book's return. What had happened to it? A scuffing sound behind her caught her attention. She straightened up and spun around.

Clifford Wedgeworth staggered into the room, grabbing his stomach. "Sick. Get my doctor." He gagged, slammed into the door and crashed to the floor.

Chapter 13

After Jennifer called for help, the scene became chaotic. She stood aside as the doctor bent over Wedgeworth's writhing form. Cynthia dropped to her knees beside her husband.

"He's choking," the doctor said. He looked up and fastened his eyes on Peabody who stood a few steps away. "Get me a sharp knife, tube, a straw, anything like that."

Peabody stood transfixed.

"Get it, now!" The doctor yelled.

Peabody turned and ran for the kitchen.

"Anything I can do, doctor?" The voice from the doorway belonged to Roger Johns, Assistant Chief of Police.

"I've got to do a tracheotomy. Hold him still. Where's that knife?"

Roger Johns knelt down just as Peabody came back with a knife and a straw. The doctor grabbed it.

Cynthia let out a gasp and reached out to stop the doctor.

"Get out of the way, Mrs. Wedgeworth," the doctor ordered.

When Cynthia remained kneeling, Jennifer stepped forward, helped the woman to her feet and moved her to a corner of the room. Cynthia shuddered, then buried her face in Jennifer's shoulder. Unable to look away, Jennifer watched the operation.

The doctor completed his task and rocked back on his heels, shaking his head. Foam slithered down the sides of Wedgeworth's face. His chest stopped heaving; his limbs went limp.

Johns released his grip on the man's head. "What would cause this?" he asked. "Allergic reaction?"

Again the doctor shook his head. "He had no allergies. Looks more like poison."

"Poison?" The Assistant Chief of Police stood. "Don't move him until I say so. I've got a few calls to make."

Cynthia drew away from Jennifer and hurried to her husband's side, falling to her knees. "Noooo." It was half-moan, half-scream. She put her arms around his still body. "Help him," she cried out to the doctor.

"I'm sorry. Not sure anything could have saved him. Whatever it was, it was potent."

Peabody had remained in the doorway. "I'd better explain things to the guests." He turned to leave, but was confronted by Assistant Chief Johns in the hallway.

"Nobody leaves," he said. "I've called in detectives from our CSI and homicide units."

"Homicide?" Peabody stuttered. "But… but…." he spluttered, but could say nothing more.

"Relax. I'm erring on the side of caution. Your boss was a very wealthy and prominent citizen, and I don't want any mistakes. Keep this to yourself for now," the Assistant Chief said. "I'll take over until my men get here." He turned and headed back to the living room where the guests milled about in confused anxiety. Peabody trailed behind like a lost puppy.

The doctor pulled Cynthia from the body of her husband. "Let's get you upstairs." He nodded to Jennifer. "Would you help and stay with her until I get there?"

"Of course." She put her arms around Cynthia's shoulders and turned toward the hall, then realized she had no idea which way to go. "I'm sorry, Cynthia. Which way to your room?"

In a daze, the woman pointed down the hall to a staircase. Cynthia seemed to gather strength and walk with firm steps with Jennifer by her side, but once in the large bedroom, she collapsed on the kingsize bed. "This is crazy. I can't believe it. It's a nightmare. Impossible."

Jennifer took off Cynthia's shoes and pulled a quilt over her. "Is there anyone I can call?"

Cynthia gave a hoarse cry, then in a voice full of despair said, "All those people are his friends. I don't know them."

Jennifer sat on the edge of the bed, not knowing what she should do or say. "Can I get you something?"

"Reset the clock. God, I can't believe this has happened."

There was a knock on the door and Jennifer stood to answer it. The doctor came in and moved to the bedside. "Mrs. Wedgeworth, I brought you a sedative. It might help you." He went to the bathroom and got a glass of water and held it out to her with a pill in his hand.

After dutifully swallowing the pill, she said in a strangled voice, "He's really dead, isn't he?"

"I'm sorry. It happened fast. We'll find out what it was. In the meantime, try to sleep. I'll come up later." As he passed Jennifer, he said, "Stay with her until she falls asleep, won't you?"

She nodded, but thought Cynthia needed a friend with her right now. Was there really no one to whom the woman could turn? While sitting on the edge of the bed, she watched Cynthia stare into space. Was she struggling to make sense of the senseless? Odd how Wedgeworth had died in his room of collectable books, the portrait of the sad clown looking down upon him. The clown's painted red tear burned into Jennifer's memory as she recalled the scene of Clifford dying before her eyes.

After Cynthia fell asleep, Jennifer went downstairs to restored order. The police had kept the guests in the living room and refused to allow anything to be moved or touched until CSI had inspected all glasses, dishes and food. Finally, under Warren Peabody's curt directions, the catering staff, like an ebb tide, vanished into the kitchen, clearing off the remaining dishes and linens as they went. Behind the closed pantry door, the clinking of glassware blended with scuffling footsteps.

The house was in lockdown. Guests milled around in shock until a short wiry man in a brown suit standing at the entrance to the sunken living room announced, "I'm Detective Cameron with the Seattle Police Department. As Assistant Police Chief Johns has told you we are investigating Clifford Wedgeworth's death. We'd appreciate it if you would leave you name, address and phone numbers with Officer Seager." He pointed to a thickset younger man in civilian clothes who stood next to him. "He'll clear you to leave. If you have any special knowledge of what led to his death, please let us know." Abruptly he spun on his heels and strode down the hall.

A man asked Officer Seager, "What was the cause of death?"

"We don't know, sir," the officer replied.

Alex, who stood next to Jennifer, leaned over, and whispered, "Why would someone murder Clifford?"

"Murder? Why do you say that?" Jennifer clutched her hands together.

He put his arm around her trembling shoulder. "What else makes sense? Poison, the doctor said. Maybe it's not a homicide, maybe he had an allergic reaction to something and the doctor didn't know about it."

"Wishful thinking." Jennifer shook her head. "It's a nightmare. Poor Cynthia. She doesn't seem to have any friends here. Alex, it was awful seeing him writhing on the floor and unable to do anything for him." For a moment she rested her head against his chest, until she noticed Emma Mae sitting alone by the fireplace. Tears streamed down her aunt's face, smudging her carefully applied makeup.

Jennifer moved away from Alex, knelt next to her, and held her hand. "I'm so sorry, Emma Mae. I know he was important to you. I saw how the two of you greeted one another."

Through her tears, Emma Mae said, "For one fleeting moment, it was as if we were the two people who had once shared so much." She paused. "At least that's how I felt." She smiled through misty eyes. "He hadn't changed much, still the lady's man."

Alex brought Emma Mae a glass of water. "It's hard to believe he's gone," he said, handing the glass to her. "He looked so healthy and seemed happy in his recent marriage. What a blow to Cynthia."

"She seems so all alone," Jennifer said.

Although everyone had reported to Office Seager, only a few people had been allowed to leave, and the crowd became impatient. The guests at first spoke in muted voices, but as their shock wore off and their thoughts turned toward their own predicaments, they became more vociferous. Snippets of conversation drifted toward Jennifer.

"What will happen to the Framington deal?" one man asked another.

"And what about the merger?" another asked.

"Don't worry," a third said, "the company will do fine. Cliff was getting tired of running it and wanted to retire. He's been handing over more details to his vice presidents."

"Easy for you to say," an elderly gentleman said. "You'll benefit, but what about those of us who are about to retire? Are our pensions secure?"

The men hunkered together in a corner, while women formed small groups near the piano. "Cynthia's going to be awfully rich," a white-haired woman's shrill voice carried across the room.

"To think I could have married Cliff and been a rich widow," a younger one said and sighed.

A woman in her forties with a swept-up hairdo barged into their conversation. "He played around a lot. I don't know how Cynthia lured him into marriage, but you have to give her credit for accomplishing what no one in Seattle could do."

The heavy woman raised her chin, revealing deep creases from ripples of fat around her neck. "Well, she'll be rich, but lonely."

"Not for long," another added. "Wealth has its attraction."

The heavy woman raised her blackened eyebrows. "I'm not easily fooled by a woman like her. A fortune hunter if there ever was one. What did Cliff see in her?"

Jennifer turned her back to the catty women. How could they make cruel comments about a woman who had just lost her husband? Mrs. Wedgeworth deserved sympathy and support.

If this had occurred in Brandon, she would have spoken up in defense of Cynthia, but this wasn't her turf. Instead, she turned her attention to Emma Mae. "Do you think you'll be all right driving home alone?"

Emma Mae squared her shoulders. "Of course, I'm just shaken." Her words were firm, but her hands trembled.

"Are you sure?" Alex leaned over. "Jennifer could drive you home. I'd follow and bring her back to get her car."

"That's an excellent idea," Jennifer said.

"If you don't mind," Emma Mae said. "I am a bit shaken, but I hate being a burden. Lord, I sound like your mother, carrying on and whining." She glanced at Jennifer. "Sorry, I didn't intend to demean Eleanor."

She was only telling the truth, but still Jennifer felt a tug of disloyalty. "You're upset. We're all upset." She stood and spoke to Alex. "I don't think I can leave my car here. They'll probably close the estate gates."

"There's a small café at the bottom of the hill, *The Boar's Head*. I met Clifford there yesterday. You can leave it in their parking lot. Emma Mae should be able to drive down the hill. We can have a bite to eat at the café after we take her home."

"You met Clifford yesterday?"

"Yes, I came to see him about his collection." He frowned. "I told you that on the phone, remember?"

Had Wedgeworth told Alex she'd appraised his collection? What would Alex say when she told him she'd found Carla's book, but now it was missing?

Jennifer was about to explain this to Alex, when her name was called. "Jennifer Frost, Detective Cameron would like to speak with you." The officer glanced at Alex and Emma Mae, looked down at his notes and said, "You both may leave."

The detective came down the hall and said, "Miss Frost, please follow me."

Jennifer looked from Emma Mae to Alex.

"We'll wait for you," Alex said with a reassuring smile.

Hesitantly, she followed the detective to a small sitting room a few steps beyond the library. Two years ago when she'd been interrogated by the police, the outcome had been disastrous. The detective held the door open for her and closed it behind them, then motioned her to a small yellow brocade sofa. Pastel-flowered wallpaper coordinated with chairs in soft jade green silk. Unlike the library's heavy masculine décor, this room was feminine and seemed inappropriate for a police interview.

The detective sat across from her, ran his hand through his wispy light brown hair and pulled out a notepad from the pocket of his gray jacket. "I understand you were the one who found Mr. Wedgeworth."

"I didn't find him. I was in the library, and he stumbled in, clutching his stomach and fell. I called for help. His doctor was one of the guests and came in immediately. Cynthia, his wife, came in shortly afterward."

"Did Mr. Wedgeworth say anything?" The detective rubbed his upper lip.

"Not really. Just, 'I'm sick. Get my doctor.'"

"What were you doing in the library?" He checked his notes. "The groundskeeper said the library was always locked. The party was in the living room."

"Mr. Wedgeworth asked to meet me in the library." How much detail should she reveal? "He had talked to his secretary and learned that it hadn't been locked during the party."

"I'll check with Mr. Peabody. Why was Wedgeworth meeting you in the middle of the party?"

"I had appraised his recent book acquisitions, and there were some matters that needed to be cleared up. He'd just gotten back from his honeymoon, and we hadn't had a chance to talk."

Jennifer waited for him to continue and worried about this private interview. Anything she had to say could have been said in front of others. She began to pick at the sofa's piping.

"Were you on good terms with Mr. Wedgeworth?"

"I guess. I mean, I only knew him through business." She hesitated and added, "I can only assume he was pleased with my work." Jennifer squirmed in her seat. She folded her hands in her lap and raised her chin. "Why these questions?"

"Routine. The doctor said Mr. Wedgeworth had no health problems, no allergies. There'll be an autopsy. My job is to look at all the angles, especially when a wealthy man dies suddenly. The doctor believes he ingested something poisonous."

The detective leaned forward. "How well did you know Mr. Wedgeworth before you appraised his collection?"

"I'd never met him before tonight."

"He asked you to appraise his collection, and he didn't know you?"

"I have gained a local reputation as a book appraiser."

"I see." His slim frame relaxed back into his chair as he eyed her. "Do you know his wife?"

"No. I just met her tonight for the first time, too."

"So how did you come by the invitation to this party?"

"I don't know. Quite frankly I was surprised to be asked."

"Odd." He wrote something in his notebook. "It took me a while to place your name, but then Assistant Chief Johns reminded me about the Carla Frost murder."

She stiffened and studied the man more closely. "I'm sorry, I don't remember you."

"Wouldn't expect you to. I was called in to review the case later. It was a difficult time for you and your family."

His understatement rankled. "Is there anything else you need to ask me?"

He searched her face then shrugged imperceptibly.

She stood, clasping her purse with both hands. "May I leave? My aunt is in shock, and I said I'd drive her home."

He rubbed the side of his jaw as if he pondered what else he could ask, then got to his feet. "I know where to get in touch with you if I have more questions."

She walked to the door but as she turned the knob, he said, "I want you to know, I've never stopped working your sister's case. I always figure something will turn up to catch the killer. I've solved a number of cold cases. I'm sorry you had to experience another suspicious death."

Her hand slipped off the doorknob, as she turned back toward him. "My sister's case is not something I discuss lightly. If you have any new information about her death, I'd appreciate knowing."

"I have nothing new yet, but I'm always hopeful, always searching for clues." His eyes narrowed. "Aren't you? Or have you put it all behind you?"

She felt her face flame red, but she swallowed her indignation.

He moved forward to hand her his card as if unaware how his remark had stung. "In case you think of anything you haven't told me."

She took his card and noticed her fingers trembled as she read: Detective Justin Cameron, Homicide Unit. "You work homicides. I gather you're convinced Wedgeworth's death was murder."

"I didn't say that. Suspicious, until we find out the cause of death." He reached around her for the doorknob and swung open the door. "Thanks for your cooperation."

Her breath was shallow, her back ramrod straight, feeling the detective's eyes on her. After leaving the room, she hesitated at the door to the library where yellow tape was strung across its doorway. Clifford's body had been removed. A photographer shot pictures, and two men dusted for fingerprints. They'd find hers, but there was no reason for them to suspect her. Still, the detective had intimidated her, and she was certain that he'd wanted her to feel that way. That's why she'd omitted explaining about the missing book that was sure to have been Carla's copy.

Chapter 14

When she returned to the living room, Alex stood with her coat over his arm. Emma Mae remained seated, her face blotchy, her eyes red and swollen. "Is everything all right?" she asked Jennifer with a quiver in her voice.

"Yes. He wanted to discuss what happened when Mr. Wedgeworth came into the library." Jennifer's smile was glued in place by sheer will-power. She slipped into her coat Alex held for her and pulled on her black kid gloves. She grasped Emma Mae's hand, helped her to her feet and hugged her, feeling Emma Mae's thin shoulders shudder. The three of them walked outside into the cold clear night and handed their respective tickets to the valet.

"Are you sure you're okay, Jennifer?" Alex asked. "You look pale."

"Cold. That's all." She wanted to blurt out that the detective had brought up Carla's murder, but restrained herself. "Let's talk later." She avoided looking at either Alex or Emma Mae, as they stood silently waiting for their cars.

When her car pulled up first, Jennifer said, "Why don't you lead the way, Alex, and I'll follow Emma Mae." She climbed into her jeep and pulled to the side until Emma Mae got into her car. When Alex's rented sedan was brought up, they proceeded down the long drive. Jennifer's headlights clung to Emma Mae's rear bumper, her confidence drained by Wedgeworth's death and Cameron's interrogation. Although the detective was merely doing his job, her nerves were shattered. The night might be clear, but she felt a dark cloud envelop her. She shivered despite having turned up the heater full blast.

At the restaurant's parking lot, she pulled in next to Emma Mae, locked her jeep, and took the driver's seat in her aunt's car. She signaled to Alex who motioned he'd be right behind her.

On the drive to Brandon, she asked her aunt, "Do you want to talk about Clifford?"

Emma Mae shook her head, but after many miles of silence she began to talk. "I can't believe he's gone. Like a dream he was there, and then he was dead. After all those years, he asked me to meet his wife. Don't you think that's odd? I mean the reason we never got together was because he was married. Then when he was free from his first wife, I called him, and he evaded getting together." She lapsed into silence again. Ten minutes later she added, "Maybe I should have known. He always had a ruthless streak, but I thought that was in business, not in his personal life."

Jennifer couldn't think of a thing to say to comfort Emma Mae, but she wondered what her aunt meant by *I should have known.*

"You know," Emma Mae began again. "I think he wanted to show off his young wife to me. Sort of his way of saying, look what a great catch I got instead of old you."

Jennifer didn't know how to react to this. Feeling sorry for herself was unusual for her aunt. "Don't get down on yourself. You're an attractive and intelligent woman. I heard Clifford tell you that."

Emma Mae stared straight ahead. "Maybe I've been stuck in Brandon too long."

Jennifer glanced at her aunt. "That thought has crossed my mind. Not about you, but about me."

Emma Mae smiled. "Yes. Perhaps we both should rethink our future. You've tied your future to clearing your name, and I've tied mine to a bookstore in a small town with little growth potential. I should never have let you buy into my business. Look what it's brought. Financial headaches and no social life. What a waste of time and energy."

Silence drifted between them. The headlights pierced the blackness of the night. She followed the road and thought about her aunt's words and how the evening's events might change things. Of course, her life twisted around finding Carla's murderer. Shouldn't it? Someone had to solve the case. It was her obligation to take the burden off her parents and prove the man she had once loved was not the killer, nor was she.

Her hope of finding out how Carla's copy came into Clifford Wedgeworth's possession would be difficult now that he was dead. But surely he'd kept records of buying, selling, and trading his rare books. Perhaps his wife or the secretary Peabody would know. She would allow a proper amount of time for mourning before contacting them. What could she learn from other sources in the mean time?

They entered Brandon's main street. Jennifer turned right at the second light and drove up the hill to her aunt's apartment complex. In the rear view mirror Jennifer saw Alex park on the street. After pulling into the detached garage, she walked Emma Mae to her door. "I'll call you tomorrow. Don't open the store in the morning."

"It's better to be busy," Emma Mae said and kissed Jennifer on the cheek.

Jennifer hugged her aunt, then turned and walked down the path to join Alex in his car.

"How's she doing?" he asked as she got in next to him.

"She's in shock and depressed. God, who wouldn't be? I thought she might want to reminisce, but instead she came down hard on herself. A little unlike her, but under the circumstances, it's probably normal." She shook her head. "And then again maybe it isn't. What's normal when you grieve? Some people babble on and on. That's what my mother did after Carla's death. She'd reminisce over and over. It drove me crazy, but her friends seemed to understand and let her go on and on. The problem is, it's been two years and she can't let go of her grief."

Jennifer stopped herself. Wasn't this what she was doing? She'd allowed her bitterness and grief to swallow her life. What future was there in that?

Alex pulled away from the curb and headed south. "As I recall after Carla's death, you held your emotions inside. Maybe that's what Emma Mae will do." They drove in silence until they were on the main road. Alex passed a motorist who dawdled in the slow lane. "Following clues is a healthy occupation, but I get the sense you're harboring a lot of anger. Oh, I know the police accused you of her murder, but they dropped all charges against both of us."

"You dumped me and ran away."

"That's not how it was at all."

"Wasn't it?"

"You believe I was responsible?"

"Don't be ridiculous." Jennifer's words came out in a rush of indignation. "Unlike you, I stood up for you when my family thought the worst of you."

"Sorry. It was stupid of me to bring up the past. It's always between us."

Jennifer shrugged, not wanting to admit to feelings that skimmed through her mind daily. She'd hidden behind anger over her sister's death, Alex's possible infidelity, and pursuing leads that got her no where. The hopes she'd pinned on Wedgeworth's book were dashed.

Alex broke into her musings. "I gather your aunt knew Clifford from an earlier time."

"Did she tell you that?"

"No. But it didn't take much to figure it out from the way they greeted one another and how she reacted to his death."

Jennifer turned, noticing his strong chin and the firm cut of his nose and brow. He acted as if nothing had changed between them. How could he be so blind to her feelings toward him? Could they be friends? Perhaps she should hold out an olive branch. "You were kind to Emma Mae tonight."

"Thanks." He glanced at her and smiled. "Almost like old times." He leaned forward and looked up toward the sky. "Say, it's a beautiful night. Why don't we eat at a restaurant overlooking the water?"

Jennifer glanced at the dashboard clock. "It's late and after what happened tonight, I don't feel like lingering over dinner, but we need to talk. The restaurant where I left my car would be quicker. Besides, Lydia's at home."

"Lydia?"

For the first time that night, Jennifer grinned. "Lydia's my best friend. She'll be waiting for me, and I can't disappoint her."

"Can't you phone her?"

"She can't answer the phone." Jennifer said, enjoying his confusion. "Come to dinner tomorrow and meet her."

"As I remember your idea of cooking was opening a few cans."

"I've improved."

He eyed her, then shifted his gaze to the road that spun on into the dark. "Does Lydia know about me? I don't want to be put through the third degree about the past."

"I assure you Lydia doesn't care about the past. She lives in the present." She smiled to herself relishing her private joke. " She has wonderful instincts about people."

"She must be very special."

"She is. I'll be interested to see what you think of her."

Chapter 15

Alex pulled into the parking lot where the neon sign of *The Boar's Head* glistened in the dark. They walked together toward the entrance to the quaint café that looked like a replica of an English cottage. In a bold move, he reached for her hand, but instead of responding to his gesture, she pretended to adjust her coat collar. Forgiving was not something she was able to do yet.

Inside they were shown to a table near the fireplace. Jennifer removed her gloves and tucked them into her coat pocket before slipping out of her coat. Alex took it and hung it on a nearby peg. The room reminded Jennifer of an English pub without the smoke.

"How about a drink?" Alex said, after they'd sat.

She nodded and avoided his wistful gaze. "I could do with a double martini."

He raised an eyebrow. "You never drank anything but wine or beer before."

"Murder does that."

"I'm sorry. This reunion has been unpleasant. Not what I wanted." He leaned closer. "What did that detective ask you?"

Before Jennifer answered, a waitress came to their table.

"Two double martinis, Bombay Gin." Alex looked at Jennifer. "Okay?"

"Fine."

He reached across the table and offered his outstretched hands to her. She clasped her hands together in her lap. He withdrew his hands and said, "You're very aloof. I thought we could patch up our relationship."

"It's been two years for crying out loud. You left to save your damn reputation. It's two years too late for regrets on your part."

"You've gotten very hard. Where's that soft Jennifer I knew?"

"It fled when Carla was killed." She looked about the room. Another time it would be romantic, but tonight it felt fake and sordid.

"Are we going to get past that or dwell on it all night?"

"You're right. Let's talk about today." She unfolded her napkin and placed it in her lap. "Roger Johns, the Assistant Chief of Police concluded Wedgeworth's death might be a homicide. Do you remember him from Carla's case?"

"Yes. He stayed in the background. His idiot detectives were the jerks who came to the conclusion that you and I were in collusion." Alex frowned. "This Detective Cameron seems a little pushy." He paused as the waitress brought their drinks. "Who'd want to kill Wedgeworth? A business rival?" He leaned forward and raised his glass. "Let's put the horrors of the evening behind us. Here's to seeing you again."

She raised her frosted glass to her lips. "And to you," she countered and sipped, feeling the liquor warm her.

"By the way, you look great in that red dress," he said without a hint of embarrassment.

"Don't," she began despite his hurt expression. "I appreciate your compliment, but I'm a little out of sync after the events today."

"I'm sorry."

"Don't keep saying your sorry. It's so…. Let's not go there."

"I'm just delighted to see you." He took another sip of his martini, fiddled with the stem then heaved a deep sigh. The chatter in the room covered their silence.

She picked up the menu and began to read it, avoiding eye contact.

He pulled the menu down. "Okay. I get it. Just two friends getting together after a long time apart." He studied her. "From the look on your face after Cameron interviewed you, it didn't go well."

She toyed with the cuticle on her thumb. "He put me on edge. I felt angry, confused, frustrated. I was the one with Wedgeworth when he died and …" she hesitated. "Cameron had worked on Carla's case."

He put down his drink. "No wonder you're upset." He rubbed his beard. "I don't remember him."

"Neither did I. He said he worked in the cold case unit and knew all about Carla's murder. Now he's in homicide."

"Look," Alex said. "I know I said I wouldn't churn up the past, but there are a few things I need to say to you."

She dreaded any more of his pleas for understanding, but sat immobile knowing he would keep on the subject until it was mush.

He smiled as if that would cover any mistakes. "I've thought of you so often. And when we do meet again, things go awry. Are we snake bit?" He hesitated. "That's one of the reasons I didn't call you after my divorce. I always thought that until Carla's death was solved, you and I couldn't get together." He looked down and rubbed his hand on the tablecloth as if smoothing out wrinkles that weren't there. "After I turned all the information about the missing book to the security fellow at the Antiquarian Booksellers Association, I was sure we'd catch someone trying to sell it."

Jennifer felt a lump in her throat and she shivered.

"Are you still cold?"

"A chill." How could she tell him that past memories pressed into present day circumstances made her cringe? She took another sip of her martini. Perhaps she could avoid his desire to renew their relationship by talking about the book she'd found. "I appraised Wedgeworth's recent acquisitions."

"You appraised Clifford's latest collection?" Alex's brow wrinkled, as he searched her face. "He didn't mention that to me." He shrugged. "But then again why should he? He didn't know that I knew you." He fingered the stem of his glass. "I don't understand why he would ask you to do an appraisal."

"Maybe you can help me find answers to a clue I've found. After you left, I studied up on rare books, talked to collectors, went to book fairs and became rather good at appraisals of books." She gave him a thin smile. "You could say you and I are competitors. I've developed a small following." He still looked puzzled, so she continued, "It was what you'd said before you left. 'Find the book and you'll find the murderer.'"

"I should have known you'd continue to search for a clue to her murderer. I'm proud of you. You always enjoyed research." He leaned back and frowned. "I go to most of the Antiquarian Book Fairs and have never seen you."

"To be honest I never went on the opening day of the events, knowing you'd probably be there with all the other buyers."

"I see. If you don't get in first thing, you miss out on some of the hidden gems." He smiled in a gentle way. "Now you can attend on the first day and not worry about running into me. I'm so pleased you got into the field. We can become partners."

"You're jumping the gun and not the game I'm interested in."

Ignoring her remark, he said, "It's such a captivating profession." He laughed. "Well, I'd like to make it my main profession, but haven't been that successful at it and still need my day job." He took another sip of his martini. "So what did you think of Wedgeworth's collection? Spectacular don't you think?"

"Yes. And surprising. I found Carla's copy of *The Big Sleep* in his collection.*" She sat back, thinking he'd gasp with surprise and excitement, but instead, he tilted his head and gave her a rueful smile. "You don't seem impressed."

"I knew he had it."

"What? How? When did you know that?"

"That's a long story, but essentially I've been doing exactly what I told you to do, searching for the book."

"That's the problem. When I was in the library just before Wedgeworth died, I noticed the book was missing from his collection."

"I know."

"You know?" She frowned, anger rising in her. "What in the hell do you mean by that?"

"I have it," he said with a smug expression.

"You? How? Where is it?" People at the next table stared at her and she lowered her voice. "Did you steal it?" Her heart raced. Her fingers dug into the edge of the table.

Alex scowled at her flurry of questions. "Jennifer, do you think I'd tell you I have the book if I'd stolen it?"

"Quite frankly I don't know what to believe with your nonchalant attitude about a book that could solve my sister's murder."

He raised his hands to ward off any further outcry on her part. "When I learned Wedgeworth had a copy, I called him and asked a few questions."

"How did you find out he had a copy? Did he advertise?" Her voice grew louder again and she tried to rein in her anger.

"Rumors mostly. You know how collectors gossip about their latest finds, who bought what."

What Alex said was true, but it didn't satisfy her. For now she'd let it go. "Did you buy it from him?"

"Hardly. I'm not that flush with funds at the moment. I suggested a trade he couldn't refuse. That's why I met him yesterday. I traded a first edition signed copy of Steinbeck's *A Cup of Gold.* Let me tell you, I hated to part with such a treasure. He was easy to deal with. I'm not sure he even inspects his new acquisitions. His tendency is to purchase books on whims. Sometimes he relies on his secretary, Warren Peabody."

"Why didn't you tell me you had it, that you found it?"

"Till now, I haven't had the chance, have I?"

She sighed. "No, sorry." She thought of all the things she needed to know. "Did you learn the book's provenance?"

"He said it came from the Jacobi estate, which both you and I know is true. But then Carla got hold of it, and whoever took it from her is the killer."

"So who did he buy it from?"

"He wasn't forthcoming, but he said he'd tell me in the next day or two. I didn't want to dash my opportunity to get my hands on the book, so I went along with him. My first priority was to get the book. In some ways he was very open and even let me roam about his fabulous collection before the party began." He grinned and sat up straighter as if he'd gotten a special gift.

"You should have pushed him on the provenance at the time you traded for it. You could have explained about Carla's murder. Surely if he was honest about his acquisition, he'd tell you."

"I doubt if Clifford could have or would have killed to get that book or any other book," he said. "He had money to do what he pleased. However, he acknowledged he had records, but wanted to check something with the previous owner first. His secretary should know where Clifford's documentations are." He paused and finished off his martini. He cautiously glanced around at the nearest tables and said softly, "But if Clifford was murdered, then Warren Peabody may be hesitant to share information about his boss's collections. We have to consider that if we start snooping around, Detective Cameron might get the wrong idea."

She had the urge to shake him after his analytical explanation. "Of course, it doesn't make sense for Wedgeworth to have killed Carla, but whoever wanted the book did. That someone could be Wedgeworth's secretary."

"Just because he's an odd duck doesn't make him a criminal."

Alex might be handsome with his new beard, but his engineering type logic drove her crazy. "Let's drop the who did it and look at the what. Have you had a chance to examine the book?" she asked.

"Enough to know it might be Carla's copy. It had H J initials on the jacket."

"Right," she said. "They stand for Helen Jacobi. Check the end page for some kind of notes. I think that whoever killed Carla didn't want the book but wanted what was in the book."

"If there is any writing in the book it could detract from the book's value. It would depend on the buyer. The fact that Helen Jacobi had written her initials in the book lessens its value." He continued to fiddle with his empty martini glass and frowned. "You're forgetting Carla let me see the book, and there was nothing stuck inside."

"She could have taken whatever was there out before she showed it to you. What about her new boyfriend? Could he have taken it?"

"What do you think was hidden in the book?"

She smiled. "I'd like you to figure that out."

"Why all the mystery?"

"No mystery. I want you to inspect the book without any prejudgements. But one thing you should know is that I found grains of sand caught in the binding."

"So, it looks like I've got the right book."

"You? What about me?"

He grinned. "I traded for it."

"I found it first." She bit her bottom lip. Putting him on the defensive was not the solution. "Will you share it?"

"Don't get upset. I'll let you see it, but I'm not letting it out of my sight." He leaned back and stroked his beard. "Have you researched the Jacobi relationship?"

"Enough. And it fits. Helen's housekeeper donated the books to the library at the direction of the executor, Mr. Arnett. Neither of them had any idea the books had any value." Jennifer's enthusiasm returned now that she could study it further. "Where's the book?"

"At my hotel."

"Let's go there now."

"Not tonight."

"Why not?"

"You said you wanted me to inspect it without any influences. I hardly think with you looking over my shoulder I could be impartial as to anything I might find."

"Could you bring it to my place in the morning, early? "I'm busy during the day. The book isn't going to disappear. I'll bring it with me tomorrow night." He picked up the menu, then glanced over it at her. "What do you know about the Jacobi estate?"

"I talked to the executor," she said. "There's a relative who lives in Israel who received the income from the sale of the house. I don't see how he's relevant."

"If it can be proved that some valuable paper came from the book, the heir might want a piece of the pie," he said.

"I hadn't thought of that. The housekeeper hinted she should get any books back if they were valuable. Maybe we're opening Pandora's box, but I have to follow this clue."

Chapter 16

The following morning Jennifer roused herself out of bed. She and Lydia jogged through the hills just as the sun peeked through the clouds. Upon her return to the house, she took a quick shower and ate a breakfast of Emma Mae's *every-grain-imaginable* granola. Unable to corral her excitement about seeing Carla's book, she jumped from one chore to another. Although it was early, she decided to walk to Books & Tea and finish the monthly accounting before opening.

With Lydia at her side, they covered the three miles quickly. A new day in Brandon with papers still on driveways, delivery trucks, street sweepers, and dog walkers gave a sense of normalcy. Turning into the alley behind the store, Jennifer noted the backdoor was ajar. She stopped, bringing Lydia to an abrupt halt. Had they left the door open last night? With trepidation, she entered the long dark hallway, stood and listened. Her heart thudded. She put down her pack, unhooked Lydia's leash and gripped the collar with one hand. Jennifer's breathing quickened as if she'd run a race. She flicked on the hall light. A crash resounded from the office.

"Who's there?" she called out. Releasing her hold on Lydia, she commanded, "Go," motioning her dog forward. The huge animal headed toward the office just as Crabapple streaked out the door.

Lydia ignored the cat, growled and barked.

Jennifer ran to the office door and peered inside as the light from the hall flooded the room. Lydia had cornered a gangly teenager.

"Please, lady, call off your dog," the teen begged. The boy's dark eyes were enormous, as he covered his groin with his hands and gaped wide-eyed at Lydia.

"What are you doing in here?" Jennifer's voice shook with a combination of fear and shock.

"Don't let your dog bite me," the boy wailed.

"What you're doing in here?"

"I just wanted to read a book."

Jennifer sneered. "Oh, right! Tell that one to the police." While Lydia remained stationed in front of the teen, Jennifer dug her cell phone from her pocket and called the Brandon police. "This is Jennifer Frost at Books & Tea. I've cornered a burglar in my store. Can you send someone right away?"

"Wow, Jennifer," Sally, the dispatcher said. "You okay?"

"Yes, but I need help ASAP."

"Officer Joe Baker is on patrol in the area. I'll page him. Want to stay on the line until he gets there?"

"No. Lydia's got the situation in hand."

There was a brusk laugh at the other end of the line and then silence. Jennifer hung up and stuck her phone back in her jacket pocket.

Every time the boy budged, Lydia growled. While Jennifer waited for Joe to arrive, she scrutinized her intruder. The teen was about seventeen with a tattoo on one forearm and five rings puncturing each ear. Not a pleasant sight when you added his acne and panicky expression.

Jennifer glanced around the room, noting that the safe was still locked. On the table next to the small fridge, a milk carton and a small orange packet had been set out. Maxie hopped up and sniffed.

When Joe Baker walked in through the back door, the boy seemed as relieved as Jennifer.

"Her dog was gonna bite me," the teenager whined.

Joe smiled at Jennifer and winked. "You're lucky. This dog is known for her bad temper."

Jennifer ordered Lydia to back off. Joe spun the teen around and spread-eagled him against the wall, checking him for weapons. Finding none, he pushed the kid into a chair. "Anything missing?" Joe asked Jennifer.

"I haven't had a chance to look in the front yet. Looks like he was about to pour himself some milk and eat some crackers."

"What's your name, son?" Joe asked.

"Matt. Matthew Garland."

"You aren't a local. Where are you from?"

"Seattle. Came up here to get out of the city. I was just hungry."

"Bookstore's not a good choice unless you were hungry for knowledge," Joe said, shaking his head. "Looks like you were after trouble."

Jennifer went over to the table and filled a cup with milk and brought it to the boy.

Instead of taking the cup, the boy lashed out, smacked the cup from her hand, splattering the milk onto the floor. Lydia lunged at the teen, but Jennifer called her off, as Joe yanked the boy up, twisted him around, and handcuffed him. "That wasn't a smart move, kid," Joe said, slamming the boy back into the chair again.

Maxie jumped down from the table and began lapping up the spilt milk. The teen's face grew pale as he stared at Maxie.

"Why did you pick this store?" Joe asked him.

The teen shrugged, but his eyes remained on the cat. "It was easy to get in," he mumbled.

Jennifer watched the teen. "Why didn't you want the milk?" she asked. "You obviously..." She stopped in mid-sentence as Maxie gagged. "What have you done?" Jennifer shouted as she leaned over Maxie, who began to convulse. "He's poisoned Maxie," she screamed.

Joe pulled out his radio and called headquarters. "Need back up at Books & Tea."

"The vet," Jennifer said. "I've got to get Maxie to the vet." She reached for the phone, but stopped. "The vet's three blocks away, but I don't have a car. Can you take me, Joe?"

He shook his head. "I can't leave here until I get back up."

Jennifer didn't argue. She brought out Maxie's cage and put the limp animal in it. "I'll run down to the vet with him. Lydia can come with me. That'll keep her safe. I don't have time to corral Crabapple. See that he stays out of here."

"Will do. I can get a statement from you later. Get going. Hope Maxie makes it," Joe called after her, as she ran for the backdoor with the cage in hand and Lydia at her heels.

Jennifer ran down the alley, her heart racing with fear for Maxie. She dodged a car at the street and kept running, lifting her skirt to lengthen her stride. One block to go. No time to check on how Maxie was doing. At the next block, she got to the veterinarian's backdoor, rang the bell, and pounded on the door. Even on Sunday, they'd have someone on duty. She looked at Maxie's still small body in the cage. "Come on, come on," she said under her breath as she waited for the door to open. When a woman appeared, Jennifer pushed past her with Lydia crowding in behind. In a rush of words, Jennifer explained what had happened to Maxie.

"Come into the back room," the woman said. "I'm Dr. Rawlings, subbing for Dr. Lovie," she explained over her shoulder.

Jennifer put the cage on the stainless steel table, and the woman removed Maxie. After a quick examination, she called for her assistant. "Randy. Help me with this." She glanced at Jennifer. "Wait outside and take your Newfie with you."

Jennifer left the examining room and sat in the outer office with Lydia at her side. Jennifer's knees quaked; her hands trembled. Why had the boy done such a thing? Please don't let Maxie die, she prayed. She should call Emma Mae, but decided to wait until she had more information. Lord, how will Emma Mae handle this after yesterday's trauma? Jennifer gripped her hands then rubbed her knuckles. Time evaporated. Waiting. Not knowing. She entwined her fingers in Lydia's fur, kneading its thickness, and murmured, "At least you're okay." Crabapple had always been fussier and more skittish than Maxie, but she worried. Should she call the store? No. Joe had his hands full without her haranguing him.

Dr. Rawlings came in and sat next to Jennifer. "Your cat's very sick. I'm not sure he's going to make it. It's hard to know how much poison he ingested."

"I'm not sure the poison was intended for the cats."

Dr. Rawlings stared at her. "What do you mean? Who was the intended victim?" She studied Jennifer's face. "My God, you?"

Jennifer shrugged. "I'm not sure. Look, I have to get back to the store. The police are there now. Could you keep my dog, Lydia, here for a few hours? At least until I know the store is safe for her. I have to check on the other cat."

Dr. Rawlings smiled and held out her hand for Lydia to sniff. "Of course. We'll put her in the side run so she won't feel caged. Check back with me in about two hours. I should know by then if Maxie will make it."

"Could you check what kind of poison it was?" Jennifer asked as she stood up.

"Absolutely! I need to know, so we can treat Maxie for any aftereffects. But the nearest lab is in Seattle, and it'll take a few days."

Jennifer left Lydia and hurried the three blocks back to Books & Tea, her mind racing with questions. Why would anyone come after me? Why now?

Two police cars were parked in the back alley. Joe had left to book the teen in at the jail, leaving Officers Mike Dallard and Lance McDuffy at the store. After Carla's death, Jennifer had become acquainted with most of the police in town.

"Sorry to hear Maxie got poisoned," McDuffy said. "How's he doing?"

"Not sure," Jennifer said, as she stood in the hall outside the office. "I'll know more in a few hours."

"You call Emma Mae yet?" Dallard asked. He wore latex gloves. After he picked up the orange packet, he dropped it into a paper bag and marked it to maintain the chain of evidence.

"Not yet. A friend of hers died yesterday, and I hate to drop this news on her over the phone."

McDuffy followed Jennifer into the main part of the bookstore. "Crabapple seems okay." He walked over and petted the cat that sat on the counter by the cash register. "Looks like she's guarding the till. We dusted it for prints. Doesn't seem to have been jimmied. Check it out."

Jennifer opened the register and after inspecting the contents, said, "Looks okay. I'm not sure money was his motive." She closed the drawer. "Did the boy say why he wanted to poison us?"

"You? I thought he poisoned the cat."

"Emma Mae and I use the milk in our tea. It's not just for the cats."

"The kid didn't know that, did he?"

"I don't know. If he's from out of town, how did he know we had animals? And why would he want to poison animals he doesn't know or people he doesn't know?" She shuddered and closed her eyes for a moment. "Perhaps I'm jumping to conclusions."

"Come down to headquarters and press charges against the kid," McDuffy said. "We'll find out if he did this on his own or someone put him up to it. I'll bet he's just a runaway who wanted to do mischief."

"It's not mischief when you poison an animal," Dallard said, coming into the front of the store. "I've bagged all the evidence and taken pictures. Jennifer, you better clean the office floor in case there's residue left."

As the two men moved down the hall, McDuffy said, "If you find anything missing or not quite right, let us know. You better install new locks, one in the back and another on the front door. Maybe an alarm system too. Never used to have much crime here, but more people means more crime." At the back door, he turned, and smiled at her. "And you better call Emma Mae. Knowing her the way I do, she'll raise Cain about this."

Jennifer nodded and swung the door shut. After she mopped the office floor, she called Emma Mae. Her voice broke as she explained what had happened.

A gasp echoed across the line. "Poor Maxie," she finally said. How about Crabapple?"

"She's okay. Shall I come get you?"

"No," Emma Mae said in a firm voice. I'll meet you at the vet's."

After hanging up, Jennifer examined the lock and shook her head. Since it was Sunday, the hardware store was closed. New locks would have to wait until Monday but she rummaged around in the back closet until she found an old padlock. Before she left the store, she slipped the padlock onto the back door's hasp and pocketed the key. Not very secure, and the damage had already been done, but it was the best she could do for now. By the time she arrived at the veterinarian's, Emma Mae was waiting in the front office.

"I'm so sorry," Jennifer said, hugging her aunt.

"Not your fault." Emma Mae's complexion was whiter than usual, and her newly dyed and coifed hair drooped around her ears. "Why on earth would someone do such a horrible thing? Maxie never hurt a soul. 'Course he did tackle every long skirt or scarf that entered the store, but that's no reason to poison him."

Jennifer didn't have the nerve to tell her aunt that she didn't think Maxie or any of the animals were the intended victims. She'd get to that later. "Have you seen Dr. Rawlings yet?"

Emma Mae shook her head. "Her assistant came out and told me to wait." Emma Mae stood, sat, and then got up again. "I hate waiting. I waited to see Clifford and look what happened." She turned toward Jennifer, her face screwed up with a fierce expression. "Never wait! Go after what you want. Life is too short to wait."

They lapsed into silence until Dr. Rawlings entered the small waiting room and Jennifer introduced her to Emma Mae. "Maxie is more Emma Mae's cat than mine, but we both love him."

"I'm sorry about Maxie," the vet said. "I couldn't save him."

Emma Mae gripped Jennifer's hand. "Oh, poor Maxie. It's not fair."

Dr. Rawlings sighed. "Animals are so innocent and precious. They break our hearts. Whatever the poison was, it was extremely potent to take effect so quickly. As I told Jennifer, I'll send fluids to a lab and let you know."

"The police took the milk carton and a packet the teen left behind," Jennifer said. "They'll learn what it was, too, but we'd appreciate hearing from you when you know."

"I want to see the boy who killed Maxie." Emma Mae raised her trembling fists. Her lips drew back into thin lines. "He needs to understand that what he did was evil."

Jennifer put her arm around her aunt, and said to the vet, "I'll take Lydia with me now."

After they arrived back at Books & Tea, Emma Mae sat in the chair in the front of the store. Her anger seemed to have seeped away, replaced by weariness. Crabapple hopped onto her lap and curled up. "I think she already misses Maxie." Emma Mae stroked the cat's fur and gazed out the window. "We won't open today."

Jennifer knelt in front of Emma Mae. "Why don't you go home? I'll take care of things here."

"I'm going down to the station and look that boy in the eye and ask him, Why?" Despite her declaration, Emma Mae remained seated.

Jennifer rose and walked around the room. "Emma Mae, he didn't know we had animals. We use the milk for tea and coffee and offer it to our customers."

Emma Mae frowned and her eyes narrowed. "You know what you're saying?"

"Yes. This boy is a stranger from Seattle. Someone put him up to poisoning the milk."

Emma Mae gave her a blank stare. "Why?"

"I don't know why!" Her hands became fists and her eyes narrowed. "But I'm going to find out."

Jennifer went to the phone and called police headquarters. Sally, the dispatcher, was still on duty. "Sally. This is Jennifer. Is Joe Baker there?"

As she waited for him to come on the line, she studied her aunt. The woman's head and shoulders were stooped, and her blue-veined hands quivered as she continued to stroke Crabapple. Emma Mae's usual calm resistance to ill winds had dissipated.

Finally, Joe came on the line. "Jen, are you all right?"

"I'm calling about the kid. Has he talked yet?"

"Not much. He said a gray-haired, old man paid him two hundred dollars to do the job. Not much of a description. He doesn't know the guy and didn't get a name. He wasn't told you had animals. Said he didn't know what it was he put into the milk. That's not much to go on."

"Do you believe him?"

"Yes, I do."

"We need to know more. Can't you force him to tell everything he knows?'

He sighed. "Jen, this is not TV."

"Sorry. But do you know what kind of poison it was?"

"We'll send the sample to the lab in Seattle. I'll let you know when I know, but the labs are always backlogged."

Her shoulders slumped. She'd hoped Joe would know what the poison was, but realized how naive her idea had been. She blurted out, "Joe, Maxie died."

"Oh God, honey, I am so sorry."

"We're going to press charges. Emma Mae wants a face-to-face meeting with the boy."

"That should put the fear of God into him."

Chapter 17

That night when Jennifer opened the door to her house, Alex stood there with the book in one hand and a bouquet of yellow roses in the other. Lydia bounded forward, barring him from entering. Alex stepped back, his mouth agape. "Whoa… .You didn't tell me you had a guard."

"Lydia, move," Jennifer commanded. "He's a good guy. Let him in."

"Lydia? This is your roommate you had to get back to?" Alex laughed. "You had me going."

"Kidding you about Lydia gave a terrible day a redeeming quality. Grandmother gave her to me. She's well-trained and a dear companion." She reached for the book, but he pulled it back and handed her the bouquet instead.

As she took them, she said, "Thank you. They're lovely. Please come in." But Lydia refused to budge. "Lydia behave." Jennifer scolded and pointed to the far corner of the room. "Go."

Lydia obeyed, but her eyes remained on Alex.

"I like dogs," he said. "Just didn't expect you to have one. Your grandmother always had interesting ideas."

She smiled at his reference to her grandmother, remembering how the two of them had discussions about antique books. She carried the flowers to the kitchen to put them in a vase. He watched from the living room while Lydia moved to stand between him and Jennifer. As Jennifer returned the vase to the coffee table, Lydia pushed at her leg. "What's the matter with you?" Jennifer said, shoving Lydia's head away.

"She's jealous." Alex stood in front of the sofa and placed the book on the coffee table.

"Don't be silly. Lydia's seen me around a lot of people, including men, and she's never acted up. She's a perfect lady."

"She's not a happy pup. You didn't see her lip curl like I did." He stared at the dog. "I bet I'm right," Alex said with his hands on his hips. "She's jealous."

"No way."

"I'll prove it to you. Come here. Close to me."

Jennifer moved toward him.

"Closer." He smiled.

As Jennifer obeyed, Lydia edged closer to her mistress.

"See?" Alex said, as he and Jennifer stood face to face. "Now you promised me she's well trained. She'll do as you command, right?"

"Yes." Jennifer frowned.

Alex put his arms around Jennifer's waist. "Put your arms around me too."

Jennifer hesitantly lifted her arms and placed them on top of Alex's shoulders. Lydia emitted a low growl.

"See?"

"That doesn't prove anything." She was about to say that Lydia never interfered when Joe put his arms around her, but instead, said to her dog. "It's okay. He's a friend, calm down."

Alex pulled Jennifer toward him and kissed her. There was a violent shove, and Alex and Jennifer found themselves sprawled on the couch with Lydia between them.

"Lydia. Bad girl!" Jennifer giggled as Lydia licked her face.

"See! I told you." Alex began to laugh, too. "Some disciplined pet."

Alex slid onto the floor, as Lydia's rump shoved him off the cushion. Then she wiggled around to settle on the couch. It took awhile before Jennifer caught her breath and ordered Lydia into the corner. Even that command had to be followed by a hard tug on her collar.

Despite her dog's behavior, it felt good to laugh. "Are you okay?"

"Full of black fur," He brushed the front of his beige sweater. "But unscathed." He eyed Lydia who continued to follow his every move. "Next time I'll bring her a bone in lieu of flowers for you. She wouldn't really bite me, would she?"

Jennifer shook her head. "I don't think so, but I realize I have some extra training to do. Alex, sit next to me on the couch and let her come to you."

Hesitantly, Alex eased back onto the couch. "Okay. Now what?"Lydia come," Jennifer commanded.

Lydia padded over to her mistress and put her large head in her lap. "Good girl." Jennifer turned to Alex. "Put your hand out and then gradually start petting her under her chin."

Lydia scrutinized him, but didn't growl. "I can see that it's peace with reservations," Alex said, moving his hand to scratch the dog behind her ears. "Okay, girl. See, I don't mean any harm to your mistress." He leaned forward and reached for the book he'd set on the coffee table. "Maybe we should talk about the book."

"Absolutely. I've been dying to see it again."

Alex nodded toward Lydia. "Can you get her out of our way?"

Jennifer laughed. "Lydia, down. Stay." With Lydia at her feet, Jennifer accepted the book.

"I studied the end pages as you suggested," he said. "Just impressions, but you were right. An old letter had been stuck or pressed between the pages. On purpose or by accident, we'll probably never know. It looks as if Einstein typed a letter, signed it, but then made handwritten notations in the margin. That's the only explanation why the writing is at an angle and reversed." Alex pulled a sheet of paper from his pocket. "This is the name you tried to decipher." He unfolded the paper. "I researched Einstein and found letters that looked like a name S … ilard. It's Szilard."

"Szilard." Jennifer read and frowned. "The name means nothing to me."

Dr. Leo Szilard discovered the neutron emission of uranium," he said, keeping his eyes on Jennifer. "Szilard detailed the method of setting up a chain reaction in uranium."

"So that makes him the man behind the atomic bomb?" Jennifer sat back in awe. "So we have two famous men with their names on a piece of paper. Does that make the book worth more?"

"I'm not sure. There was a disagreement between these men. In 1939 Einstein wrote a letter to President Roosevelt recommending that he and his scientists look into the making of an atomic weapon. Years afterward, Einstein implied that Szilard had drafted the letter and he, Einstein, had signed his name to it. Later in his life, Einstein said that his connection with the letter was the biggest mistake of his life."

"You figured all this out from those fragments on the back page?" Jennifer asked with a raised eyebrow.

"Of course not. I just wanted you to understand the connection between Szilard and Einstein." Alex hesitated, then continued. "I checked to see if any new Einstein papers had been found. So far nothing, but the Hebrew University of Jerusalem has the archives of Einstein's papers. I need to contact the curator."

"It doesn't matter to me what the letter was about, except that the value could be important. If a letter was in the book, the murderer may have taken it and sold it. What I need to learn is who." She rubbed her chin and stared at the book. "If we can't find the paper or if it doesn't exist, I'm back to square one. Still, I need to find out who had the book before Wedgeworth."

"A step is a step." Alex leaned back. "You promised dinner and not out of a can. And a drink?"

"Wine will have to do."

"Fine." He relaxed back into the couch as Jennifer headed for the kitchen. "Have you ever thought about the eerie connection of what you and I are doing now that correlates to the scene in *The Big Sleep*?"

Jennifer came to the archway separating the kitchen from the living room. "What are you talking about?"

"Don't you remember when Marlowe wants to find out if a book dealer is legit or not? He goes in and asks if she has a third edition of an 1860 *Ben Hur*. When the clerk tells him, she doesn't have it, he knows the store isn't legit, since any book dealer in 1939 would know the book wasn't published until 1880 and would have corrected him."

"And that tells me what?" Jennifer frowned.

He shrugged. "I just thought it was quirky that this book has a scene like that."

"I guess." She started to turn back to the kitchen, then stopped. "Sorry. It is interesting. My mind's on too many things lately." There was a hissing sound on the stove, and she went to take a pot off the burner.

"Can I help?" he offered.

"Open the bottle of wine that's on the table. Everything's ready and not burned, thank goodness." She dished out the food and put the plates on the small pine table in the living room. Over Szechuan chicken and a fruit salad, they chatted about mundane things, trying to ease into the camaraderie they had once shared.

Their conversation became stilted, and she pushed her plate away. "Something happened today at the store. I'm not sure whether it's related to Wedgeworth's death. Our cat was poisoned by a Seattle teenager, who broke into the shop."

"Poisoned? God, that's terrible. I'm sorry." He laid down his fork. "I know how you and Emma Mae love animals. Why would a kid do something like that?" He took a sip of wine and studied Jennifer. "Wait a minute. If the kid was from out of town, how did he know you had animals?"

"Exactly!"

"He was after you?" He started to reach across the table for her hand, but after a glance at Lydia, he stopped. "What do the police say?"

"They suggested we change the locks."

"They're right, of course, but a little late for it." He studied her for a moment. "Will the police start checking on your place more often? Are you safe here? Maybe you should go to your island for a while."

"I have Lydia and, as you saw, she can be intimidating."

Before Alex could argue the point, the phone rang. Jennifer rose to answer it and heard Emma Mae's curt voice. "Turn on your TV to channel five. Clifford was murdered. Poisoned."

Chapter 18

On Tuesday Detective Cameron walked into Books & Tea, trailed by stocky Officer Seager. Jennifer wasn't surprised, but hadn't expected them so soon.

"Afternoon, Miss Frost," he said, approaching her as she stood at the front counter. "I'd like to speak to you and Emma Mae Langdon about Clifford Wedgeworth's murder."

"My aunt's in the office resting." She glanced at nearby customers.

"I'd like to speak with both of you privately." He nodded toward the back of the store.

Jennifer hesitated. "She's had a bad time with Mr. Wedgeworth's death, and then her cat was poisoned."

"I was sorry to hear about that."

"You heard about Maxie?" Jennifer asked.

"If that's the dead cat's name, yes." He drummed his fingers on the counter.

"How?"

"How what?" He frowned.

She leaned forward keeping her voice low. "How did you learn about Maxie?"

"I keep in touch with the local police." He looked around the store as if assessing its worth. "Any ideas about who would put the kid up to such mischief?"

"Killing a pet is not mischief."

"Poor choice of words, sorry. Question stands. Who has it in for you or Emma Mae?"

"I don't know of anyone." She bit at her lower lip.

"Take us to your aunt." He acted as if he planned to arrest them.

"Wait here." She didn't add a please, since he'd been too pushy. She walked down the hall to the office, wondering if Joe knew they'd be coming and if so why hadn't he alerted her? Lydia lay across the threshold to the back exit door and raised her head when Jennifer went into the office. Emma Mae reclined on the small sofa, one arm crooked over her face. "You awake?" Jennifer asked quietly.

"Yes." She moved her arm and stared at the ceiling.

"Are you okay?" Jennifer was uncertain as to how badly the recent tragedies had affected her aunt.

Emma Mae let out a sigh. "Thinking about that awful boy."

"Detective Cameron is here. Are you up to seeing him?"

"About time." Emma Mae sat up, threw off an afghan, and swung her feet to the floor. "I have questions, don't you?" She pushed at her hair and straightened her blouse. "Were Clifford and Maxie killed by the same poison? Why can't our police department tell us what that boy used? Everything is so hush-hush."

"I want to know, too." Jennifer stepped back from the sofa. "The vet will tell us when she gets the report even if the police don't."

Jennifer stepped into the hall and motioned to Cameron and Seager. Lydia got up and sniffed at them as they passed.

"Is he yours?" the detective asked.

"Yes, she's mine. Don't worry, Lydia's well-trained." As she said this, she recalled Lydia's reaction to Alex and smiled.

The detective nodded and both men entered the office, giving Lydia a wide berth. Emma Mae sat at the desk like a schoolmarm waiting for her students. Jennifer smothered a chuckle. Leave it to Emma Mae to take the seat of authority.

"I'm sorry about your cat," Cameron began, then glanced at Jennifer. "Would you leave us alone, Miss Frost?"

"Jennifer can hear anything I have to say." Emma Mae sat erect, her thin chin pointed upward.

Cameron pursed his lips. "I'm sure that's true, but I'd like to talk to you alone, then I'll talk to your niece. Bear with me." He raised his hands and gave what Jennifer thought was an insincere smile. "Police procedure," he added.

Jennifer bit off a retort and left. Seager closed the door, preventing any eavesdropping. Even as she returned to help customers, her mind drifted to the past few days. Detective Cameron had already interviewed Jennifer after Wedgeworth's death. What else could he ask her?

Mrs. Perkins, one of her mother's friends, entered. Jennifer groaned inwardly. Not a good time to have a know-it-all rumormonger in the store.

With a purposeful set to her receding chin, the woman approached like a hen ruffling its feathers. "I just heard about Maxie from your mother," Mrs. Perkins said, peering around the store, then toward the back. "How's Emma Mae taking it?"

"It's been difficult on her." She forced a smile. "May I help you find a book?"

"No." The woman fidgeted; her pale hands with their bright red fingernails kneaded her purse as if it were dough. "I want to offer Emma Mae my condolences. Where is she?"

"Busy. In the office." Jennifer moved in front of the woman to block her attempt to walk down the hall to the office. Trying to be pleasant, Jennifer added, "I'll tell her you came by."

"Surely she can drop what she's doing and see me."

At that moment Officer Seager came out of the office and beckoned to Jennifer.

"Who's that young man?" Mrs. Perkins asked, pointing.

"Excuse me," Jennifer said. "Emma Mae needs me right now. Why don't you write her a note, and she'll give you a call?"

Jennifer left Mrs. Perkins standing at the counter, but she knew the woman wouldn't budge until she'd learned everything about the "young man."

Emma Mae stood as Jennifer entered the office. "The detective doesn't want us to speak to each other until he's talked with you." She waggled a finger at Cameron. "Don't you dare give my niece a hard time."

Only Emma Mae could get away with doing that to a policeman. As her aunt walked by, Jennifer whispered, "Mrs. Perkins is here."

"Oh, my. She's such a buttinski." Emma Mae turned toward the detective. "Everyone's talking about Maxie's death, so the sooner you give us the details, the better it will be for this town." She shut the door firmly behind her.

Jennifer moved toward the desk, but the detective rolled a chair in front of it and motioned to it. No seat of authority for her.

A trapped fly buzzed against the window, searching for an out.

"Tell me about your relationship with Clifford Wedgeworth," he said before she was seated.

"I already told you." She sat, her back rigid.

"Indulge me." He eased himself into the chair behind the desk. Seager sat on the edge of the sofa, taking notes on a laptop.

Cameron's practiced smile irked her, but she repeated what she'd told him earlier, trying to remain cooperative.

"That's it? Nothing to add?" He looked up from his notes.

"What else do you want to know?"

"We're checking phone records of the Wedgeworth's and all those involved. Did you call him?"

"No."

"Email him?"

"No."

"I'd appreciate some cooperation, Miss Frost."

"I thought I was being very forthright."

She waited. Silence. He waited, staring at her. The fly swooped by.

"Did you check the catering service?" she finally asked.

"Why would I do that?"

"I hadn't thought of it before," she said. "I mean before I heard Mr. Wedgeworth had been poisoned. One of the waiters offered him cheese crackers that Mrs. Wedgeworth had baked. Mr. Wedgeworth mentioned the flavor was different. I didn't think too much of it at the time." She thought of Cynthia's reaction. "His wife seemed surprised. Could those crackers have contained the poison?"

"Interesting," Cameron said. "Do you know what the poison was?"

"The news didn't say. Could it be the same thing that killed our cat? I'm sure you realize that Emma Mae is anxious to know."

"As I told your aunt, I don't have that information, Miss Frost." The detective leaned back and crossed his arms over his chest. The fly buzzed around the room. "Why do you think a waiter would want to kill Mr. Wedgeworth?"

Jennifer glanced at Seager, who was inputting everything she said into his laptop. Had she said too much? "Two poisonings within a few days seem too coincidental. The boy who poisoned Maxie said an old man paid him to do it. The waiter was old."

"Can you give me a better description, other than that he was old?"

Jennifer thought for a moment then shook her head. "I'm afraid not. It happened quickly, and he was dressed like the other caterers. He was old. The rest were relatively young." The soft click of the laptop keys made her acutely aware of every word she spoke. The fly continued to buzz. "The poison that killed Maxie was potent. He got sick immediately, and Mr. Wedgeworth seemed fine one moment, and then fell dead. Doesn't the similarity seem odd?"

Cameron said, "Your aunt said you took a trip to Baja this past winter. Is that true?"

"What's that got to do with what we were talking about?"

"*You* were talking about poison. *I* asked if you went to Baja." The detective shooed the fly away with a wave of his hand.

"Emma Mae already told you I did. It's not a secret." She stared at the ticking clock on the wall. The minute hand moved. She folded her hands in her lap.

Detective Cameron tapped his pencil on his notepad. "Two years ago you, your aunt, and Alex Glidden were on the island when your sister was murdered. Now we have another murder, and you, your aunt, and Alex Glidden are again on-scene. What should I make of that?"

"I have no idea," she said.

He glanced at the file before him. "You inherited your sister's share of your grandfather's estate."

Jennifer clasped her hands together in her lap. "That's correct. I'm sure that information is in the police file from Carla's case."

"What did you do with her money?"

"Her money?" His insinuation was obvious. "I've invested two years of my life looking for my sister's murderer, so don't pull the old police refrain that I killed her."

"That's not what I'm saying." Cameron voice held a cloying smoothness. "What did you do with the money you inherited?"

"I don't know what that has to do with Wedgeworth's murder."

He nodded. "I'm trying to put together all pertinent facts."

She toyed with the cuticle on her thumb. "I bought half ownership in this business and put the rest in securities. My investment kept the store going."

"Bookstores aren't moneymakers these days. Why invest in it. Why keep it?"

How much should she explain? She'd thought that finding Carla's book would be easier if she were in the book business. And it had been. She'd found the book, but everything hadn't fallen into place as she thought it would. With Joe leaving town, she had doubts about staying in Brandon.

"I asked you a question," the detective said.

"The answer to your question isn't simple. The book business seemed a way to learn about Carla's missing copy of *The Big Sleep* by Chandler, the copy was in Clifford Wedgeworth's collection. I'm sure you already know about that."

"It's general knowledge that the Wedgeworth book collection goes to a foundation, so the book you supposedly found isn't likely to be a motive," he said.

Jennifer gnawed on an idea. If the book wasn't the reason for Clifford's murder, then Cynthia might have killed him to get control of the estate. Was the woman capable of murder? But why try to kill Emma Mae or me? Cynthia Wedgeworth now went on the top of her people-to-see list.

"We're interviewing everyone with a motive." The fly landed on the desk. He thwacked at it with his notepad.

Startled, she pushed her chair back, scraping it on the wood floor.

The fly continued its harried flight.

"According to Warren Peabody, there's no record that you appraised Wedgeworth's collection, no contract, no check issued, and he was unaware of such a decision made by his employer."

"I was paid cash."

"Isn't that unusual?"

"Yes. I thought so at the time. Our initial contact was a message on my answering machine. I'm not sure who left it." She hesitated. "You said you were checking phone records. Wouldn't it be listed?"

"Male or female?"

She shrugged. "Hard to tell. A deep voice. I presumed Mr. Wedgeworth had his reasons for not wanting any documentation of our arrangement."

He leaned forward. "Why?"

"I don't know. I sent Mr. Wedgeworth a disc. It must be among his possessions."

"Do you have a copy?"

"No. At his request, I agreed not to keep a copy."

Cameron's practiced smile again. *God, he was insufferable.* "The groundskeeper, Harold, can attest to my being at the estate to do the appraisal. He let me into the library. Ask him."

"I will." He turned a page of his notebook. Then as if somehow he had discovered an amazing clue, he said, "We matched your print to ones found on the glass case in the library."

"I told you I appraised the collection."

"Peabody said the bookcases had been thoroughly cleaned before the party."

Jennifer began to perspire. "Before Mr. Wedgeworth came into the library, I looked for Carla's copy I'd found in the collection during my appraisal. It was missing."

"Alex Glidden said he got it from Clifford Wedgeworth in a trade."

"Yes, he told me, but I didn't know that at the time."

"I see. So you found Carla's book, the one you said she had at the time of her death. Now Alex has this copy, but neither of you know how Clifford Wedgeworth got the book. Is that correct? And you think your sister and Wedgeworth might have been killed for the book. A book that's worth a mere eighteen thousand dollars."

If he didn't know about the imprints of a document signed by Einstein, she wasn't about to tell him.

He turned to Officer Seager. "Make a note to check with Peabody about the book in question, then get it from Alex Glidden."

Jennifer froze. *No. You can't do that. I need it.* Instead, she clasped her hands tighter.

"The idea that Clifford Wedgeworth's murder ties back to your sister's case is disturbing."

The fly landed on the desk again. Cameron smashed it with his notebook. He grinned and brushed it into the wastebasket at the side of the desk. "I'm giving you the same warning I've given to the others. Don't leave the area without contacting my department." He smiled. "It wouldn't look good for your credibility."

Seager closed his laptop and the men left without a goodbye.

So much for good manners. Jennifer remained seated in the office, fuming. She didn't like Detective Cameron and didn't want him to have Carla's book, even though the police had a right to take it as evidence. She had to warn Alex. It felt as if a fishhook dangled just outside her mouth, ready for her to bite. One false move and she'd be hooked. A suspect again. Becoming the scapegoat for an overzealous detective was not going to happen to her. She needed to see Wedgeworth's records of his collections before the detective confiscated them as evidence. To do that she needed Cynthia's permission.

Chapter 19

Before the brunt of a threatening storm hit, Jennifer drove up the coast and hiked on the bluffs. Gusts whipped her hair and plastered her sage-colored corduroy pants and green windbreaker against her body. Below the cliff, angry waves smashed against the rocks, and in the distance, steel-gray clouds frowned over the turbulent ocean. Wind raced across the sea, spewing the pewter-colored water into white, frothy foam. Soon, the storm would howl its fury onto the coast.

Lydia trotted ahead, her nose quivering at smells emanating from the sea. Errant blasts of frenzied air splayed her black fur and lifted her ears like birds in flightThe hour long hike helped Jennifer gain a semblance of order to her ideas and her options. Her house, the town, and even the store felt claustrophobic. Events past and present were an unsolved puzzle: when she picked up one piece, another was shoved out of place. Would Alex's search for the seller of the Einstein letter lead to the killer? Unless the police found another motive for Wedgeworth's death, her theory that he was killed to prevent him from disclosing the previous owner of Carla's copy made sense. Alex had been evasive about how he'd learned Wedgeworth owned the book. He was usually meticulous, yet he'd ignored the most important element of acquiring a valuable book—its provenance. Alex knew this information could lead to the identity of Carla's killer.

The police wanted her to stay in the area. Was her island considered part of "the area?" Alex had urged her to go to her island to be safe, but Carla hadn't been safe there. Even if she wanted to flee to her island, a dash across open water in this gale would be foolhardy even in Clarence's sturdy trawler. Besides, she needed to find answers, not hide.

Was the old man, who hired the boy, Wedgeworth and Carla's killer? If so, who was he and why would he want them both dead? Had the same man tried to kill her or Emma Mae or was it an anomaly?

There were too many threads with no center spool. All she was certain of was that the killer was close. Perhaps her meeting with Cynthia Wedgeworth tomorrow would answer some questions.

Whistling for Lydia, she turned back the way she'd come and spotted a man coming toward her. She recognized his easy saunter from the way he'd approached her on the island, when he'd called himself Rick instead of Ken. What was he doing out here? With the wind whipping across the treeless bluff, Lydia hadn't picked up his scent. When Ken drew nearer, Lydia noticed and trotted in front of her mistress.

Ken and Jennifer stopped a few feet apart. His black watchman's cap covered his forehead and tufts of gray hair spilled out on either side near his temples. His blue windbreaker was zipped up to his neck. "We meet in lonely places," he said.

"How did you know I was out here?"

"Your aunt. Seems you have a problem with a Detective Cameron. She thinks I might be able to help."

She eyed him with suspicion. "I can't imagine how."

"Miss Langdon hired me as a private detective."

"She what?" Jennifer took a step back.

"You heard me. I'm as surprised as you are. But let's discuss it while we walk to the parking area." He gazed at the threatening sky. "It's going to cut loose soon, and I don't want to get drenched."

As Ken moved next to Jennifer, Lydia nudged between them.

"Whoa! She's shoving me to the edge." He pushed at the dog's shoulder with his knee, but Lydia didn't budge.

"Sorry." Jennifer moved over and snapped on Lydia's leash. "She's been overly protective of late."

"From what I hear, that's not a bad idea." He stuck his hands in his pockets as he strode next to her. "Your aunt doesn't like Cameron. Thinks he's interested only in facts that will help his career. I ran a check on him." He leaned close to Jennifer, so his words wouldn't be lost in the wind. "Seems two years ago he was in the cold case unit, got lucky and broke a case that had been on the books for a couple of years. That got him a raise and a transfer into the homicide unit. He became their 'fair-haired boy,' despite some legal challenges. The district attorney liked the results, because they made him look good. But lately cases have backfired due to Cameron's mishandling evidence and his heavy-handed approach with witnesses. The tide's turning against him, and he needs to solve another case."

"That doesn't sound encouraging, but shouldn't you be telling my aunt this instead of me?" She stopped and faced him. "She's your client, not me." Why did Ken bring out the worst in her? Although Emma Mae wanted to protect her, the idea of having a private detective, especially Ken, checking out the evidence she and Alex had already collected annoyed her. She picked up her pace and he matched her stride.

"I'm doing what my client wants, and that is to inform you of everything I learn." He stopped and took her arm, preventing her from moving on. "Why won't you trust me? You should have pulled in outside assistance after your sister was killed instead of going at it on your own. Have you got something against a helping hand or what?"

Jennifer stared out at the forbidding sea. She and Alex had joined together against the onslaught of the police, friends, family, and the press. It had been them against the world, but despite giving them a sense of control, they hadn't succeeded, and Alex had abandoned her. Why not accept help now? Her hair whipped around her face as she turned to study Ken. "Okay. You win."

He gave a curt nod. "Good. Let's talk about what you know and what you don't and go from there."

They moved on as Jennifer told him about the crime and what she and Alex had learned since, about the book and the possibility of a paper written by Einstein being left inside it. By the time she finished explaining, they'd arrived at the parking area. The earlier spritz of rain turned into a heavy deluge. The small confine of his Porsche was out of the question, so they got into Jennifer's jeep with Lydia in the back. The car swayed from heavy gusts and water streamed down the front windshield.

Even before they'd settled into their seats, Ken asked, "How does Alex fit into the picture?"

"What do you mean? I told you he's been searching for the book like I have. It just happened that he was at the party when Wedgeworth died."

"Don't jump all over me, but his sudden appearance seems coincidental."

Jennifer's view out of the window blurred. Joe had implied the same thing, but she'd chalked up his reaction to a case of jealousy. But if she was honest, she too had similar thoughts; however, his confiding in her about the book had dispelled her misgivings. Alex's explanation of his reappearance seemed so rational that she hadn't questioned him. She felt a nudge at her elbow and looked down to see Lydia's large head between the bucket seats. "You want to investigate Alex, don't you?" she asked Ken.

"It makes sense to find out if everything he's told you is true. If so, no harm's done. If not, we need to find out why."

She shivered. "It all sounds so...so slimy."

"That's why I told you not to play detective."

"Yes, you did."

Ken's jacket rustled as he half-turned toward her. "For two years, no new clues appeared about your sister's death. Then Alex appears. You find the book and clues to a missing paper. The one man who can tell you the former owner of the book is poisoned. Your cat is poisoned. Why? Is someone trying to scare you or kill you?"

Jennifer stroked Lydia's neck. All he said was true and the questions he asked were the same she'd asked herself. However, the one fact Ken failed to mention was that he, himself, had been brought onto the scene by Wedgeworth. Could she trust him?

"Ken, how did you get to know Wedgeworth?"

"The ever cautious Jennifer." He smiled. "I'd done some investigative work for him in the past."

As a careful businessman, Wedgeworth would have checked on Ken's credentials. She nodded, somewhat satisfied. She didn't trust people; thought everyone had a hidden agenda. Paranoid, Emma Mae would say. But was she paranoid or cautious? She'd keep her appointment with Cynthia Wedgeworth to herself.

"I can almost see your wheels cranking," Ken said. "I've learned if you think too much about a puzzle, you lose the main picture. Keep it simple and the pieces fall into place."

There was a roar behind them. Jennifer peered out the rearview mirror and saw Alex's rented sedan. Dressed in a tan raincoat, he got out, and slammed his car door. He hurried toward her side of the jeep and rapped on the window. She cracked open the window.

"Are you all right? What's going on?" he yelled over the thundering rain.

She motioned for him to get in the backseat. When he opened the door, Lydia met him with a slobbering lick. "Geez! What's worse, your growl or your kisses? Give me a break." He shoved his way into the back, pulling his coat around him. After shutting the door, he glared first at Ken and then at Jennifer.

The group sat in the car with the rain pounding on the roof and the smell of wet dog permeating the air. Neither man seemed pleased with the presence of the other. Jennifer introduced them and watched the male dance of intimidation.

"You're visiting, I understand," Ken said. "Bad timing."

"It's always a good time to see Jennifer." Alex put a possessive hand on Jennifer's shoulder. "Emma Mae said you'd come up here to walk. She was worried about you in this storm."

"A woman who likes to live on a deserted island can handle a little storm," Ken said. "Did she tell you that's where we met?"

Alex frowned, his mouth narrowed into a grimace. "She hasn't mentioned you."

"No wonder. You've only been here a short time and a lot has happened. Murder makes one forget other matters." Ken stroked Lydia's fur.

"Give it a rest, fellas." Jennifer shook her head. "I'm driving back to the store before the road becomes impassable."

"Good idea," Ken said. "I'll be in touch." He put his hand on the door handle. "Keep me posted." He gave Alex a hard look. "Maybe you should think about heading back to sunny California. It can be rough up here for visitors."

Alex snapped back, "I can handle the elements. I've lived here before."

"So I've heard. Just remember, times change, people change, circumstances change." Ken leaned forward, kissed Jennifer on the cheek, gave a pat to Lydia, and got out of the car.

Jennifer watched him run to his Porsche and climb in. Within seconds, he had the motor purring. Skidding out of the muddy parking area, he sprayed globs of muck onto Alex's sedan. He was as good at driving as he was at sailing. The jeep remained unblemished.

"Idiot!" Alex said under his breath.

Jennifer covered her smile with her hand. Both men had turned up in peculiar circumstances. She wished she could be certain that they had her well-being in mind and not their own.

Alex began to shove Lydia aside, but when she resisted, he gave up. Clasping the back of Jennifer's seat, he leaned forward so that his mouth was close to her ear.

She twisted around to look at him. "Why did you really come up here?"

"Emma Mae said you were walking on the bluffs. She failed to mention you were with someone. Despite distrusting me, she asked me to deliver the latest news to you."

"Since Maxie was killed, she's suspicious of everyone. She even hired Ken to investigate."

"Investigate what? What are you talking about?"

"Ken's a private detective. I thought I told you about him."

"Well, you didn't, and it's a crazy idea. What can he do that you and I haven't done?"

"I don't know, but we'll find out, won't we?"

Alex's eyes narrowed. "I don't trust him and I don't like him."

"Nobody asked you to." His sulking was tiresome. "Did you come up here to spy on me?"

"I didn't come here to fight, but to tell you the vet called about the poison that killed Maxie. It's really strange, but now I know why Detective Cameron asked about my trip to Florida."

Jennifer gripped the steering wheel. "What was it?"

"The Barbados nut."

"What's that?"

"I asked the vet for an exact clarification. She said it comes from the tropics. It's the seed from a small tree called *Jatropha curcas* and has the similar toxic properties to snake venom. Apparently, it has a pleasant taste, but it's deadly."

"Why would they allow it to be sold?"

"It's used to process biodiesel fuel. Reaction time after eating it is about fifteen to twenty minutes. The vet said in the case of a small animal like Maxie, it would take less time."

"Is that what killed Wedgeworth?"

Alex shook his head. "I don't know. The police aren't talking. But why ask everyone where they've traveled recently if it wasn't that particular poison?"

They sat in silence. Jennifer stroked Lydia's head and stared out at the rain streaming down the windshield. "What did Emma Mae say?"

"She was grim. She didn't want to tell me where you were, but I convinced her that it would be better if you knew as soon as possible." He pursed his lips. "Your aunt never believed I was innocent of Carla's death." His shoulders slumped. "Maybe, I should never have gotten in touch with you again. When I learned about the book, I thought I could help. Instead things seem to be getting worse."

She stared into the rearview mirror and watched his face sag in despair. "Your return speaks to your innocence." Why was she always defending him to herself and others? "You're here and you said you'd help. Have you found out anything about the Einstein paper?"

"Cameron wanted the book as evidence."

"I warned you."

"Thank goodness you did. I put it in the mail addressed to myself at a Tacoma post office box. I told him I'd sent it to Hebrew University in Israel. So what could he do? If he wants to get a court order to get it back, the paperwork will take forever and by then things might have been resolved."

She smiled and patted his hand. "You're brilliant."

His dark eyes sparkled, but he said, "Brilliant enough to be put in jail for withholding evidence. I contacted the curator in Jerusalem. He admitted an Einstein paper had been recently recovered. When I said I had the book that the paper had been lodged in and it had an imprint of Einstein's signature, he was interested in meeting me. Wants a look at the book. He'll be in Boston this weekend. I just hope the mail delivers the book in time before I fly out."

"But you can't leave the state unless you notify the police," she said.

"Yeah. Well, I'll take my chances."

"That might not be a good idea. Cameron has his eye on both of us. What if you don't find out the name of the person who sold the paper to the museum?" Her eyes met his.

"Maybe I can come up with another idea," he said. "I'll let you know."

Chapter 20

Throughout the night, the wind and rain tore across the land, stripping golden-brown leaves from limbs, uprooting saplings and slinging refuse into the streets. By dawn, nature, like a child calmed after a temper tantrum, settled into a cold, raw day.

She called Joe, knowing he'd be up early. When his voice came over the line in a groggy rasp, she said, "Hi, sleepy head."

"Ha. Easy for you to talk. I was up late assisting firemen getting people out of a house where a tree had fallen through their roof."

"Oh, Joe. I'm so sorry. Was anyone hurt?"

"No. Lucky thing." He paused. "What's up?"

"A lot. Can you drop over? I have an appointment with Cynthia Wedgeworth and I wanted to ask you a few things before I go."

"You sound anxious."

She smiled at this. "A little ruffled. When do you have to go on duty?"

"I've got some time. If you fix breakfast, I'll swing by in a half hour."

"Deal. See you," she said and hung up.

Jennifer gazed through the kitchen window pasted with fall leaves, thinking of how much she depended on Joe. She set to making french toast and placed a few strips of bacon on the griddle. When Joe's truck came up the driveway, Lydia perked up her head.

He entered the front door wearing his uniform and scratched Lydia behind the ears. Jennifer welcomed him with open arms. Perhaps her kiss was more fervent than usual, since his response turned into more than just a morning embrace.

"You smell of lavender," he murmured into her ear as he nuzzled her neck.

"Joe," she said, "Breakfast is ready."

He burst out laughing. "God, you certainly know how to break the spell."

She held him tighter. "I am a pain, aren't I?"

"A wonderful pain." He kissed her lightly.

As they parted, their fingers traced each others' palms. She smiled into his blue eyes, knowing her longing for him was written there. "Sit down," she said more abruptly than she intended. He drew up a chair to the table, and she placed coffee, juice and a plate of bacon and french toast in front of him.

"I like the service, especially the welcome."

"I only do that for special guests." She winked and sat opposite him, watching him devour breakfast.

"Tell me what's going on," he said between mouthfuls.

"So much. I don't know where to start." She took a sip of coffee before beginning. "The poison used on Maxie was from the Barbados nut. Apparently it contains a very toxic chemical."

His fork paused in midair. "How did you hear that? The Seattle police haven't notified us of the lab's results yet."

"The vet called Emma Mae and told Alex. From the questions the police are asking, I think it may be the same poison used on Wedgeworth."

"Jesus, Jennifer. That's crazy. Aren't you jumping to conclusions?" He stared at her. "No, I take that back. It could be, but that means you're involved in some nasty business."

Not wanting to talk about her own danger, she asked, "What do you know about Detective Cameron?"

He wiped his mouth with a paper napkin. "A good man. Overly obsessive about his old job on cold cases. It's understandable in a way." He took a last bite of bacon.

"Why?"

"His wife and daughter were murdered about five years ago. Never found the killer. He went on a drinking binge, then got his act together and worked his way into the Cold Case Unit. He's cracked one or two difficult cases. A promotion led to the Homicide Unit."

She sat back and twirled her cup. "Interesting. That's a variation of the scenario I heard from Ken Sullivan."

"Oh? Ken isn't exactly enamored with the Seattle police department and vice versa. He got himself in an awkward situation on a case that riled the police. But he's legit. Only oddity is that he has a lot of money for someone who only has a small P.I. practice." He shrugged. "Maybe he inherited money."

"He said he came into money a few years ago."

"Possible. I could look into his financial records if I had cause. I can ask Cameron."

"Please don't. Cameron brought up the old investigation into my sister's murder and implied that I was still a suspect."

"That's ridiculous."

"He doesn't seem to think so."

"I can set him straight."

"As you said, he has a hangup on cold cases and the last thing I need is to be put in Cameron's crosshairs any more than I already am."

"Is there anything I can do to help?"

How much should she tell him about Alex and the missing book? After all he was a policeman. If he knew that Alex had deliberately mailed the book to himself, trying to avoid Cameron from obtaining their discovery, he might feel legally bound to tell Cameron She reached across the table for his hand. "Be there for me like you always have been."

Chapter 21

When Jennifer left for her appointment with Cynthia, Lydia remained behind in the large enclosed backyard. Her dog should be safe, but as a precaution she asked a stay-at-home neighbor to check on her.

Driving south on wet pavement littered with debris took longer than she'd anticipated, and she was a half hour late for her appointment with Cynthia Wedgeworth. When she arrived at the gate to the estate's entrance, she reached out and pushed the button in the lion's mouth. Cynthia's voice told her to drive in and park in front of the main entrance. Jennifer couldn't detect any hint of disapproval for her being late.

Even here on the estate, the storm had left its mark. At the far end of the large green lawn Harold was dragging a large limb to a pile of dead branches. After she parked at the front of the manor, Jennifer zipped up her fleece-lined jacket and stepped out into the cold. She took in the austere stone of the house in contrast to the shiny rain-cleaned green of the surrounding bushes. Shutting her car door, she walked up the steps and rang the bell.

Cynthia opened the door and stood in the archway, her eyes red-rimmed and swollen, her hair disheveled, her slacks wrinkled, and her wool cardigan baggy.

"Mrs. Wedgeworth," Jennifer began.

"Please, call me Cynthia." She beckoned Jennifer inside and offered a weak handshake. "I'm glad you called."

Even through Jennifer's glove, the woman's hand felt cold.

"We'll be more comfortable in the kitchen," Cynthia said, closing the front door.

As Jennifer followed her hostess through the living room where the party had taken place, she removed her gloves, but kept her jacket on.

Cynthia must have noticed, for she stopped and said, "Warren keeps the heat off in parts of the house that I don't use. The kitchen is warmer."

Jennifer thought it odd that Warren Peabody had control over the use of the house. They went through a door leading to a pantry and continued on into a modern kitchen with stainless steel appliances. The wallpaper's pattern of strawberry plants and vines gave a cheerful feel to the room despite the dismal weather visible through a large bay window. Cynthia motioned for Jennifer to sit at the table in a breakfast nook while she went to the gas stove and turned on the burner.

"Black tea okay?" she asked.

"Fine." Jennifer studied Cynthia as she stood at the burners waiting for the water in the blue teakettle to boil. Strands of blonde hair escaped from a ponytail and straggled down the sides of her plain face. Her sweater stretched down to her hips. She scuffed about the kitchen in fur-lined mukluks. Jennifer wondered where the servants were and whether Cynthia, now an heiress, was alone in the huge house.

As if reading Jennifer's mind, Cynthia said, "The servants are gone."

"But it's only been what…a week?"

"Warren let them go. Said I didn't need them. Harold's the only one who stayed." As she poured the boiling water into a white ceramic teapot, her large diamond engagement ring sparkled. "Of course, Warren comes and goes as he pleases." She sighed and shuffled to the table with two mugs and turned back to get the teapot. "The memorial service is tomorrow at St. Martins." She set down the pot of steeping tea on the table and sat across from Jennifer. "There's a reception in the annex afterward. I couldn't stand to have a gathering here after what happened." She poured tea into the mugs and cupped her cold hands around hers. "I haven't talked with anyone in three days, unless you count Cliff's lawyer and Warren."

Jennifer reached across the table and laid her hand on the woman's forearm. "I'm so sorry. I had no idea. I thought you had friends here."

Cynthia shrugged and Jennifer withdrew her hand. In silence they sipped their tea and looked out the window at the green landscape that melted into the shroud of fog. The refrigerator whirred. When Jennifer cleared her throat, the sound echoed through the kitchen.

"I'm from Las Vegas," Cynthia said. "In Seattle, that's like having your forehead stamped, 'Gold Digger.' You know why Cliff married me?" She smiled wryly. "I made him laugh. Can you believe it? A man with all his wealth, and his life had become a drag. He said he was tired of business, tired of holding onto an empire, tired of being serious." She slumped in her chair, her lips trembling. "Maybe he was just tired of life. But he said when he met me, he felt alive again." Cynthia rallied and raised her head. "He made me feel special. I hadn't felt special to anyone in years, except maybe the kids." She rubbed her fingers along her thin lips.

Surprised, Jennifer blurted out, "I didn't know you had children."

"Not mine exactly. I taught kindergarten in Vegas. Hardly the *femme fatale* Cliff's friends make me out to be."

"You must have loved him a great deal to move to Seattle without knowing what you were getting into."

"We met at a clown convention." Cynthia's lips drew back in a smile. "Yeah, I know what you're thinking. Clifford Wedgeworth a clown! No way. But he loved the idea that when he was in makeup he could be someone else."

Wedgeworth as a clown was at odds with Jennifer's impression of him, but she recalled the painting above the door in the library.

Cynthia shook her head. "His makeup wasn't excessive. He used it subtly to hide his identity."

"Did his friends know about his hobby?"

"I doubt it. He said clowning was his private passion. It was no one else's business." She looked around the kitchen and out the window at the manicured estate. "At my age, I should have known better than to marry a man out of my social league and twenty-four years my senior. But I thought I'd be able to fit in." She wadded up a tissue and clenched it in her hand. "Sailing is a big thing here. He owns a yacht. I'd never been on a boat. Got seasick the one time he took me out. I would have tried real hard to make him happy, make a life here. That'll never happen now." She dabbed at her eyes with the tissue. "We were married only four months."

"You must feel confused and lonely. At least that's how I felt after my sister died." Jennifer noticed that Cynthia drifted in and out of using the present tense and past tense when she spoke about her husband. "It's hard to grasp the enormity of what's happened to you. Like a dream."

"I'm in a fog." Cynthia stared down at the table. "We got married in Vegas and came here afterward because Cliff had to tend to business. Everything went smoothly until I made a big mistake. I thought I was doing something nice for him, but I realized the day he died, actually it was when he introduced me to you, that he was furious with me." She pulled out a tissue from the sweater's side pocket and dabbed at her red eyes.

Jennifer frowned. "Why?"

"Because I hired you to appraise his recent acquisitions."

"I don't understand. You hired me?" Jennifer blinked. It was like having all the right colors in a Rubik cube fall into place. "Then you have the disc."

Cynthia nodded.

The typed letters and the handwritten notes on Clifford's desk circled through Jennifer's mind. Of course, *C Wedgeworth* could have stood for Cynthia or Clifford. "But why was an appraisal a problem? And how did you decide to hire me?"

Cynthia blew her nose. "I overheard Warren and Cliff talking about his recent acquisitions. Warren said Cliff should get another appraisal for estate purposes. I heard your name mentioned. So thinking I was real smart, I asked you to do it on the sly, while we were on our honeymoon, as a surprise. Yesterday Warren told me that when Cliff found out what I'd done, he became irate and suspicious."

Jennifer shook her head. "Cynthia, it doesn't make sense. If he wanted to get an appraisal and I did one, why was he angry?"

"I signed a prenuptial agreement. I didn't read it thoroughly. I wasn't after his money, even though his friends thought I was. He said he'd take care of me and that was good enough for me. There's a meeting with the lawyer on Monday. I have no idea what to expect." She kneaded her brow with her fingers. "Let's see. I guess I got off track. My mind jumps from one thing to the next."

"That's understandable with everything that's happened."

"Oh, I know. The prenup agreement." She hesitated and took a sip from her mug before she explained. "Warren said that Cliff thought I was trying to undermine that agreement. If I'd known what Cliff thought, I'd have told him why I had the appraisal done. But he was killed before I could make it right." Tears trickled down her cheeks, but she didn't make a sound.

Jennifer reached out and held Cynthia's hand. "It was a misunderstanding. He would have understood."

"But he's gone, and I can't tell him!" She pulled her hand away from Jennifer's, folded her arms on the table and cradled her head in them. Her body heaved with heavy sobs.

Jennifer waited, unable to help.

Finally after a few audible gasps, Cynthia lifted her head and sighed. "You must think I'm crazy."

"Hardly. You're miserable. Perfectly understandable." Jennifer wondered how she would react to her request to see her husband's records. She'd have to tell her about Carla. Perhaps shared agony would make her willing to help. "I need to explain why I came to see you. What I have to say may shed some light on your husband's death, but I'm not sure. Are you up to listening?"

A hint of a smile crept over Cynthia's face. "I don't have much else to do. More tea?"

Jennifer looked about the kitchen. "Do you have any honey or sugar?"

Cynthia's hand flew to her mouth. "What a dunce. I should have thought to ask. Honey, yes." She rose and rummaged through a cabinet until she found a plastic jar of honey. Holding it up like a trophy, she walked back to the table, set it in front of Jennifer, and poured more tea into both their mugs.

Over honey-sweetened tea, Jennifer told Cynthia the story of Carla's murder, the missing book, how she found it in Clifford's collection, and what had transpired since. When she'd finished, Cynthia said, "I'm sorry. I didn't realize how much trauma you've been through." She frowned. "You think Cliff was murdered because he had your sister's book?"

"As I said, it's an assumption. It's not that he had the book. It's who he got it from that's important." Jennifer hesitated and studied Cynthia. "I'd like to see his records to check the book's provenance."

"Warren keeps Clifford's records locked in the library desk."

"I don't understand all the circumstances about your affairs, but aren't you in control of Clifford's estate?"

Cynthia gave her a blank look. "I haven't given it much thought. I've just been sitting around moping. I haven't thought much about who does what." She straightened up. "Maybe it's time I asked some questions."

Cynthia's flash of insight gave Jennifer the courage to ask, "Could we take a look at the records now?"

Cynthia shrugged. "Why not? You'll have to wait while I get the key to the library door. It's upstairs in Cliff's closet. Warren has the only other key." She stood. "I'll be back in a minute."

While she waited for Cynthia to return, Jennifer wandered around the kitchen. Why had Warren asked the servants to leave? As Wedgeworth's personal secretary, he seemed to have total control of everything—a little too much control. Under the circumstances, Jennifer wanted to know more about the man. Maybe Ken could find out.

The kitchen seemed too clean, as if no one had cooked in days. Did she dare open the refrigerator? She edged toward it, opened it and peeked inside. Seeing it was stocked with food was a relief. She'd just shut the door when Cynthia returned.

Side by side they walked along the hall to the library. While Cynthia fussed with the lock, Jennifer thought of the first time she'd been here when Harold had admitted her. After Cynthia swung the door open, she and Jennifer stared in the direction of the bathroom where Clifford had died. There was no sign that anything remarkable had happened, but Jennifer replayed the tape of the incident in her mind. Realizing Cynthia was doing the same thing, she put her arm around the woman's shoulders.

"Thanks." Cynthia put a fist to her lips. "I haven't been in here since…." Her voice trailed off. "I felt kind of shaky for a second." She moved behind the desk, sat in the large leather swivel chair and unlocked the top drawer. After she slid the drawer open, she pulled out a small wooden box with four keys inside. "Three are for the glass bookcases," she mumbled. "He keeps ledgers in the file drawer." She unlocked the bottom right drawer with the fourth key, pulled out two ledgers, and put them on top of the desk.

Jennifer looked over Cynthia's shoulder as the widow opened one for general accounts. Cynthia slipped it back into the drawer. Jennifer itched to grab the green ledger that contained information on Clifford's books. Each page held information on one book. Cynthia turned the pages, inspecting each one by one.

Unable to wait, Jennifer said. "The entry for *The Big Sleep* should follow the George Washington book entry."

Cynthia flipped forward several pages. Jennifer gasped, reached forward and fingered the ragged edges of a torn out page. The entry information of *The Big Sleep* was missing.

"What do you think you're doing?" Warren Peabody stood in the doorway with his hands on his narrow hips.

Chapter 22

Warren's sallow face grew taught, his eyes glared, and his body quivered like a cat ready to pounce on its prey. "Those are Mr. Wedgeworth's!"

Cynthia recoiled in the desk chair.

"They are kept under lock and key for a reason." He moved forward, his jaw set. "You have no right to…." His right hand reached out as if to grab the ledger, but Cynthia pulled it away.

"I have every right. I'm his wife." Her words came out slowly, then a hiss escaped her quivering lips. Somehow Cynthia had gathered strength from her recent conversation with Jennifer and their discovery of the missing page. Sitting erect with her chin up, she seemed to reassess Warren.

"Damn it! I'm his widow. Cliff is dead. Murdered." Cynthia pounded her fist on the desk with tears welling up in her eyes. "You come and go like you own the place. You dismissed the servants without asking me. You're managing the memorial service." Her eyes grew flinty. "But you will no longer manage what I do in this house."

Warren's face reddened and his prominent Adam's apple bobbed, as he took a step back and drew in his breath. "I'm his secretary. I've been with Mr. Wedgeworth for twelve years. I know what he'd want done. How would you know? You've been here only a few months."

Cynthia's hands trembled as she tapped her index finger on the ledger. "If you were in charge of this, then you must have torn out the page. Why?" Her blue eyes grew smoky. "Did you kill Clifford?"

Warren's face drained white. "How can you say that after all the years I've worked for him?" He stuck out his narrow chin. "I was his confidant, his right hand man, his true friend. I understood him." He stepped back to stand by the leather chair at the far table, his body rigid, as if he were expecting to be physically assaulted.

Both shared grief and anger, but Jennifer's disappointment in the lost page made her less sympathetic. "It's a difficult time for both of you.

Under normal circumstances, I'd walk out and let you argue. But Clifford Wedgeworth was murdered, and the reason may be related to the lost page in the ledger." Her body stiffened. "Mr. Peabody, did you take it?"

Warren took a halting step forward. "Who do you think you are barging in here and making accusations?"

"She's my guest," Cynthia said. "The page has been torn out."

"You're wrong. Mr. Wedgeworth prided himself on keeping exact reports." He moved toward the desk and thrust out his hand. "Let me see."

Cynthia shoved the ledger forward, facing it toward him. He picked it up and ran his bony fingers through the pages, stopping where the page had been removed. "Impossible." Frowning, he flipped through more pages.

Jennifer walked around the desk to his side. "Alex Glidden traded him a copy of Steinbeck's *A Cup of Gold* for the Chandler book. Has that trade been posted?" Jennifer peered over Warren's shoulder as he thumbed through the pages. There was no such entry. Had Alex told her the truth? She closed her eyes for a second to regain her poise, then looked at Warren. "The book exchange has to be on the missing page unless Wedgeworth didn't have time to enter it or decided not to enter it."

Warren slapped the ledger down on the desk. "What does any of this have to do with Mr. Wedgeworth's murder?"

Jennifer wasn't happy about giving Warren any more information than necessary, but if she was going to get information, she needed to concede something. "My sister was murdered and her copy of *The Big Sleep* was a clue to her murderer. Learning the provenance of Wedgeworth's copy could lead to the killer."

Warren glared at her, his face flushed. "Mr. Wedgeworth would never have bought a book from a questionable source, much less a…a murderer. The idea is preposterous."

"He might not have known, but if the seller was the murderer, he would need to keep Wedgeworth quiet." She pointed to the ledger. "And get rid of evidence that could incriminate him." Warren let out a long sigh, and his spine lost some of its rigidity. "I see. Is that why he was killed?"

"I'm not sure," Jennifer said. "It's an assumption that makes sense."

"Do the police agree with you?" Warren asked.

Jennifer hesitated, "I don't know."

"How could anyone get at the ledgers?" He glanced at Cynthia. "I came over the evening before he died. He spoke of a recent addition, but didn't say what it was. It wasn't like him to put off entering a transaction."

"Was the ledger out during the party?" Jennifer asked.

"Absolutely not. He asked me to unlock the room." He studied Jennifer. "You were there at the time. You must remember. I told him that I hadn't locked it because his guest had spent an extraordinary amount of time looking over the collection. I became too busy with arrangements for the party."

"Who was this guest?" Jennifer asked.

"Alex Glidden."

"Alex?" Jennifer's heart lurched. She covered her mouth with her hand to avoid letting out the gasp that nearly choked her.

"You know him?" Warren asked.

"Yes."

"Maybe he did it. He spent a lot of time in here alone." Warren sagged into the leather chair as if a great weight hung about his narrow shoulders. "But the ledgers were locked away." He looked at Cynthia. "Mrs. Wedgeworth, you had access to this room and you knew where he kept the key to the drawers."

Her eyebrows arched. "I didn't kill Cliff. I loved him."

"Cynthia, you got the library key from your husband's closet," Jennifer said. "Harold unlocked it for me when I did the appraisal."

"What appraisal?" Warren asked. "I don't know of any appraisal."

"You weren't supposed to know," Cynthia said. "It was a surprise for Cliff."

"Not at all proper," Warren said. "It was Mr. Wedgeworth's special collection. You shouldn't have interfered."

"It had nothing to do with you," Cynthia said.

"I should have been informed."

"Then it wouldn't have stayed a surprise, would it?" Cynthia said.

The two seemed ready to have a bitter argument. "Let's get back to the keys," Jennifer said. "Did Harold have an extra key or was that key your husband's?"

Cynthia said, "I gave Cliff's key to Harold."

"Harold could have made a copy," Jennifer said. She turned to Peabody. "Or was it yours?"

Warren's dark eyes smoldered. "I didn't give mine to Harold. I keep my set of keys with me at all times. I never give them to anyone."

"Could the drawer have been pried open?" Jennifer asked. "Are there marks on the drawer?"

Cynthia bent over and rubbed her fingers along the drawer's edges, then looked up. "I can't see or feel any marks. Besides, the police never said anything about the drawer being jimmied."

"What does all this key business have to do with his death?" Warren asked. "Mr. Wedgeworth was poisoned. It could have been food poisoning. Something the caterers served. All these insinuations about murder and a killer are blown out of proportion. Pure speculation by the police and you, Miss Frost."

"The poison was the Barbados nut," Cynthia said. "Hardly a common item. The caterer didn't serve it and Cliff wasn't allergic to any foods, not even nuts."

Jennifer whirled on Cynthia like Maxie going after a skirt. "Who told you about that particular nut?"

Cynthia's fingers played along her upper lip. "I don't know. Someone, not the police. They consider me a suspect and wouldn't tell me anything." She looked at Warren. "Was it you?"

"I don't know what you're talking about." He kneaded his temples with his fingers. "The police have been treating me dreadfully, too. It's not fair. It's a nightmare."

Jennifer's mind spun. Cynthia's grief appeared genuine and made it improbable that she was the murderer. "Think, Cynthia. Who could have told you about the source of the poison? It might be important."

Cynthia fiddled with her diamond ring while Warren and Jennifer waited. Finally, she looked up. "Harold must have told me. Other than that awful detective, what's his name, Cameron, I haven't talked to anyone but Warren, Harold, and Cliff's attorney." She relaxed back into her chair as if that explained everything. But of course, it didn't.

Like a dog gnawing a bone, Jennifer continued to query Warren. What would he gain by his boss's death? "Mr. Peabody, have you traveled out of the country lately?"

"Where do you get off asking questions?"

"You sound worried. How come?"

"Well, it's the same stupid question the police asked. Sure. I went to Acapulco when Mr. and Mrs. Wedgeworth went on their honeymoon to the Bahamas. So what?"

"The Barbados nut comes from the tropics. Obviously, the police want to know who had the opportunity to get it." Jennifer said.

"I didn't kill him!" He threw up his hands in disgust. "You can probably get that nut in any specialty market. How do you know you can't? And what motive would I have? Where else am I going to get a job with the salary he gave me? Who's going to hire a fifty-two-year-old secretary? No one. That's who."

Maybe Warren didn't have a motive, but Cynthia might, depending on the prenup. "How would someone doctor the cheese crackers and know Mr. Wedgeworth and no one else would eat them?"

"The crackers? That's how he was poisoned?" Cynthia asked.

"I'm not sure," Jennifer said. "But it seems likely, don't you think?"

Jennifer turned to Warren. "What about the catering service?"

"We always use Blakely Catering." Warren glanced at Cynthia. "I didn't check the caterers out with you, since I didn't think you were interested in taking charge of the party."

Cynthia motioned with her hand. "You did a good job. I was too nervous meeting Cliff's friends."

Jennifer wondered if the police had checked with the catering service about its employees. How could she find out if they had without getting in Cameron's crosshairs?

"There was an elderly server who brought the crackers to Wedgeworth," Jennifer said.

"I'd forgotten that," Cynthia said. "I couldn't understand why the man said I'd baked them. I hadn't and I tried to explain that to Cliff, but he ignored me."

Jennifer looked from one to the other. "Did either of you tell the caterer those were his favorite crackers or that they'd been baked especially for him?"

Both shook their heads.

"Who else might have known about your husband's fondness for the crackers?" Jennifer noticed their interest perked up.

Cynthia looked at Warren. "His friends?"

"Could be, but I wouldn't know who." Like a snake, Warren ran his tongue over his lips as he studied Jennifer. "How did you know he liked those crackers?"

"Harold offered them to me when I was doing the appraisal."

"See," Warren said. "That damn appraisal caused all this."

Jennifer ignored his reaction. "It's obvious that the police think one of us is the killer."

"Well, it isn't me," Warren announced, folding his arms across his narrow chest. "I had no motive." Then he pointed a bony finger at Cynthia. "But you did."

Cynthia's eyes narrowed. "You didn't like the idea that Cliff married me. Did you expect to inherit all his money? Perhaps you even influenced Cliff to draw up a special codicil to his will."

"Ridiculous." Warren's upper lip glistened with sweat. "Of course, I expected something for my devoted service. He often said he'd take care of me."

Jennifer doubted that Warren's expectations of a large inheritance had any bearing on the case, but she couldn't rule it out. "Carping at each other isn't going to help. That's what the police like to do, divide and conquer. We need to share our information. Maybe that way, we can find clues the police can't."

"What if the killer is one of us?" Warren asked with hooded eyes.

"Then the other two can protect each other," Jennifer said.

Warren plucked at the sleeve of his tweed jacket. "I think we should stay out of the police business. It'll only get us into trouble."

Cynthia's face flushed, and her new sense of self seemed to energize her. "I don't see how we can go wrong confiding in each other. I'm in, but I'm not sure how I can help."

"Oh, all right. I'll go along," Warren said, brushing a piece of lint from his lapel. "I've dealt with the catering service, so I'll see if they hired anyone new for the party. But that's as far as I'll go."

Cynthia turned to Jennifer. "And you?"

"I'll keep trying to find the previous owner of my sister's book. To me that's the key." And, she thought, I'll talk to Alex.

Cynthia closed her eyes for a moment and leaned back. Finally, she glanced at the ledger, put it away, locked the drawer, and returned the key to the small box in the top drawer. "Your visit's been an eye-opener, Jennifer. I'm too tired to continue this conversation." She stood and walked toward the library door, but stopped in front of Warren. "I'd appreciate it if you left your keys belonging to the manor on the desk and call me before you come next time."

Warren's mouth gaped open. "But I need to be here. It's my job. Mr. Wedgeworth relied on me. He...." Warren crumpled into the leather chair and put his head in his hands.

"I'll show you out," Cynthia said to Jennifer. With her head held high, Cynthia walked out of the library, no longer shuffling along in her mukluks, but stepping forward with assurance.

The new plush oriental rug running the length of the marble hall hushed their footfalls. At the front door, they hugged. Jennifer felt a bond with the bereft woman, but was she letting her empathy play her for a fool?

Chapter 23

Back outside Jennifer glanced at the gray sky and inhaled the damp air and the fresh scent of cut grass. She buttoned her jacket and pulled on her lined leather driving gloves. As she tossed her purse into her car, she noticed Harold bending over a flowerbed a short distance away. She hesitated, then closed the car door and walked across the expanse of wet grass toward him. He was raking a rose bed he'd pruned. Thorny green branches and brownish-red maple leaves lay atop a burlap ground cloth.

He looked up as she approached, put his rake up against the maple's trunk, and removed his weather-beaten hat. Grabbing a blue handkerchief from his overall pocket, he wiped his wrinkled brow. "Nice to see you again, Miss Frost. It's been gloomy around here since the party. Mrs. Wedgeworth needed a friendly visitor."

"She did seem lonely. We talked about the party and her husband."

"That'll help some." He shoved the blue cloth back into his pocket.

"Warren came in while I was there."

Harold nodded and raised an eyebrow. "Saw him drive up. He's a piece of work." He rubbed the stubble on his chin. "But Mr. Wedgeworth seemed to put great store in the fellow. Even though he seemed a bit…. " He made a rocking motion with one hand. "Well, you know what I mean. I just do my job and live my life."

Jennifer nodded. "You probably see everyone who comes and goes."

"Just about." He pointed to a small house hidden back amongst a copse of pines. "Living on the estate makes that inevitable, and me a bit invisible. I've been here for…" He thought a moment and started counting on his fingers. "Twenty-two years."

"That's a long time. You must love the place." She didn't say it, but thought that he must also have liked his boss.

"Can't beat what I do. I've worked outdoors my whole life in some way or another. I like working with nature, and plants are a lot easier to tend than people." He chuckled at his own words, showing a row of stained teeth.

Jennifer pushed a lock of hair off her forehead. "Mrs. Wedgeworth said you told her what poison killed her husband. I thought the police wanted that kept a secret."

He grinned and winked. "Yeah, I know. That detective thinks he's so smart. Asked me all kinds of questions when he came back a few days ago. Treated me like a dummy. It got my dander up, so when that Officer Seager put his laptop on a table and stepped away, I took a look see."

Jennifer smiled, thinking how great it was that someone had gotten the better of Cameron. "You outfoxed him."

"You bet. People think old guys who do gardening are dumb. Hell, I have a computer. Doesn't everybody?" He cocked his head. "I bet you know what poisoned him, too."

How had he learned what the poison was? Jennifer folded her arms across her chest, trying to keep warm. "Our cat, Maxie, was killed with the same poison."

"Miss Langdon's cat? Oh, I'm sorry to hear that. I hope they catch the murdering son-of-a-gun."

Had she understood Harold correctly? "You know my aunt?"

He smiled. "I didn't know she was your aunt, but sure. I knew Emma Mae Langdon when she worked for Mr. Wedgeworth years ago. She was a beauty, and when I saw her the other day driving in looking so pretty, well, it sure took me back."

Jennifer noted a flush on the old man's face. She would have to question her aunt about her younger days. It seemed there was a lot Emma Mae had never mentioned. She became aware of the dampness through the soles of her navy blue shoes and looked down.

Harold took note. "The ground's like a bog after last night's storm. I'll walk back to your car with you." He pointed at her shoes. "Hope they aren't a total loss."

"Me too." As they walked, Jennifer asked, "Did my aunt remember you?"

"Well," he gave a quick shrug. "She had her mind on getting to the party and all."

"That night did anyone leave early or look out of place?"

"Police asked me the same thing." He shook his head. "Everyone who came had an invitation."

They stood on the gravel path next to Jennifer's car. "What about the catering service? Anyone look unusual?"

"Blakely's Caterers have been here lots of times. I recognized most of them, except one older guy, but he left early. Didn't feel well."

Jennifer gripped Harold's arm. "That's gotta be him!"

"Who?"

"There was an older waiter who knew Wedgeworth liked those special spicy crackers. He inferred that Cynthia had baked them, but she hadn't. Don't you think it's odd that a waiter from a catering service said that?"

Harold screwed up his lips in a disgusted look. "Could be they'd been told. Heck, Blakely has been here so often, any of them might have known that and maybe the guy was told that by someone." He shook his head. "Funny that someone would use such a strange poison like that Barbados nut. You know, I read that poison is a woman's choice of a weapon. I did some research on the Web." He winked at her and tapped his head. "You'd think if there were so many of those Barbados plants in the tropics, they'd do something about getting rid of them. Plus, bringing fruits and nuts back into the country would be kinda difficult these days. It had to be someone who got hold of the stuff locally." He raised his hands and waggled his index finger. "Or maybe someone had their own boat. You know how many of Mr. Wedgeworth's friends sail back and forth to Hawaii and Mexico? Those places are tropical. And then there are all those boats for hire."

Jennifer marveled at the old man's acuity, thinking his ideas weren't far off the mark. "If you come up with any more ideas, give me a call." Jennifer got out her purse from the car seat, extracted her business card, and handed it to him. As she climbed into her car, she asked, "By the way, do you still have the key to the library?"

"Heck, no. Mrs. Wedgeworth gave me her husband's before they left on their honeymoon and I gave it back when they got home."

She thought about the keys and if they were important, then started her engine. "I'll remind Emma Mae that you knew her when."

"That'd be great. Give her my best." He tapped the side of her car and walked back to his work.

On the way home she pondered the morning. None of the new information seemed to lead to a killer, yet the implication that Alex had both opportunity and motive to tear out the ledger's page gnawed at her.

The road crews had cleaned up the storm's debris, allowing her to make good time. By three in the afternoon, she pulled into her drive, expecting to be greeted by Lydia's barking. Nothing. Silence. She parked, got out and hurried to the backyard. Jennifer opened the gate and whistled. Still no Lydia. In the distance she saw a black body lying against the fence. A vise settled around her heart. Panic seized her.

"Lydia," she called. The dog turned her massive head toward her mistress, but didn't get up. Didn't bark. Jennifer ran through the long wet grass. *Oh, God! Please, not Lydia.* Her heart hammered. When she stood over Lydia, her loving companion looked up beseechingly. "Are you sick?" Jennifer knelt and cradled Lydia's big muzzle in her hands, gazed into the animal's deep brown eyes and stroked her head. A blob of white fur burrowed into the dog's black furry chest.

Gently, Jennifer reached down and pulled out a scrawny white kitten. "Ah ha!" Jennifer let out a sigh of relief. "So you've become a surrogate mother while I've been away." She got to her feet holding the kitten. "I think we'd better feed the poor darling." Lydia scrambled to her paws and pushed her nose at Jennifer's hands that held the kitten. Seemingly satisfied, the dog shook her thick black fur and followed her mistress into the kitchen.

After placing the mewling kitten on the floor atop a terrycloth towel, Jennifer heated a bowl of milk. While it warmed, Lydia kept watch over her foundling, licking the stray's rumpled coat. After testing the milk, Jennifer put it down for the little creature to lap up.

Perhaps the kitten had been separated from its mother during the storm. If Lydia hadn't rescued it, it might have succumbed to the cold and wet. "I think we should call her Stormy."

Lydia didn't voice an objection.

Jennifer had to go to Books & Tea and wondered about taking the kitten with her. She doubted if it would be a good idea until she, or was it he, was older. And how would Crabapple react to a new cat? While she dithered about leaving Lydia and the kitten in the house until she returned, the phone rang.

"Miss Jennifer Frost?" the voice asked. "I'm secretary for George Raven at Raven and Crowell law firm. Mr. Raven is the attorney for Clifford Wedgeworth's estate. There's a reading of Mr. Wedgeworth's will on Monday at his estate. According to Mr. Wedgeworth's wishes, all those mentioned in his will are requested to be present at an oral reading. Will you be able to attend?"

Jennifer frowned. "There must be some mistake. I couldn't be in his will. I only met him the night he was…the night he died. Perhaps, you're trying to reach my aunt, Emma Mae Langdon."

"Miss Langdon has already been contacted and has agreed to attend. According to Mr. Raven, your name is in a recent codicil Mr. Wedgeworth wrote. It's important that you be present. The reading will be held at the Wedgeworth estate at four."

"I see." But of course, she didn't. "Thanks for the call. I'll be there." After she hung up, she wondered why Clifford Wedgeworth would have wanted her presence at the reading of his will.

Chapter 24

Emma Mae remained truculent over Jennifer's hesitation to attend Clifford Wedgeworth's memorial service. While sitting in the passenger seat of Jennifer's jeep, she once again scolded her niece. "I know you weren't keen on coming, but it's only fitting that we pay our respects." She smoothed out wrinkles in her black wool dress.

"I understand. You convinced me, okay?" For spite, Jennifer added, "Perhaps you want to attend because Harold will be there." Jennifer grinned as her aunt's cheeks turned rosy.

"That's enough of that kind of talk. You know very well I didn't remember him until you mentioned him." Emma Mae turned to study the landscape while her long fingers curled around her beaded purse.

Jennifer had a lot of questions about Emma Mae old relationship with Wedgeworth. She'd never considered her aunt might have a secretive past. "Harold said he knew you when you and he worked for Wedgeworth. What was his job?"

The stare Emma Mae gave Jennifer might have dissuaded someone else from questioning further, but not Jennifer. The wall of silence Emma Mae had built surrounding her youth had shown signs of cracking ever since Clifford Wedgeworth's death. Her aunt had always been stoic, kind, and practical, but with the revelation of a past love affair, Jennifer saw her anew. In her youth was Emma Mae a flirt like Carla?

"Harold was a surveyor for Cliff's company, working in the back country with the lumberjacks. We dated a few times, but my heart was full of Cliff." She smiled. "I must have made life miserable for every other man who might have been interested in me."

"I can't believe I'm hearing this," Jennifer said. "Your feelings for Cliff influenced your life that much?"

Emma Mae straightened in her seat and stared at the oncoming traffic. "Why is it that the young always think they know all the answers? And besides, look at your own life the past two years."

"I've been trying to find a murderer." She hesitated, thinking about the past years. "Maybe I have let Carla's murder dominate my life, but if there's a chance to find the killer through a lost book, shouldn't I search for it?"

"See!" Emma Mae tugged on her seat belt as she shifted around to gaze at Jennifer. "You're still obsessed with Carla's murder."

"And you with Cliff."

"Yes, I was, but Cliff is dead, and I can get on with my life. You should too, before it's too late. I've made my mistakes and paid with loneliness. You don't have to make the same mistake." An edgy silence prevailed until Emma Mae said, "I want to find who killed Carla and Cliff, and who was behind poisoning Maxi, but sometimes we have to let things go. I haven't wanted to throw cold water on your assumptions, but the murderer may not be the same for all three."

Jennifer gripped the steering wheel tighter. She refused to believe that possibility because then her entire theory about the book and the missing document could be wrong. "Why do you think there could be two murderers?"

"Why not? Maybe even three." Emma Mae said. "Just because Cliff had Carla's book doesn't mean he was killed by the same person who killed Carla."

"I don't think I'm wrong." Jennifer murmured as she checked the cross street. "We must be close to the church." She slowed down. "Look for Lime Street. That's where we have to turn."

After checking the instructions she held, Emma Mae said, "It's a few more blocks."

Jennifer sped up, but her mind raced faster than the car's engine. There had to be a connection between the murders. "Do you know how Harold became Wedgeworth's groundskeeper?"

"You're nosey about everything lately. Of course I know. A crane fell on Harold and broke his hip. He could have sued Wedgeworth and his firm but he didn't. Cliff took care of things and Harold's had a good life."

"What reason could Harold have had to sue?"

"Safety had been neglected. Profits were important if the company was to grow. Things weren't always done within the law in the forest. And …

and those activities made the situation dicey. Most of the employees knew, but we kept quiet."

"Are you telling me that Wedgeworth's company logged illegally?"

Emma Mae leaned forward and peered out the front window. "Lime Street's next."

Jennifer turned at Lime and drove into a lot filled with cars. She squeezed her jeep between a Mercedes and a Miata, turned off the engine, and stared at her aunt. "You can't leave me dangling."

"What I just told you is in the past. All I'm saying is that Cliff gave Harold a job and that Harold didn't sue." Emma Mae got out of the car, shut the door, and began to walk toward the building, her black dress swooshing around her thin calves.

After locking the car, Jennifer hurried after her. "Wait!" She grabbed her aunt's arm. "Do other people, like his friends, his competitors, his business associates know how he ran the company?"

Emma Mae pulled her arm away. "It was a long time ago. This is not the time to criticize Cliff. But yes, I'm sure they knew. I didn't leave him only because he wouldn't divorce his wife and marry me. I left because I knew too much company business and didn't like what I had learned. Why do you think he lent me money? It wasn't love on his part; it was payoff!" She glared at Jennifer, her face flushed, her eyes flinty. "I paid him back every penny. I told you that. And yes, if he'd asked me, I would have married him. So, now you know I compromised on my ethics." She turned quickly and walked up the stairs into the church, her beaded purse swinging at her side.

Jennifer followed her into the crowded sanctuary with her mindset about Clifford Wedgeworth and his murder transformed. People hadn't stayed with the man out of loyalty, but out of fear. Had he been blackmailed by Harold, and yes, even Emma Mae? What about Warren? Were there others? Was Emma Mae correct that Wedgeworth's murder may have nothing to do with Carla's? Could his murderer have been a disgruntled employee? Her mind swirled.An usher showed them down the side aisle. As they passed one row, Jennifer looked sideways and stopped. Alex? He was supposed to be in Boston meeting with the curator. She hesitated, but Alex didn't notice her, and she continued after Emma Mae. The usher waited, handed her a program, and she scooted in next to her aunt. As she rubbed her hands on her chocolate brown skirt, she thought what a stupid choice it was. Then it dawned on her. She'd worn the same outfit to Carla's funeral. She was about to say something to Emma Mae, but noticed she was deep in thought or prayer.

Jennifer gazed at the assemblage and spotted Cynthia, wearing a long sleeved, navy blue dress and a matching cloche hat, sitting in the first pew — alone. Warren and Harold sat across the aisle. Cynthia had to handle her loss without support. Jennifer felt a stab of pity.

Two Episcopal priests came to the center pulpit, and the rite began.

Jennifer tried to concentrate on what was being said, but heard only what was left unsaid. The men who spoke about Clifford Wedgeworth talked of his business acumen, his reign at the helm of a large and powerful logging company, and of his ability to deal with state and federal officials. There was no mention of his personal life, his charity, his love of life, his friends. Only a man from the Findley Foundation, an organization dealing with antique books, spoke of Wedgeworth as a patron. Clifford Wedgeworth seemed to be less of an individual in death than he'd been in life. Her impression of him had been that he was charming, strong and handsome. Now she began to wonder what he was actually like.

Didn't anyone know the personal side of the man? Cynthia had talked about his secret interest in clowns, so he must have had a sense of humor. Sometimes people use the act of being a clown as a cover for their own sadness or insecurity.

After a time, Jennifer's mind turned to Alex. He couldn't have flown east to meet with the curator and be here now. Had Wedgeworth been more than a business acquaintance? When the music began, she drifted guiltily back to the present.

After the service, Cynthia walked down the aisle while other mourners followed behind. No one offered her an arm for assistance or for comfort. How small and cruel Wedgeworth's friends were to snub his widow. Surely a hand, an arm, a shoulder to lean on would have been appreciated and helpful even if they didn't know Cynthia very well.

The crowd moved out of the church to make its way to the reception in the annex. Emma Mae and Jennifer followed others as the crowd moved forward, but when Jennifer was even with Alex's row, she waited for him to exit while Emma Mae walked ahead. As he stepped into the crowded aisle, she confronted him, hands jammed into her suit jacket. "This doesn't look like Boston to me."

"Jennifer." He took her arm. His dark eyes sparkled. "I'm so glad I found you here."

"You didn't find me," she said through compressed lips. "I found you. I thought you'd left for Boston."

He nodded, smiled at a nearby couple, then turned back to Jennifer. "Let's talk outside."

The crowd swept them along until they were on the steps of the church. People milled around looking for friends, greeting each other with the re-petitive phrases often heard at funerals and memorial services. "It's so sad …. He was too young … . I haven't seen you since …. What a nice service."

She remembered how she and her family managed to withstand the well-meaning but fatuous words of those attending Carla's funeral. She clutched her brown purse with its strap slung over one shoulder and wished it were a teddy bear.

Alex, still holding onto Jennifer's arm, steered her to the far side of the church patio. "I should have called you," he began.

"Yes, you should have."

"Don't be this way, Jennifer. I've had all I can take from everyone. Coming back to this area has been hell."

"Hell? You left me to handle the flack from Carla's murder, so don't whine to me about hell." She sat on the three-foot high slump stone wall that separated the church from its school and playground.

"Sorry," he mumbled, his shoulders slumping. He rubbed his neck and looked out across the yard. "Ever since I told Cameron I sent the book to Israel, he's pegged me as his number one suspect and refused to allow me to leave town." He wiped his brow with the back of his hand. "If he finds out I still have it, I'm in real trouble."

She chewed her lower lip. "Everyone is the detective's number one suspect. Me, Cynthia Wedgeworth, Warren Peabody and … I could go on and on." She stood and paced in front of him, her heels clicking on the cement. "Frankly, I don't think he has a clue who killed Wedgeworth any more than he has a clue who killed Carla or, for that matter, Emma Mae's cat."

Alex put his hand on her forearm. "You've had it rough. And here I've only been thinking of myself." He moved closer, his breath whispering against her hair. When she refused to accept his gesture of reconciliation, he dropped his arm and stepped back. "God, what a mess."

Perhaps his nerves were as raw as hers, but she'd run out of patience. "If you can't leave to find out about the Einstein document, we are stuck."

"Give me some credit." He jammed his hands in his trouser pockets. "I took care of that. I sent an emissary. He gets back Sunday."

"Who did you send?"

"Your private detective, Ken Sullivan."

"What? I can't believe you did that." Jennifer shook her head. "You were at each other's throats the last time I saw you together."

"Believe me, he wasn't my first choice. But on such short notice, I didn't have many options."

"Does Emma Mae know?" she asked. "She's the one who hired him and will have to pay him."

"Not to worry. I'm picking up the tab for his trip and expenses." He hesitated, before continuing. "The curator wanted to see the book, but I'm not letting that book out of my possession. Earlier I had photographed the back pages with the imprints and gave them to Ken to show him." He studied her and frowned. "You do trust Ken, don't you?"

She shrugged. "I guess. At least as much as I trust anyone at the moment. Don't you think it's a conflict of interest for him to take on your assignment and still be employed by Emma Mae?" Her own ethics were being stretched, knowing Ken was investigating Alex. Did ethics matter when you're out to catch a killer? She'd play the game she was dealt and muddled through.

Seeing others walk to the church annex for the reception, she said, "I want to pay my respects to Cynthia." She turned and began to walk away, then asked over her shoulder, "You coming?"

He nodded and caught up with her. "I want you to know that I will not run out on you this time. I'm here for the long haul, no matter what the outcome."

She stopped and looked into his eyes. Should she believe him? When would be the right time to bring up his affair with Carla, his access to Wedgeworth's collection? "Alex, we have a lot of unfinished business to talk about."

"Wonderful." He took her arm and they moved on. "We should both get away for a while."

"That's not what I meant."

"What about going sailing or …." He smiled. "Sea kayaking?"

"Lydia would love it."

He blinked. "She gets in the kayak?"

"In the front cockpit and sometimes leaps out to swim."

Alex shook his head. "You and your dog!"

Surprised by his dismissive tone, she felt her unease deepen. He didn't seem to realize how his attitude toward Lydia affected her.

They followed the gathering crowd into the annex. Jennifer wanted to overhear conversations to learn if anyone might have had a grievance against Wedgeworth. The Blakely company catered the reception, manning the buffet stations. She tugged at Alex's arm and whispered, "Look for an elderly server. Most of Blakely's employees are young, so he should stand out."

After scanning the catering crew, they moved through the crowd toward Cynthia, where a few people were offering their condolences. Noticing Jennifer, Cynthia reached out to her and they hugged. When Cynthia drew back, she continued to grasp Jennifer's hand. "Could you stay with me for a few minutes? Please."

"Of course." Jennifer nodded toward Alex. "This is Alex Glidden, a friend of mine who also knew your husband."

Cynthia let go of Jennifer's hand and shook Alex's.

"I met you at your party," Alex said. "Cliff was an interesting and vital man. I'm sorry for your loss."

"I remember you. We met before the party. Cliff kept the library open for you."

"Yes. It was a special treat."

Alex must not know about the missing page in the ledger, because if he had, he would realize that admitting his presence at the library prior to the party made him the prime suspect for tearing out the ledger's page.

Cynthia tugged at the cuff of her jacket and toyed with the gold band of her wristwatch. "I don't think I was very cordial toward you then. Cliff and I had a misunderstanding."

"Actually, you were very polite."

"I told her about Carla's book," Jennifer said. "Cynthia showed me her husband's records, but unfortunately the page about *The Big Sleep* and the book you traded for it is missing."

"Missing?" Alex stared at Jennifer. "Why didn't you tell me?"

"I just found out. And if you were the last person alone in the room, then …."

"God." Alex put his hand to his mouth. "No wonder Cameron thinks I'm guilty."

"You too?" Cynthia raised her eyebrows. "It seems everyone is suspect."

"Did the detective ask about the ledger?" Jennifer asked Cynthia.

"Not yet. He hasn't been around for a few days, thank God."

Jennifer wondered how long it would be before the police put the clues together about the Chandler book and Wedgeworth's ledger. Perhaps they didn't believe her theory that the book linked Carla's and Wedgeworth's murders.

Harold walked forward with Emma Mae and said to Cynthia, "Anything I can do for you just let me know, Mrs. Wedgeworth. Your husband was a good employer."

"Thank you for all you've done at the estate, Harold. I know Cliff depended on you." She gave him a wan smile. "You'll have to suggest what needs to be done. I'm over my head when it comes to horticulture."

"No problem. When the seasons change there's planting, and in between, the beds need to be kept neat. I'll bring in the usual crew when necessary. Mr. Wedgeworth liked everything trim and neat, and I'll keep it that way. You just have to pay the bills." He let out a soft laugh.

Emma Mae introduced herself. "I knew your husband when I worked for the company many years ago. He was a fine man, and his death is a terrible loss."

"Thank you," Cynthia said. "Cliff spoke warmly of you when we made out the invitation list. Said you were a true friend. May I call you Emma Mae?"

Emma Mae blinked and raised her chin. "Well, everyone else does. Certainly."

"And please call me, Cynthia."

Jennifer, Alex, Emma Mae, and Harold stood in a ring around Cynthia until Warren came over and asked Cynthia to accompany him to meet the man from the Findley Foundation. Before leaving their company, she gave Jennifer a pleading look.

"I'll be here if you need me," Jennifer told her.

As their small group remained together, Jennifer overheard two men behind her, talking about the tragedy. At first she thought they were speaking about Wedgeworth until she heard the name Bjorn. Turning, she said, "Excuse me, I overheard you mention Bjorn. Is that Bjorn Halverson?"

"Why yes," the elder of two said. "Did you know him, too? "

"Did?" she asked. "What do you mean?"

"It was on the radio. He died in a fire at his boatyard this morning. He was beloved by the entire boating community."

Jennifer's hand flew to her mouth. "Oh, no! He was such a nice man."

Alex moved to her side. "How do you know him, Jennifer?"

"He gave me some information."

"It's a terrible thing to happen to anyone," the younger man said. "What a way to go."

"It seems strange," the elderly gentleman said. "Bjorn was careful with all his solvents and rags, and he always smoked his pipe out by the dock, never inside. He was no fool."

"Yeah, but he was getting old, and he could have tripped or fainted. You never know. His craftsmanship will be missed. At least he died doing what he liked. It makes you think though, doesn't it? One mistake is all it takes," the younger man said, nodding knowingly as if he'd spoken the wise words.

Emma Mae and Harold had stood on the fringe listening, but now Emma Mae touched Jennifer's arm and said, "I remember you told me you went to talk to a boat builder, Jennifer, but I had no idea it was Bjorn. I knew him."

Jennifer rolled her eyes. "You know everyone."

Emma Mae pulled in her pointed chin. "That's what comes of living in the same area all your life, but I'm not the only one who knew Bjorn." Emma Mae turned to Alex and tapped his arm with the back of her hand. "You knew him, Alex, and so did Jennifer's parents."

"I knew him?" Alex asked, frowning.

"Men! What kind of a filing system do you have in your brain?" Emma Mae said with her hands on her hips. "Bjorn was the fellow you chartered the boat from the summer Carla was killed."

Chapter 25

On Sunday afternoon Jennifer and Alex waited for Ken Sullivan at the Monaco Kimpton bar. His plane was due in at one o'clock. They'd agreed to meet at two o'clock, but it was now past two-thirty, and Ken remained a no-show.

Jennifer sat at the low cocktail table, rolling the edges of her napkin over the base of her wine glass. Alex's dark eyes narrowed as his call to Ken's cell went unanswered. "Flight was on time. Where do you suppose he is?" He folded the newspaper he'd brought with him and slapped it on the table. "It still rankles me that I had to hire the guy. If Cameron weren't such a stubborn idiot, I'd have gone to meet the museum curator myself."

Despite her own misgivings about Ken, she grinned at his agitation. "You don't like him much, do you?"

"Damn right."

Jennifer was surprised at his vehemence and avoided further comments. "You had little choice, considering the time restraints, and Ken is a private detective. Still, we probably should have met him at the airport." She crossed her legs and waggled her foot back and forth.

"The hotel was his idea, not mine." He checked his watch. "He should have been here by now." He clasped his hands and cracked his knuckles. "At least he could have called. He's got my cell number."

She disliked Alex's habit of cracking his knuckles, but understood his frustration.

"I'm worried," Alex said.

She nodded. "Me too."

"I hate waiting." Alex adjusted his blue blazer and gazed at the entrance. "If he doesn't show, you could stay in town, and we could have dinner together."

"This is not old times, Alex. Besides, Emma Mae's at my place tending my dog and a kitten Lydia found abandoned in the storm." Jennifer noted his frown. "Please understand, Alex. I couldn't bear to leave them alone after Maxie was poisoned. And we're closing the bookstore on Sundays from now on. We both have to attend a meeting on Monday, so we'll be closed then too. I need to get another dog sitter for that day as well." She grinned and added, "How about you?"

"With Lydia? Alone? Do you really think she'd stand for my company?"

"She'd get used to you."

"I appreciate your trust, but I can't accept. What if something happened to her? You'd never forgive me, and you and I are still dealing with fallout from Carla's death." He leaned forward. "I don't want Lydia to come between us any more than she already has."

She realized with a jolt that she'd been willing to put Lydia's life in his hands. In the past she'd only trusted Emma Mae and Joe. Part of her was pleased Alex hadn't agreed to her request, but another part of her wanted to trust him again.

"Joe might be able to take her. I'm not sure of his schedule," she said.

"I hear he's leaving Brandon." His eyes studied her. "You're fond of him, aren't you?"

"Yes."

"Real fond?"

"Alex, you're behaving like a jilted lover. Remember, you left me and got married. I stayed and began a new life. And you weren't exactly faithful to me while we were engaged."

"What are you talking about?"

"Carla."

He frowned and leaned forward. "You don't believe that story about Carla and me, do you?"

"While on the island, you and she often went off together, just like you did that last night."

"Oh, for God's sake, she was a flirt. How many guys did she shack up with?"

She bristled. "Don't talk that way about her. You aren't answering my question."

"I'm not going to. I thought you trusted me more than that." He sank back in his chair, his face sagged. "So you and Joe are an item. I didn't expect that."

"Why? Did you think I'd sit around and wait for you?" Was Alex that egotistical?

"He's a cop. Maybe he can protect you, but he's not around all the time."

"I'm not with him for protection."

Alex seemed unfazed by her rising anger. "The two of us could go to your island. Get away. You'd be safe there."

"Carla wasn't." After a curt ironic laugh, she asked, "Do you think Cameron would permit it?"

"It's not like you'd be leaving the state. Last I knew Beastly Island was still part of the state of Washington and in the jurisdiction of the Seattle Police Department." He traced the sweat on his beer glass with his index finger. "When Joe leaves Brandon, are you going with him?"

"That's none of your business."

"Okay. Let's put it this way. Have you thought about selling the store, moving out of Brandon?"

"Emma Mae and I have talked around it, but we aren't ready to make a commitment one way or the other. Maybe after Carla's murder is solved," she added as an afterthought.

"Everything comes back to that, doesn't it?" He leaned back, a scowl on his face.

She fingered her green beaded necklace and stared past him toward the entrance. "Nothing's changed about that."

As an elderly couple walked into the bar, she glanced at her watch. "What about you? Will you head back to San Diego after this is settled?"

"After what's settled? Wedgeworth's or Carla's murder?"

Replaying the old tape of their problem was futile, so she switched the subject. "How's your business doing while you've been away?"

He nodded as if letting her know he understood the topic shift. "It's getting more difficult to handle from long distance. Clients like to have their hands held even when it's not tax time."

Her lips pouted in mock sympathy. "The difficult life of a CPA."

He shook his head. "People laugh about CPAs, but when taxes are due, we are doctors for acute IRS distress."

"But you'd rather spend your time dealing with rare books."

"Absolutely. Trouble is, I can't make a good living at it." He glanced toward the door. "Finally, here he comes."

Ken walked through the room toward their table with his self-confident swagger. He always acts like he knows more than everyone else, she thought. Was that what annoyed her?

Alex ignored Ken's outstretched hand. "We were getting anxious." He motioned to the extra chair.

"Sorry. I had a tough time getting out of the airport."

"You could have phoned," Alex said.

Ken placed his canvas overnight bag on the floor and shook Jennifer's hand, holding it a moment longer than necessary. "It's good to see you, but I didn't expect you at this meeting."

Once again she noticed the smoothness of his palm. Even Alex's hands were rougher, and he didn't lead an outdoor life. Ken's khaki trousers and blue polo shirt were rumpled, yet his gray eyes sparkled and held no hint of redness from his overnight travels. "You look rested," she said. "I expected you to look exhausted."

"Healthy living." He grinned, dropped his raincoat across the back of a chair and took a seat in the remaining one. "Boston on Friday and back on Sunday with a stopover in Chicago." He turned to Alex. "I hope you appreciate that I took the cheaper flight to save on expenses." The waiter came over, and Ken ordered Twelve Bowmore on the rocks.

Alex raised his eyebrows. "I suppose you expect me to pay for your expensive scotch."

"If you'd like, thanks," Ken said.

"Do you want something to eat?" Jennifer asked.

"I grabbed lunch at O'Hare. Not many decent eating places there." He relaxed into his chair and ran a hand over his closely cropped black hair. "O'Hare's restaurants didn't live up to your tastes?"

Ken ignored Alex's dig and just smiled.

"All right, let's get on with your report," Alex said. "What did you find out."

"Remember our agreement. No matter what I learn, you pay."

Alex nodded. "Agreed."

Ken settled back and began. "I had to wait around Saturday to see your man from the museum. The curator gave me only fifteen minutes between his meetings. It was a painful fifteen minutes, like dragging the East River for a nail. No wonder you couldn't get him to tell you anything over the phone. Despite your letter of introduction, Alex, he was closed-mouthed. But he was interested in how the newly discovered Einstein document might relate to a murder. I showed him the pictures of the imprints from the book you gave me. He wanted to keep them." He studied Alex. "I gave them to him. Hope that was okay?"

"No problem with that. They were copies."

"He said the document he bought through an agent was authentic, but the seller wanted to remain anonymous. He refused to explain any details about the contents of the letter, but eventually the information will be released. As instructed, I told him what you both believed to be in the letter. He acknowledged that the letter mentioned Szilard. At some time in the future, the museum will notify the media that a new document signed by Einstein has been found." He hesitated and bit his lower lip. "However, I think that if the document damages Einstein's reputation, they'll keep it under wraps."

The waiter put Ken's drink down on the table, and Alex said to the man, "Put it on my tab." He looked at Ken and added, "You'd probably bill me for it anyway, wouldn't you?"

"I'm not that mercenary." Ken picked up the drink and took a sip. "Smooth as a summer night." He set his glass down. "Okay. Let's get down to the nitty-gritty. The museum paid the agent a little over $550,000 for the document."

"Wow," Jennifer said. "That's a hefty sum."

Ken ignored her outburst and said, "Obviously, the agent must have taken a cut."

"That doesn't get us anywhere." Jennifer stared at Ken. "Who was the agent?"

"Heinrich Stolz in New York."

"I know of him," Alex said. "He owns a rare bookstore in Manhattan."

Ken raised an eyebrow. "You seem to know a lot of people in the business."

"I should. I've been dealing in rare books most of my adult life. Did you contact Stolz?"

Ken shook his head. "No, I didn't. I thought I'd leave that to you."

"Another name, another merry-go-round," Jennifer said. "It's an endless circle."

"Not necessarily," Alex said. "I'll call Stolz tomorrow." He looked down at the table, then at Jennifer. "But he's legitimate. Giving a client's name away is considered unethical. I can press him with the urgency of the matter."

"I'd think finding a murderer would loosen his tongue." Jennifer said.

Ken took another sip of his drink before he said, "Alex is probably right. Giving out a client's name who asked to remain anonymous isn't professional." He smiled at her and cocked an eyebrow.

She knew he was referring to his refusal to tell her that Clifford Wedgeworth had been his client. "So, we're back to square one." She drained her glass and firmly set it on the table.

"Maybe not," Alex said. "I have the book. The missing page from Wedgeworth's ledger about the book's former owner gives credence to the idea that it relates to the murderer. We'll find the answer. I'm not giving up."

"Neither am I," Jennifer said, but inwardly she felt defeated.

Ken leaned forward. "What's this about a missing ledger page?" He stared at Jennifer. "You didn't tell me anything about that."

She folded her arms. "I didn't think it was important to your investigation."

"Damn certain it's part of the investigation." He lowered his voice. "Why are you holding out on me?"

She lifted her chin and decided she might as well let him in on all they'd learned. After all, Alex had trusted him enough to talk to the curator, so why shouldn't she? "Alex bought the book from Wedgeworth. His ledger should have shown the previous owner, but when Cynthia and I examined the ledger, the page had been torn out."

"Does Cameron know about this?"

Jennifer glanced at Alex and said, "No."

Ken leaned back. "I see." He turned to Alex. "Cameron wanted the book as evidence, right? But you still have the book."

Alex shrugged.

"Okay." Ken nodded. "At some point Cameron is going to find out about the missing page, and that won't make you look good, Alex."

"It can't be helped."

Jennifer studied Ken, trying to determine how involved he should be. Finally she asked, "Any ideas?"

"Since you're both on his suspect list, turning the book over to him probably won't work in your favor. But what if someone told Cameron about the missing page?"

"That would make Alex more of a suspect, since he was in the library with the collection right before the party," Jennifer said.

"Not necessarily. Mrs. Wedgeworth and Warren Peabody had an opportunity to take the page. And it might be better to give him that information instead of having him learn about it on his own." Ken took a swallow of his drink and turned the glass in his hand. "If Cameron learns that both of you as well as Mrs. Wedgeworth know about the missing page and haven't told him, it could look bad for all of you." He glanced from Jennifer to Alex. "So, what are you planning to do now?"

"We'll decide after I contact Stolz." Alex stared into the distance and sat in an uncomfortable silence until he turned to Jennifer. "I think you should go to the island for a while."

"No."

Alex ignored her response and explained to Ken, "Emma Mae's cat was poisoned, and we think it's the same substance that killed Clifford. The police refuse to tell us anything."

"I heard about the cat," Ken said. "Alex might be right about going to your island. I know how you feel about Lydia. You wouldn't want her to be the next victim."

A cold vise tightened around her chest. Both Alex and Ken had articulated her worst fear. Because of her devotion to Lydia, her dog could be in danger, too, since the killer seemed to have no compunction about killing animals to make a statement. Or had it been more than that? Going off to her island wouldn't help find Carla's killer.

"So you're considering going to the island." Ken sat back nonchalantly staring into the glass of Scotch.

"I have too many things to do on the mainland. I have a meeting with Wedgeworth's lawyer tomorrow afternoon. Apparently, Emma Mae and I are mentioned in a codicil to his will."

Alex raised his glass. "You said you had a meeting, but I had no idea it concerned Wedgeworth's estate."

"A complete surprise to us," Jennifer said. "I can't imagine why, although, as you know, Emma Mae worked for him years ago."

Ken rubbed his cheek and studied her. "He was a very wealthy man. You should be delighted."

"I probably should be, but I'm more curious than anything else."

"Jennifer, you never used to be so skeptical," Alex said.

"I never used to be a lot of things … before Carla was …."

Alex's face reddened, and he turned toward Ken. "Thanks for your effort, but there isn't much else you can do for us now."

"Miss Langdon hasn't fired me. I hope I didn't miss something while I was back east."

Jennifer frowned, realizing he wouldn't have heard about Bjorn. "Bjorn Halverson died."

Ken had been about to take a swallow of his drink, but stopped. "What? He's the fellow who helped me refurbish *The High Life*. What happened?"

"He died in a fire at his repair yard yesterday morning," she said.

He took a gulp of his scotch, then slowly set his glass down. "He was a nice old guy. How did you find out?"

"We learned of his death at Wedgeworth's memorial service. It's in the paper." Alex picked up the Sunday paper from the table and paged through it until he came to the article and passed the paper to Ken.

As Ken read, Jennifer watched Alex. Here was another connection between Alex and Ken; they both knew Bjorn. And now Bjorn was dead. Jennifer knew the article had speculated the fire was arson. Had someone wanted to kill Bjorn or was his death a result of the arson and not the reason behind the crime? The possibility that Bjorn might have started the fire accidentally didn't sound like the man she'd spoken with.

Ken put down the paper and folded it. "What a lousy thing to happen to him. You're eyeing me with a far away stare, Jennifer. Want to explain what's going on in that analytical mind of yours?"

"Connections between all the murders and the Einstein letter."

"If you start believing that every death is connected to your sister's murder, you're going to go batty," Ken said, then turned to Alex. "You knew Bjorn?"

Alex nodded. "Emma Mae reminded me that I'd chartered a boat from him the summer Carla was killed." Alex's eyes narrowed. "Bjorn repaired your sloop?"

"Right. He was a great carpenter. The best. A lot of boaters knew the old fellow. interesting coincidence that we both knew him." Ken stood and picked up his raincoat. "I took a taxi from the airport." He looked at Jennifer. "Could you drop me off at the dock on your way to Brandon?" After a quick glance at Alex, he added, "That is, if you're headed that way now."

"It's on my way," she said, as she and Alex stood.

Alex put his hand on her shoulder. "Stay in town, Jennifer. We have a lot to talk about."

"I have to get back." She kissed him on the cheek.

But he pulled her into an embrace and whispered, "Someday Lydia will play second fiddle to me."

Jennifer leaned back and studied his face. "Lydia's loyalty has nothing to do with us." She slid away from his arms and followed Ken out of the bar.

Chapter 26

Ken gave Jennifer directions to his boat's mooring. On the way, Jennifer realized they would pass the road leading to Bjorn's boatyard.

"I'd like to stop by Bjorn's place," she said. "Do you mind?"

"Odd thing to do." His brusqueness surprised her.

She glanced at him and noticed a narrowing of his eyes and tightening of his jaw. "We don't have to."

He shrugged. "I didn't think you were into ghoulish sights."

"I'm not, but I feel I have unfinished business there." She turned onto the dirt road that led to Bjorn's. As they approached the site, she could smell wet burned wood. She pulled up short of the yellow police tape strung across the road and turned off the engine. When she got out, Ken stayed in the car. The blackened struts of the building stood out against the glistening blue water beyond. Part of the metal roof rested next to the partially burned charter boat sign. Even the dock had been scorched. As she stood surveying the scene, she heard the crunch of gravel as Ken walked up behind her.

His voice almost purred in her ear. "What are you thinking?"

She hunched her shoulders, wary of his presence. She moved a few feet forward, separating herself from him. His attitude toward her was like a cave entrance, mysterious and somewhat scary. Without turning around, she murmured, "I don't know why I needed to come here. Perhaps to pay my respects."

In some odd way, she felt responsible for Bjorn's death, and yet, she didn't understand why. Had her asking him about Ken caused this or was it Alex's connection to Bjorn? Were these circumstances in a patchwork of random events?

She studied the charter boat sign. Bjorn had said something about charter files at home. Could they be significant? He'd mentioned a sister.

She must be grieving. Jennifer decided to visit the woman to convey her sympathy. Yet, she understood that her visit would have an ulterior motive. "Let's go," she said and brushed past him to return to the car.

They drove out the rutted lane, and Ken guided her to a small paved lot about three miles away. After she pulled into a parking space, she spotted the shining black hull among the other boats painted white.

Before they got out of the car, he asked, "Want to come aboard?"

She studied the dock and noted the workmen within shouting distance. "I can't stay long."

They walked along the docks, stopping at *The High Life*. Ken boarded, placed his canvas bag down, and held out his hand to Jennifer as she stepped onto the polished teak deck.

"Welcome to my kingdom." Ken opened his arms wide and beamed with pride at his world on the sea. "I once offered you champagne if you'd come aboard. How about a glass of wine?"

"I have a long drive home, so I'll take a rain check."

"You're a careful woman." He moved toward the companionway door with his bag in his hand. "How about hot tea?"

She smiled. "That would be nice."

"Come see the interior. Most of it is Bjorn's work." He ducked down and disappeared into the cabin and Jennifer followed.

She was amazed at the quality of the workmanship. She ran her hand over the pristine mahogany countertops and noted the wood joinery. Drawers and cupboards filled every niche in the galley and nothing was out of place. "Wonderfully done," she said.

He pointed to the ceiling. "Okume plywood panels with teak battens at the seam. Bjorn's idea. Its tan texture gives more light to the cabin." He moved toward the navigational center, took a white cloth and wiped a speck of dust off one of the instruments. "I moved the radar to the cockpit bulkhead and fitted it with a wood-trimmed transparent door." He gestured at the cabin. "Take a look around."

Pride in his boat was understandable, but he had an overly fussy obsession, like a doting mother. The innovations were not only useful but installed with superb craftsmanship. The aft sleeping cabin had a large bed with a neat navy blue coverlet trimmed in white. Jackets hung from wood pegs. Her eyes stilled at a picture of a clown hanging on the wall. She drew in a breath and returned to the galley and accepted a mug of steaming tea.

"Jasmine. Hope you like it," he said.

She took a sip, enjoying the clean refreshing taste, but after seeing the clown painting the cabin now felt claustrophobic. Coincidence? She doubted it. "The interior is handsome, and I appreciate you letting me see it. It's a beautiful day. Let's go on deck."

"Of course." He grabbed two maroon canvas cushions and went up the steps.

She held her tea in one hand and grasped the handrail with the other. Up top the sun shone and the cool fall breeze curled the water into small waves. "I wonder how much longer we'll have this glorious weather?" she said, keeping the conversation light.

He placed the cushions on the seats at the helm and motioned for her to join him. "If it holds, you should take advantage of it. Come sailing with me or get in some kayaking off your island."

She took another sip of the soothing tea. "You and Alex seem to have the same idea. You've been investigating him. What have you found?"

"Wondered when you'd ask." He leaned back and lifted his tanned face to the sun. "Haven't had too much time, but I did learn he lost a big client when he got his divorce, and his business is on the skids." He turned toward her and took off his sunglasses. "I've been wondering how he can afford staying at the Monaco under his current financial situation."

"That proves nothing."

"Maybe not. But you're so close to him, you might not see the inter-twining clues."

"Clues?" What had she missed?

"All right." His gray eyes studied her. "Let me put it this way. The circumstances surrounding Alex's behavior during the time of the murders infer that he had some connections with one, if not both crimes."

"So did I. It's the same evidence the police had harped on after Carla died and now Cameron seems to be following their line of thinking."

"True, but there's more. Do you want me to list them?" He didn't wait for her reply. "He avoided being the main suspect of your sister's murder by putting the monkey on your back and skipping town."

"That's nothing new." She tightened her grip on the mug.

"Okay. But think about it. He had motive and opportunity."

"What motive? The desire for a rare book worth no more than $20,000 is hardly a motive. And at the time he didn't know about any document or letter inside the book."

"Are you sure about that?" His eyes held hers.

She dropped her eyes. "No. But from his reaction to Einstein's letter it doesn't seem that he did."

"But you aren't sure." He put his hand on her forearm as if to comfort her.

She put her mug down, stood, and moved to the rail.

"Of course, there's the big question that you've brushed aside, or have you?" He asked.

"What are you talking about?"

"You know damn well. You're afraid to admit he had an affair with your sister. Did you ever confront him about that?"

"Yes." Her hands clenched at her side.

"What did he say?"

"Well, he … he was evasive." She shrugged and swallowed, feeling her throat close. "How did you learn about that story?"

"It's in the police report. Your mother's statement."

She glared at him. "Mother has an acid tongue. She never liked him. And besides, even if he did, how does that give him a motive?"

He shrugged. "Maybe Carla wanted more. Marriage, for instance, yet he was engaged to you."

"Then he would have killed me, not Carla."

He shook his head. "They could have had a fight. Any number of things could have happened on the beach that night."

"Any number of things does not mean he killed her." She knew her face was red.

Ken took a sip of tea before continuing. "All right. Let's strike that one. But he was present when Clifford died; he's an avid book collector which ties him to both cases; he got Wedgeworth's copy that belonged to Carla; the page is missing showing the previous owner; right before the murder he was in the library alone with free access to the collection; he's living beyond his income."

"But he sent you to find out about Einstein's paper."

"Could have been a ruse to throw me and you off guard, and let me remind you, it led to nothing." He stood and leaned against the rail next to her. "I'm sorry to be the one to have to make you face all this. I admire you for sticking up for him."

"I need more than circumstantial stuff."

"The evidence is overwhelming, and some of what I've stated are facts."

She shaded her eyes when she looked at him and shook her head. "This isn't getting us anywhere. I have to get home to rescue Emma Mae from animal sitting. Thanks for the tea."

He shook his head. "You and your animals. I'd say you were perfect except for your allegiance to Lydia."

"I'll take that as a compliment and not a slight."

He placed his mug on the cushion. "Animals don't fit my lifestyle."

"But your lifestyle includes clowns."

He hesitated and cocked his head with a slight scowl. "You spotted my clown picture. Forgot about that." He waggled his finger at her. "You're perceptive. Yes, I enjoy pictures of clowns and circuses."

"Did you know Wedgeworth was also interested in clowns?"

"We talked about it." He stood next to her. "If I thought my hobbies interested you, I'd have told you." Ken walked with her down the dock. "How did you learn about Clifford's interest in clowns?"

"There's a picture in his library and his wife told me they met in Vegas at a clown convention. Do you attend those?"

"No. I'm not into large groups."

At her car he took her hand, but she pulled it away and took her car keys from her pocket.

"Tell me," he said. "Do you want me to keep you informed about what I find out about Alex or not? Your aunt hired me to find information that could help you deal with the police. I need to investigate everyone close to you."

"As I said, I need facts that lead somewhere other than more suppositions."

"Okay. We're talking the same language then." He stood very close to her. "One thing though. I've always made it a policy not to get involved emotionally with my clients. But you're a secondary client, so I'm making an exception."

His hand cradled her cheek and his lips sought hers. She turned her head and his kiss landed on her cheek. Slowly she disentangled herself from his embrace.

His brow creased. "Wrong time, wrong place?"

She nodded.

He lowered his arms, but remained standing close. "Someday, Jennifer, you'll realize you can't hide from your desires. And I hope I'm there when that happens."

She felt his warm breath on her face. "You think you have me all figured out, don't you?"

He shook his head. "Oh, no. I wish I did. Unfortunately for me, you're a very complicated woman. Normally, I try to avoid the type, but you've gotten under my skin."

She turned and unlocked the car door. "I think of myself as simple, yet dedicated."

"Simple, no. Dedicated, yes. And the combination could be deadly to the wrong person." He reached up and touched her hair.

She flicked his hand away.

Unfazed, he continued, "Underestimating you could be the worst mistake a man could make. I wonder if that isn't what happened to Alex."

She slipped into her car, shut the door, and lowered the window. "Flattery from you seems strange, Ken."

He tapped the side of her car and eyed her. "An intriguing and complicated woman inspires a man to do outrageous acts." He chuckled, then added, "You might just be the death of me."

Chapter 27

On the drive home, Jennifer thought about Alex and Carla being lovers right under her nose. It stabbed her to the core. She pounded on the steering wheel, tears flowed, blurring her vision. "Damn you, Alex." She flipped on the radio to her favorite jazz station, trying to dispel her anger. Slowly she ratcheted her emotions down until she began to think logically. The murders formed a web with Alex and herself at the center. Bjorn's death only complicated things. If Carla's lost book wasn't the key, what was?

Ken remained an enigma. He was attractive, but there was something about him that spooked her. Joe said he was legit, but Ken's interest in clowns seemed an odd coincidence and made her uneasy. His explanation of why he entered her life remained suspect, and she had no way to verify that Clifford Wedgeworth had actually hired him to investigate her. However, if he hadn't, why come out to the island? She made a mental note to ask Cynthia and Warren if they knew Ken.

When Jennifer drove up to her house, Lydia barked, the front door opened and Lydia ran to Jennifer, butting against her thigh and mouthing her forearm. She scratched her dog behind the ears, and ruffled the fur. "I missed you too."

Emma Mae stood on the porch, her long skirt flapping around her ankles. "She's been looking for you for the past hour."

"Sorry I'm late." Jennifer followed Emma Mae into the house with Lydia prancing at her side. "I went aboard Ken's sloop." She dropped her purse on the table by the door.

"Oh." Emma Mae folded her arms.

Jennifer laughed, then said, "It was nothing special. Well, his boat was special, not the meeting."

Emma Mae grinned and raised her eyebrows.

"The fact I went aboard means nothing, so don't give me your 'tell me all' look." Jennifer put her jacket in the hall closet and went into the living room.

Emma Mae sat on the couch and leaned forward. "Did you learn anything that would help solve the mystery letter?"

"A little. We got the name of the agent who sold the book to the museum. Alex will contact him." She headed for the kitchen. "Have you fed Lydia?"

"No. Figured she'd be happier if you did. She looks plain mournful when you're not around." Emma Mae picked Stormy up and settled the cat on her lap.

Jennifer scooped kibbles into Lydia's bowl, pulled out a can of dog food from the fridge, and stirred in small chunks. After the dish was placed on the floor on the porch, Lydia dove in.

"You spoil her," Emma Mae called out from the other room.

Jennifer came back into the living room, sat at her desk and grinned. "And just what do you do with the cats, may I ask?"

"Cats don't need babysitting," Emma Mae said. "That reminds me. I asked Joanna Roberts to tend the store tomorrow afternoon."

"Good idea. She worked out well last Christmas," Jennifer said.

"Right. She knows the store and needs the income. I told her we'd need her part time from now on."

"I'm glad you hired her. We were getting stretched thin. I've got too much on my plate right now to think about the business." Jennifer bit on her lower lip. "I'd love to take a few days off and go to the island." She thought about Joe and how lovely it would be for the two of them to spend time there together.

Emma Mae interrupted her thoughts. "Are you sure that would be wise?"

"The weather should be lovely the rest of the week," Jennifer said.

"That's not what I meant," Emma Mae said.

"I know." Despite her family's angst about Beastly, Jennifer longed for the island's peace, and Lydia would be safer on the island. Alex and Ken's suggestion of her retreat niggled at her. She rose, picked up the morning paper and returned to her desk. "Have your heard anything about a service for Bjorn Halverson?"

"It's too early for a notice. Aren't you tired of going to funerals?"

Jennifer eyed her aunt with a pained expression. "I'd like to talk to his sister. Bjorn told me he kept some of his files at home. Maybe she'll let me see them."

"What do you think you'll find?"

"I'm not sure. I keep feeling that the answer to both murders is close." She shook her head and rubbed her temples. "I must sound loony."

"You sound just like you always have about Carla's murder. I hired Ken Sullivan to help you, so why don't you let him talk to Bjorn's sister?" Emma Mae stroked Stormy's white fur absentmindedly, while she kept her gaze on her niece.

"I need to do it myself." She glanced up from the paper. "It's important to me."

Emma Mae cocked her head to one side. "Don't you trust Ken?"

Jennifer continued perusing the paper without looking up. She didn't want to speak of her ambivalent feelings toward Ken. "Please, understand that I have to do things my way."

"Are you going to tell him you're going to the island?"

"Why should I? You hired him. If he finds out anything, he can tell you, and you can reach me on my cell phone. If it's urgent, I'll come home." Jennifer flattened the newspaper on the desk and read the headline — *Arson Suspected in Boat Fire.* Obviously her aunt hadn't read the article. "You probably want to get home."

"Trying to get rid of me, aren't you?" She cradled the kitten in her hand, stood, and put Stormy on the floor next to Lydia. "I hope you find whatever it is you're looking for when you see Bjorn's sister." She went to Jennifer and hugged her. "Don't do something stupid and get hurt. You know I can't run the store without you." Her eyes misted. "And I love you, child."

Jennifer smiled. "I know you do. And you've always been there for me. Tomorrow we'll go to the reading of Wedgeworth's will together." She patted her aunt on the shoulder. "Trust me. I have no intention of becoming another victim."

"Just don't put yourself at risk." Emma Mae waggled a finger at her niece. "And stay away from Alex. In this one thing, your mother and I agree. He's not to be trusted."

Ignoring her aunt's nagging, she said, "I'll pick you up at three o'clock. That should get us to the estate on time."

She stood in the doorway, watched Emma Mae stroll down the path and get into her car, then she returned to the living room. Lydia hadn't budged, but her eyes followed her mistress's every move. Jennifer noted her watchfulness and smiled. "It's a good thing Emma Mae isn't as attentive as you are, or she'd never leave me alone."

Back at her desk, she searched through the white pages and found Bjorn's name and a Ruth Halverson listed at the same address. Without hesitation she punched in the numbers and waited.

When a woman answered, she said, "Hello. My name is Jennifer Frost. I'm trying to locate Bjorn Halverson's sister, Ruth."

"I'm Ruth, Bjorn's sister."

"You don't know me," Jennifer continued, "but I spoke with your brother, Bjorn, awhile back and...."

"I remember," the woman interrupted. "Bjorn spoke of you and your lovable Newfoundland."

"He did? That makes me feel special," Jennifer said. "He was such a nice man. I'm so sorry for your loss. I wanted to know when a service will be held."

"Thursday at two," Ruth replied. "At the Congregational Church on 4th Avenue."

"Would it be all right if I attended?"

"I'd be most grateful if you'd come. And you're kind to call." After a slight hesitation, Ruth continued. "I hate to impose on you, but could I ask you to visit me before the service?"

"Of course," Jennifer said, pleased at the opportunity to talk to Ruth so soon. "Even though I spoke with Bjorn for only a short time, I felt he was a very good man."

"I almost called you right after his death, but then I had to take care of all the arrangements and time got away from me. Bjorn's death has shaken me so. Could you come tomorrow?"

"I have an appointment in the late afternoon, but I could come by before around two. Would that be all right?" As she asked this, she knew Emma Mae might be upset about driving to the estate alone. She certainly was testing her aunt's patience on many fronts. After Ruth gave Jennifer directions to her house, she hung up.

The following morning heavy fog hovered along the coast. Jennifer took Lydia on a short walk through the hills behind the house and managed to arrive at Books & Tea early enough to catch up on paperwork.

When she told Emma Mae that she'd set up an appointment to visit Ruth Halverson before the meeting at the estate, her aunt's face flushed.

"Joanne can't come into work until two thirty." Emma Mae drummed her fingers on her folded forearm as she stood next to the office desk where Jennifer had spread out order forms. "This will probably be another wild goose chase just like that letter." She threw her hands up in the air. "Oh, all right, I'll hold the fort with the store and the animals until Joanne arrives. I hope you know what you're doing," she said over her shoulder as she strode out of the room.

"I hope I do, too," Jennifer murmured to herself. The hours passed quickly as Jennifer took care of book orders and paid bills. At one thirty she left Lydia and Stormy with Emma Mae and drove south. The fog had lifted, but the weather forecast was tentative. Sunny skies would prevail unless the jet stream shifted and sent the storm hovering over Alaska south into Washington.

Ruth's directions to her house were easy to follow, and Jennifer pulled up in front of a neatly kept wood frame bungalow a little after two. She walked up the brick pathway to the front door that opened before she had a chance to ring the bell. An elderly, angular woman with deep blue eyes stood in the archway. Her white hair, pulled into a chignon, accentuated her pale skin.

"Please, come in," Ruth said as she looked behind Jennifer. "I thought maybe you'd bring your dog. Bjorn and I were animal lovers, but we never had a pet of our own." She smiled. "I don't know why."

She ushered Jennifer into a cheerfully furnished room with bookcases and cupboards stained with a pale blue wash and painted with Scandinavian designs. Ash wood floors glistened around a beige throw rug. She beckoned Jennifer to sit on a sofa covered with a yellow canvas slipcover while she remained standing with her hands folded in front of her paisley skirt. "Can I get you a cup of tea or coffee?"

"Coffee, black, would be lovely," Jennifer said.

"I just brewed some fresh. I'll be right back." The woman hurried away and returned with a tray laden with a pot, two cups, and a plate of cookies. She obviously had everything primed for Jennifer's visit. After placing the tray down on the coffee table, she sat in a white wicker chair across from the sofa.

"I'm glad you asked me to visit," Jennifer explained. "My visit with Bjorn was brief, but he was so helpful. He had a good sense of humor and we hit it off."

"People are like that, aren't they," Ruth said as she poured coffee into a cup and handed it to Jennifer. "Bjorn seldom was effusive about anyone, so when he came home and talked about you and your Newfoundland, I knew you must be special." She poured a cup for herself and offered Jennifer a cookie. "Homemade butter cookies. Bjorn loved them." She became teary-eyed, took out a tissue from her skirt pocket and blew her nose. "Sorry. I'm still so upset."

"His death was tragic," Jennifer said.

"His death was murder!" Ruth's hands shook as she clasped them in her lap.

Jennifer stifled a gasp then nodded. "I read in the paper that the authorities suspect arson." Jennifer gathered her thoughts and sipped her coffee, then asked, "Couldn't he have tried to put out the fire, fallen and hit his head?

Ruth's blue eyes clouded as she shook her head. "It was murder."

"You're thinking someone wanted to kill him and used the fire as a cover up?"

"Exactly." The old woman didn't blink as she stared at Jennifer.

"Do you have any idea why or who?" If Ruth was right, did Bjorn's death relate to Wedgeworth's or Carla's death? "Do the police have any idea who did it?"

"Not yet." Ruth sat up straighter. "That's why I needed to talk to you. Bjorn was very upset the last few days before his death. He wanted to help you solve your sister's murder and went to his favorite bar where local dockworkers hung out. I've been wondering if all his talk about that murder made someone nervous. I want to show you something." She left the room and returned with a file. "Bjorn had left this on his desk here at the house. He kept deliberating whether he should call you, and then of course, it was too late." Ruth placed the file in Jennifer's hands and sat next to her on the sofa.

The file label read: "August Charters." The date was two years ago. Jennifer leafed through the sheets, until Ruth pointed to several papers. "This is what you need to see, I think. They're application forms to charter one of Bjorn's boats."

At first Jennifer was mystified. She noted Alex's name and date of the charter. But Jennifer knew he'd chartered a boat for himself and her family, so that gave her no new information. But the next form stumped her. Carla had chartered another boat the day before, with Alex co-signing as the responsible party and captain. She thought back. Both Alex and Carla were on board when Jennifer and the family sailed to the island on Alex's chartered boat. "This must be a mistake." Jennifer pointed to the line where Alex had co-signed. "They wouldn't charter two boats one day and then the next too."

"For insurance purposes, you needed to be twenty-five to charter a boat," Ruth said. "How old was your sister?"

"Twenty-three." Jennifer flipped the forms back and forth comparing them. Carla didn't know how to pilot a boat and would have had to hire a captain. "I don't get it," Jennifer frowned as she studied the paper. "Why two boats within two days? Perhaps the dates got mixed up."

Ruth shrugged. "Bjorn had a young man helping with his charter service back then. Maybe that fellow didn't pay attention to the paper work. I don't know, but Bjorn thought it might be important. He checked his accounting and two charters were paid for, one by Alex Glidden and one by Carla Frost."

Ruth's blue eyes gazed at Jennifer with interest. "Do you think any of this has to do with my brother's death?"

"I have no idea." The idea that two boats had been chartered strengthened Jennifer's theory that someone else had come onto the island and killed Carla. Although no other boat had anchored nearby, there was the northern point where a good sailor could have found safe harbor. But the police had checked and no other boats were in the area. Could Bjorn's files point to the answer?

Jennifer compared the two rental agreements. "Look at this! The signatures are totally different. I know this is Carla's signature," she said, pointing to one form. She turned the page back. "But Alex's signatures are different. Someone must have forged his name." Jennifer took a deep breath. "Can we contact the man who worked for Bjorn?"

"Bjorn didn't know how. He had the man's name and social security number of course, but he didn't know how to trace him. I wouldn't know where to start, would you?"

"I might know someone who could find him," Jennifer said, thinking of Joe.

Ruth took a sheet of paper out of the file that had the information about the man, and handed it to Jennifer. "The police claim they'll solve the case. But Bjorn told me your sister's murder has never been solved, so I wonder." She crumpled her tissue and opened the file again. "Do you know this Alex Glidden?"

"We were engaged once. He and I found my sister's body. I don't know what this double entry of Bjorn's charter boats means, but I'll ask Alex and my family if they remember Carla talking about chartering a boat for herself. I can't imagine why she would. She and Alex sailed with us to the island. If Bjorn's other boat went to sea, it couldn't have been manned by Alex or Carla."

"Then someone else took a boat out and used their names," Ruth said. "I sometimes helped Bjorn out at the docks, especially during his busy chartering season. I don't remember anything amiss. There were so many people who came and went."

She wondered if Ruth would remember Alex. "Have the police shown you any pictures of possible suspects?"

"No. Not yet," Ruth said.

Jennifer dug into her purse and took out an old photo of Alex. As she did so, she wondered why she'd kept it all these years. "Do you recognize this man?" she asked, showing the snapshot to Ruth.

Ruth squinted and studied the picture, but shook her head. "Usually, I need something special about a person before I'll remember him, like a scar or an unusual trait." Ruth stopped and stared at the wall as if thinking about the past. "There were a lot of young men hanging around during that time."

Jennifer patted the women's hand. "It was a long time ago. Did you mention the files to the police?"

"No. I've been too confused about everything that's happened. Besides, the police think a local gang, who have been shaking down small boatyard owners, started the fire. Bjorn talked about retiring because of them, but I knew he couldn't stay away from the marina. He loved boats, woodwork, and sails. They were his life. Take that away, and he'd have died of frustration and boredom."

Jennifer glanced at her watch. "I've got to leave." She dug out her business card from her wallet and handed it to Ruth. "Call me, if you find anything else in the files that might relate to your brother's or my sister's death. And I'll let you know what I find out, if anything." She moved forward on the couch as if to rise, but Ruth put her hand on Jennifer's arm.

"May I ask a favor?" Ruth said. "It has nothing to do with recent events. But I was wondering if you'd come by with your Newfoundland." She looked down at the floor as if embarrassed about her request. "It's just … I don't know … Bjorn talked about your Newfie and well …."

"I'd love to bring Lydia to visit, and the three of us could take a walk together." Jennifer covered the woman's hand with her own. "Maybe go to the beach. Lydia loves to swim."

Ruth smiled. "Bjorn said you were like a steady ship. It was his supreme compliment."

Jennifer swallowed hard; her eyes grew misty. "He was a good man. I'll see you at his memorial service."

Ruth smiled. "If you learn anything that relates to Bjorn's murder, please call me or let a Detective Cameron know."

The name Cameron stopped Jennifer cold.

Chapter 28

On her drive to Wedgeworth's estate, Jennifer called Alex at the Monaco, eager to learn his thoughts on the two boat charters. The hotel operator told her there was no one by that name registered. "That's impossible. Would you please connect me to the front desk?"

When the man came on the line, she asked, "Mr. Alex Glidden stayed at your hotel. He was to leave me a message and a forwarding number where I could reach him. Could you check your records?"

"Just a minute," he said.

She drove up the hill to the estate and through the open gate, while holding her cell phone to her ear. The manager came back on the phone. "Mr. Glidden stayed here two nights, but didn't leave a forwarding address or a message."

Jennifer's heart sank. "Thank you." She clicked off her phone, put it in her lap and parked her car. Alex had run out on her again and with the book, too. "Damn." So much for his promise to see things through this time. Did the police know he had skipped town? After stuffing her cell phone into her purse, she got out and walked past several cars, including Emma Mae's.

Harold opened the door soon after she rang the bell. "Welcome, Miss Frost. You're the last to arrive. The group is assembled in the study. It's on your right past the living room." A heavy-set man with bright red hair stood behind a desk. Chairs were arranged in a semicircle; Emma Mae sat in one of them. The man from the Findley Foundation, whom Jennifer had met at the memorial service, stood next to the fireplace speaking with a woman and a man she didn't recognize.

Cynthia, who'd been talking to the red-haired man, excused herself and took Jennifer's arm, leading her to a corner of the room. "I wanted to warn you. Warren told Cameron about the missing page from Cliff's ledger and the detective confiscated it as evidence."

Jennifer glanced over at the lanky secretary. "For heaven's sakes, why would Warren do that? I thought we'd agreed to work together."

Cynthia grimaced and shook her head. "I think Warren got scared and wanted to deflect suspicion away from himself. Of course, we had to tell the detective about your visit. I think we've gotten you in trouble. I'm sorry."

Before Jennifer could respond, the red-haired man moved to the desk. "I believe we're all here now. Would everyone be seated, please."

"We'll talk later." Cynthia moved away and took a seat to the right of the desk.

Jennifer sat next to her aunt.

"You're late," Emma Mae whispered to Jennifer as Harold sat on the other side of Emma Mae.

"My name is George Raven," the red-haired man said after everyone was seated. "I was Clifford Wedgeworth's lawyer and am acting as the executor of his estate. Mr. Wedgeworth requested that all inheritors of his estate be present at the reading of his will and codicil." He glanced around the room. "You've all met Mrs. Wedgeworth, but I'd like the rest of you to introduce yourselves." Each in turn stated their name and affiliation: Warren Peabody, Norman Babcock of The Nature Conservancy, Robert Stewart of the Findley Foundation, Grace Knowland of the Seattle Unified School System, Harold McBain, Emma Mae, and Jennifer.

"Thank you." George Raven looked at the group as he held his reading glasses in his hand. "Clifford Wedgeworth made several codicils to his will in the last weeks of his life. But before I explain his wishes, I will read a letter, written by him."

He put on his glasses. "I, Clifford Wedgeworth, want to make amends for the life I have led. I have not always treated my friends kindly. I have abused the land in many of my business dealings and sometimes have acted out of greed instead of integrity. I cannot change the past, but I can financially reward loyalty and give restitution to those I have wronged."

Mr. Raven took off his glasses and again looked at the group. "I'll explain Mr. Wedgeworth's wishes and later I'll discuss details of his bequests with some of you in private."

He continued and referred to notes from time to time. "This house and the adjoining lands go to The Nature Conservancy with some provisos. Harold McBain shall retain the right to live in the carriage house located on the grounds as long as he desires, and he shall continue as groundskeeper with his commensurate salary as long as he so wishes. Cynthia Wedgeworth may live in the Wedgeworth manor for one year from the date of her husband's death. This is in accordance with their prenuptial agreement. All taxes and utilities shall be paid by the Conservancy from the date ownership is transferred to them." Mr. Raven looked at Norman Babcock. "Mr. Wedgeworth left monies for this purpose."

Mr. Raven then smiled at Cynthia. He again donned his reading glasses and picked up another letter. "My wife, Cynthia Evans Wedgeworth, will receive two million dollars. My portfolio, consisting of stocks and bonds, will be sold to pay distributions I have designated and any remaining sums will be used to pay for my company's encumbrances."

Cynthia put her hands to her cheeks. Was the woman embarrassed or shocked? Had she expected more or less?

Again Mr. Raven glanced over his glasses and spoke to Grace Knowland. "Clifford Wedgeworth had a great interest in clowns. I understand from Mrs. Wedgeworth that a room in this house was reserved for his costumes and other clown paraphernalia. He left his clown collection including clown suits, memorabilia and makeup kits to the Seattle Unified School District. He also left a $250,000 fund to be used by the district to further an interest in clowns and maintain the collection."

"As to the Findley Foundation," Mr. Raven continued. "Mr. Wedgeworth made recent changes." Robert Stewart sat straighter. "I now quote: 'My book collection in the library goes to the Findley Foundation, except for recent acquisitions I have designated, which I give to Jennifer Frost.'"

Jennifer felt her cheeks glow hot. What had the man been thinking? Did he know he'd bought *The Big Sleep* from Carla's killer and this was his way of making amends? When had the codicil been written—before or after he made the trade with Alex?

"He has listed the books in a particular bookcase," Raven continued. "I'll give you the list, Miss Frost, and a copy will go to Mr. Stewart."

Cynthia and Emma Mae stared at Jennifer, their mouths agape.

Mr. Raven continued reading. "To Harold McBain, I give the sum of $500,000 for his devoted service and his trustworthiness."

Harold smiled but showed no other reaction to his inheritance.

To Warren Peabody, who has served me well for many years, I give the sum of $500,000."

Warren shifted in his seat, cleared his throat and glared at the lawyer. Had he expected more?

"To Emma Mae Langdon, who was a dear friend, loyal and true through many years, I give the sum of $250,000." Mr. Raven put down the paper and took off his glasses. "The rest of Mr. Wedgeworth's estate deals with matters regarding his business." He turned to Cynthia. "Mrs. Wedgeworth, if you'll allow me to use the library, I'd like to have private discussions first with Mr. Babcock, then Mr. Stewart and later Mrs. Knowland."

Cynthia nodded, and Raven walked out of the living room with a briefcase in hand. Mr. Babcock followed him to the library.

"Can you believe it?" Harold said to Emma Mae. "He always said he'd take care of me, and he's honored his word. And you must be feeling good about it, too."

A soft laugh came from Emma Mae. "I never dreamed he'd remember me in his will." She turned to Jennifer. "He gave you the books you appraised for him."

"I appraised the books for Cynthia, not for her husband."

"What are you talking about?" Emma Mae asked.

"Cynthia wanted to surprise him with the appraisal as a gift." As Jennifer mulled the inheritance, her thoughts were interrupted by Cynthia.

"Excuse me Emma Mae, but I need to talk to Jennifer in private."

Jennifer followed Cynthia to the same sitting room where Detective Cameron had interrogated her the day of the murder. Cynthia sat on the sofa, her hands clutched together in front of her. She let out a long sigh as if she'd been holding her breath. "I'm glad Cliff gave you the book collection."

"Do you know why he did?"

"I'm not sure. If he knew the origin of that book you found, we'll never know." Cynthia slumped back in the couch. "Cliff wasn't perfect, but he wouldn't murder your sister for a book he could have bought. He must have learned about my asking you to do the appraisal and took it the wrong way. Why else would he have given those exact books to you?" She held up her hands as if to ward off Jennifer's rebuttal. "He only left me the exact amount stated in our prenup. I sound like the gold digger everyone thought I was, don't I?"

Jennifer's thoughts had gone in that direction. "The books were always destined to go the Findley Foundation and not to you."

"I realize that. I meant the stocks and bonds."

"It might depend on when your husband drew up the codicil," Jennifer said.

"Yes, that's true." Cynthia paused, then said, "You've been kind to me. Actually, you're the only one who's given me any support." She paused, then blurted out, "Warren told Cameron of your suggestion that the three of us pool our information and not tell the police what we learned. Warren made it sound like you wanted us to withhold evidence. I tried to tell Cameron that wasn't so, but I think he believed Warren and not me."

"I never said to withhold evidence from the police." Jennifer moved to the edge of her chair.

"I wanted to call you earlier, but that detective warned me not to trust someone who was a suspect in another murder. Warren said you've been kind to me because you wanted to gain my confidence. I don't know what or who to believe. But now that you have the collection, I've got to ask. Were you using me?"

For a nanosecond, Jennifer was speechless, then said, "I haven't been faking my empathy. I'm sorry you'd think that."

"Thank you. I believe you and I'm glad."

Jennifer stood and paced the room. "Warren seems to want to shift blame away from himself, yet he's a logical suspect. He had access to the room, the keys, knowledge of your husband's tastes in food and information about the Blakely Catering staff."

Cynthia had tears in her eyes. "I know you think I'm an ingrate, but I don't know who to believe. And I'm scared they'll think I killed Cliff. I didn't."

"No, I don't think you did. You said you gave Cliff's library key to Harold. I opened the bookcase with a key left on the desk, then left it there. Harold checked everything before I left, but he could have made duplicates."

"But that was only to the library not the key to his desk where the ledger was kept."

"True. So who does that leave as a guilty party?"

Cynthia frowned. "Warren had all the keys, but why would he kill the one person who paid him an exorbitant salary?"

Jennifer's mind raced, trying to think of anything that might have relevance to the case. "Do you know Ken Sullivan? He's the private detective your husband hired to investigate me."

Cynthia thought for a moment, then said, "The name isn't familiar. Perhaps Warren might know. I'll ask him. Is it important?"

Jennifer sighed. "I have no idea. I'm just groping for clues." She walked to the door, turned and asked, "Are you going to stay in the house?"

"Probably for a while. At least until I can figure out where to go." She shrugged. "Back to teaching I guess."

Jennifer smiled. "If you enjoyed it, do it." Her words stopped her. She hadn't taken this advice. Was it about time she did?

"If you need help, I'll be there for you," Cynthia said. "I mean it. No matter what Warren or that detective say."

"Thanks. I'm sure the police are just gathering evidence and are as muddled as we are."

Jennifer left the room and hurried down the hall. With her thoughts spinning scenarios, she collided with the portly Mr. Raven as he came out of the library.

"I'm so sorry," he said, putting out a hand to steady her. "Are you all right?"

"No harm done," she said. "Actually, I'm glad I ran into you before you left, but I don't mean literally." They both smiled. "Can you tell me the exact date when Mr. Wedgeworth wrote the codicil including me in his will?"

"Of course, but I'll have to look it up." He walked into the living room, set his briefcase on the table and pulled out a file. As he thumbed through pages, Cynthia appeared at the living room entryway. "Ah, here it is," Mr. Raven said and gave Jennifer the date.

Jennifer glanced at Cynthia as she said, "So, he included me in his will before the Wedgeworths went on their honeymoon."

Mr. Raven smiled. "Well, I don't know when they went on their honeymoon, but I do know Mr. Wedgeworth was most explicit that his codicil be signed before he left town."

Jennifer turned to Cynthia and said, "I appraised the collection while you were away. Your husband must have known you hired me and that's when he had me investigated. You said he was angry with you. Could he have believed you wanted the collection for yourself?"

Cynthia's lips quivered. "He might have given you the collection out of spite, but it was always going to the Findley Foundation."

"He might have done it out of guilt for his past crimes. Perhaps he knew *The Big Sleep* belonged to my sister and if so, he knew her murderer."

"Never."

Jennifer gazed at Cynthia. "Well, until we get the murderer, we won't know, will we?"

"Be careful," Cynthia said. "I heard about your cat."

Chapter 29

As Jennifer headed toward her red jeep, Cameron and another police officer walked up to her. "Miss Frost, do you know where Alex Glidden is?" Cameron asked.

"No. I called his hotel right before I drove here and he'd checked out."

"I'd like to ask you a few questions. The police station would be best."

She thought of the torturous interview she'd been subjected to after Carla's murder that had resulted in the police accusing her of murder. "Am I under arrest?"

"No." He glanced at the manor house. "Mr. Peabody claims you asked him to withhold evidence. Did you?"

"I've answered all your questions truthfully."

"That's not what I asked." He gave her a hard stare. "It would be helpful if you could clear up some matters."

"Do I need a lawyer?" She put her hand in her jacket pocket to prevent him from seeing how she was shaking.

"If you'd like, but it's not necessary. However, I wouldn't want you to refuse my invitation. You can drive your car and follow us."

She nodded, but her stomach squeezed tight. After getting in her car, she began to hyperventilate. Calm down, think, she told herself and took several deep breaths. Digging into her purse, she got out her cell phone and called Joe. When he answered, she said, "Joe, the police want to question me at the Seattle station. I don't trust Cameron. Two years ago a similar session didn't go too well. What should I do?"

His voice was clipped, but steady. "Where are you?"

Wedgeworth's estate. In my car."

"Damn, Jen. You've got to go with them or it won't look good. Which precinct?"

"West, I think."

"Don't say anything without a lawyer."

"I don't know one in Seattle, do you? I don't want to sit around in that bilious green room staring at the four walls until I get legal counsel."

"It'll be tough finding someone good at the last minute." He paused then said, "Amanda Crawford might be available. She's retired, but knows the ropes. I'll give her a call. If she can't meet you there, I'll let you know. I'll come down as soon as I can and be there after the interrogation."

"They call it questioning," she said.

"That's what they call it, but I know better."

"Me too." She gripped her phone tighter. "You don't have to come."

"I'll be there."

"They're letting me drive my car."

"Don't put too much store in that favor. Do not answer any questions until Amanda gets there. If she can't make it, tell them you don't have anything to say until you get a lawyer."

"Thanks Joe." She hung up and sat in her car digesting Joe's suggestions and warnings. She wished he could be with her during the interrogation. A lawyer she didn't know might be uncomfortable. She put her cell phone on the passenger seat and started her car. She glanced at the manor and saw Warren Peabody on the front steps with a smirk on his narrow face. Cynthia peered out a window, holding a handkerchief to her mouth.

Driving behind Cameron's car drove her crazy. She had an overwhelming desire to ram it. She laughed at the idea. That would put her in good graces with the police. The Seattle traffic slowed the twenty minute trip to thirty minutes. For all Jennifer cared it could be five hours. More time to get a lawyer, more time to avoid Cameron's sleazy questions, but more time for her mind to play out haunting scenarios of being dragged off to a cell.

Her phone's buzzing brought her back to reality. It was Joe. "Amanda will meet you there. Do as she says. Be brave. It'll be okay. See you soon."

At least one problem solved. She followed Cameron's car into the parking lot where a policeman motioned her to an empty slot. Once inside the station, she was shown down a hall with institutional linoleum and pale green walls. She wrinkled her nose at the smell of old socks combined with a pine-scented antiseptic spray. The policeman opened a door to a room she remembered too well—pale green walls, one door to freedom, a one way viewing window, and a metal table with four stiff-backed plastic chairs.

For about thirty minutes she waited, then Cameron entered and set a file on the table. Soon afterward an officer admitted an elderly woman.

Her face was wrinkled, but tan, and despite a slight dowager's hump, she stood with her chin raised. Her intelligent blue eyes sparkled with energetic interest. Jennifer liked Amanda Crawford immediately.

"Nice to see you again, Detective Cameron," she said and nodded to Jennifer. "I represent Miss Frost."

Cameron was obviously taken by surprise. "She doesn't need a lawyer. I'm merely questioning her about matters that can help solve Clifford Wedgeworth's death."

"Nicely put. So you aren't arresting Miss Frost?"

"This is merely a formality."

"I've heard that song before." The woman gave a reassuring smile to Jennifer and sat next to her. "I advise you not to say anything, my dear."

"I'd like to hear what the detective wants," Jennifer said, "but I won't submit to a grilling."

"I'm here to see that doesn't happen." The crow's feet by Amanda's eyes deepened.

Cameron sat in a chair on the opposite side of the table. "We've interviewed your cohorts, Miss Frost."

"What are you talking about?" Jennifer frowned.

Amanda said, "Explain what you mean by cohorts, Detective."

Cameron leaned forward. "Both Warren Peabody and Cynthia Wedgeworth said you badgered them into withholding evidence. Did you?"

Amanda looked at Jennifer and shook her head.

"Okay. Let me put it this way," Cameron said. "There was a book missing from the Wedgeworth collection. Your friend Alex conspired with you to take it."

"What specific book are you talking about Detective?" Amanda asked.

"*The Big Sleep* by Raymond Chandler." He pointed at Jennifer. "She knows all about it."

"Nobody took it," Jennifer said. "Alex Glidden traded another book he owned for it. You already know that."

"You appraised Wedgeworth's collection. You had access to the house with keys you used that day. You were present when Wedgeworth was killed, and you were present when your sister was killed. What do you have to say?"

"I did not have access to the house or his library until Harold let me in. He even searched my belongs before I left."

Amanda smiled, giving her client a slight nod of approval.

"There's more to the book than you told me." Cameron said. "I've learned there were imprints in it that might be useful to the investigation. You hid this information from the police?"

"I didn't hide anything. You didn't ask. In fact, you said the book had nothing to do with Wedgeworth's murder."

"That's beside the point. You withheld evidence."

Amanda broke in. "She can't withhold evidence that she doesn't or didn't know was evidence."

"I'm asking now for you to tell me about these imprints."

"Off the record," Amanda said.

Cameron used his practiced grin. "Hey, this is just a friendly visit."

Amanda laughed. "You still using that shopworn line?"

He leaned back. "Off the record."

Amanda nodded to Jennifer. "Okay, go ahead."

"Alex and I wanted to find out more about the prints. It looked as if a letter or some kind of document had been signed by Einstein."

"Albert Einstein?" Cameron's eyes widened.

"Yes. The letter could be priceless. We think Carla's killer didn't want the book, but what was in the book. If we could find out who sold the book to Wedgeworth, we might learn who took the letter and killed Carla." She turned toward Amanda. "He should know all this because he followed up the investigation into my sister's murder."

Amanda raised an eyebrow. "Detective, exactly what case are you questioning my client about?"

"Both."

"You think my client committed both these murders?"

"He drummed his fingers on the table. "I sympathize with her about her sister, but she and her fiancé were at the scene of both crimes."

Amanda gave him a rueful smile. "That's the first time I've ever heard you use the word, sympathy. My, how you've changed."

"Don't be sarcastic, counselor. Your client is up to her ears in this. I'm only trying to get to the bottom of her involvement."

"I'm a bystander," Jennifer said.

Cameron shook his head and opened a file. "You received $50,000 from your sister's death."

"I told you that already."

"You, Alex and Carla had a fight before she died."

"It wasn't a fight. It was a discussion."

"You had a fight with Wedgeworth before he died."

"I did not. I hadn't even met him until the night he was murdered."

"Okay," Amanda interceded. "I think this is enough. What do you want to ask that you don't already know?"

"Where is Alex Glidden?"

"I don't know."

"This is what I think. You're holding out on me. You're still in love with Alex. He's guilty of both Carla and Wedgeworth's murder and you are his accomplice."

"That's crazy. I loved my sister. I've put my life on hold for two years searching for her killer."

Amanda put her hand on Jennifer's arm and shook her head.

Jennifer glared at Cameron.

"I'll spell out the facts," Cameron said. "Alex lives above his means. Needs money. He killed Carla and took the book, probably knew about the Einstein letter. When Wedgeworth found out the book was obtained from a murder victim, Alex killed him. You're covering for Alex. Admirable, but ill-placed."

Jennifer erupted. "I am not covering for him. He's no longer my fiancé. Someone else landed on the island that night; Alex heard an engine."

Amanda tried to restrain Jennifer's tirade to no avail.

Instead, Jennifer continued. "Bjorn Halverson's murder could be related to Wedgeworth's death. Check his files concerning the charter of two separate boats that show Alex's signature had been forged on one of them. And what about our poisoned cat? Alex had no reason to do that. Someone's setting Alex up."

Cameron shook his head. "Nice try, but Bjorn's files were burned in the fire."

"Not all of them. Talk to Ruth Halverson."

Cameron stared at her, then said, "Bjorn's files are probably shoddy bookkeeping. He was killed by a waterfront gang. We have them in custody. Only Alex claimed he heard a boat engine the night of your sister's murder. You stated you didn't hear anything."

"What about our cat?"

"A subterfuge to confound the investigation."

Jennifer sat back and shook her head at Cameron's litany of skewed reasoning.

"I think we're though here," Amanda said and stood. "You want Alex, not my client." She motioned to Jennifer.

For a second Cameron barred the door. "You're in a lot of trouble, Miss Frost. It would be better if you told the truth."

"Detective, your actions are close to harassment," Amanda said, inserting herself between Jennifer and Cameron. "You don't have a scintilla of evidence linking my client to either crime. It's all supposition." Amanda took Jennifer's elbow and they left the station.

When they emerged from the building, tears sprang to her eyes when she saw Joe and she moved into his open arms. After a moment she stepped back and wiped her cheeks with her finger tips.

He kept his arm around her shoulders and said, "It's okay, Jen."

She swallowed hard and murmured, "Thanks."

Joe slid his arm around her waist, turned toward Amanda and shook her hand.

"Jennifer handled herself very well," the feisty lawyer said.

"Cameron believes I killed my sister." She couldn't help but sniffle. "He's an ass."

Amanda shrugged. "Of course he is, but he's like a hound once he gets the scent. Cameron has a habit of overlooking details, jumping to conclusions. Alex Glidden should get himself a lawyer if he hasn't done so already." She paused. "It didn't sound like the police have much to go on. All bluster symbolizing nothing," she paraphrased Shakespeare.

"How long have you known Cameron?" Jennifer asked.

Amanda's eyes twinkled. "We've butted heads before."

"I appreciate your help." Jennifer dug into her purse for a business card. "You can send your bill to this address."

Amanda took the card and gave Jennifer one of her own. "If Cameron pulls you in for questioning again or comes by for small talk, call me. Do not say anything until I get there." Amanda smiled, patted Jennifer's arm, and walked up the street.

Jennifer turned to Joe. "She's wonderful. How do you know her?"

"Long story. I learned how to read attorney speak and their body language from her. She teaches at the University now."

"Do you use Cameron's tactics?"

"You do what you gotta do." He hesitated, then took her arm. "Come on. Time to take your mind off crime and have dinner. We'll go to a restaurant on the Wharf, then drive back to Brandon."

Chapter 30

When Jennifer got home that night, she hugged Lydia and fell into bed with dreams hounding her throughout the night. When she awoke the following morning, she lounged on her couch in pajamas under a down quilt, remembering the time before Carla's murder, years when she'd been guiding outdoor groups and enjoying the sweet smell of the forest and the sea.

She called Emma Mae and said she was ill and wouldn't be in. Apparently her aunt didn't buy her excuse, for within the hour she was at Jennifer's front door and then inside the house, standing over Jennifer who lay on the couch. With her brow creased she demanded, "What's really going on?"

"Everything's a mess. Alex skipped town." She didn't add that Joe was leaving.

"You aren't the first person to learn a man you trusted betrayed you."

"The police want him for Carla's murder."

"That's old news."

"They want him for Wedgeworth's murder, too."

Emma Mae shoved the comforter aside and sat next to her niece. "I've never seen you like this. I called Ken. Told him how Detective Cameron pulled you in for questioning."

"I wish you hadn't done that."

"Why? I hired him to help you. He obviously likes you."

"I wonder," Jennifer mumbled.

"Alex has disappeared, leaving you holding the proverbial bag. Again. The police know he withheld evidence."

"So did I," Jennifer said. "Kind of."

"I have questions for Alex, don't you?" Emma Mae sighed heavily and put her hand on her niece's arm. "Carla was always a handful, getting into small troubles here and there. Haven't you ever wondered about Carla and Alex?"

Jennifer gritted her teeth. "Stop bringing that up." She glared at her aunt. "Instead of putting out an arrest warrant on Alex, Cameron should take another look at all the evidence, but he's so hung up on Alex and me he won't check out anything else." Jennifer pulled the quilt tighter around her. Lydia moved toward her mistress and pushed her nose under Jennifer's hand.

Emma Mae eyed her niece. "What about poor Lydia? Have you walked her lately?"

"She'll be okay." Jennifer stroked Lydia's big head and scratched her behind the ears.

"She might, but will you? I shouldn't say this, but something has to get your spine straight. Go to your island. Do what you love: kayak, hike, bask in the sun. And when you come back, you'll be able to face Alex, Detective Cameron and testify at the trial. For God sakes child, show some gumption."

"I thought finding Carla's murderer would lead to peace, to getting things back to normal."

"A jury will decide if Alex killed Carla and Wedgeworth."

"It can't go that far!"

"Okay," Emma Mae said. "You think Alex didn't commit the crimes. Then who did?"

"I don't know." Jennifer wailed and threw her arms around Lydia's head.

Emma Mae smiled. "At least you're getting angry. That's a good sign."

Jennifer huffed. "You are such a pain, Emma Mae. I could strangle you, if I didn't love you so much."

"Well, that's a good sign, too." Emma Mae patted Jennifer's hand. "The world is full of knuckleheads. Don't let them win."

Jennifer started to sob and laugh at the same time. Emma Mae smiled, and soon the two of them were in each others arms, rocking with laughter and tears. Lydia barked, then settled down by the front door.

Jennifer hiccuped. She and Emma Mae sighed in unison, and the room grew quiet. Jennifer leaned her head back on the couch. "The island sounds like paradise. Would you really mind if I went off for awhile?"

"Of course not. Go ahead. When you come back, you can start over."

"Im not sure starting over would include the bookstore. Would you mind terribly if we severed our partnership?"

"No." Emma Mae leaned back. "I've been thinking it's time for me to move on to something else."

"Would that something else include Harold?"

"You're impudent." She straightened her skirt. A smile played on her lips. "Well, it might." She stood and looked down at her niece. "What will you do if we close the store? Go back to guiding adventure tours?"

Jennifer snorted. "Adventure. That's a laugh. I've had enough of adventures, all the wrong kind."

Chapter 31

The day before Joe left for Bellingham they spent the day together walking in the woods with Lydia happily at their heels. The leaves were turning, the air was crisp with the hint of winter on its breath but the sun shone. Glorious weather, yet Jennifer's heart ached with loss. She couldn't bear to have him leave without her. It was as if everyone she cared for had abandoned her. Joe had turned in his badge last week; the first step to private life and the role of security adviser to a company in Bellingham. She wasn't ready to leave and go with him.

He strode over a large rock, his jeans tight against his muscular thighs as he scrambled up the side of a steep hill. She followed as Lydia loped ahead. On the top of the crest there was a small meadow with a lone fir tree in its midst. He flung out his arms and turned his face to the sky. "Let's take a break," he said and sat on the ground, his legs crossed. Jennifer joined him. They each pulled out a water bottle from their small daypacks and Jennifer passed him a package of trail mix. Lydia plopped down under the tree, rolling and squirming on her back.

"She loves to be outside," Jennifer said.

"So do you."

She nodded. "Yeah, maybe that's my trouble. I've stuck my head in books for the past two years. Too bad life can't be one lovely hike after another. I used to feel all I needed was to be surrounded by nature. Now my life's upside down and I don't know how to straighten it out."

"You'll have to accept that Alex committed the murders. If you don't, I'm not sure you'll be able to get on with your life. I know you loved him. Perhaps you still love him." He shook his head. "I'm not sure where you and I stand. Was I just an interim lover, taking Alex's place in your life?"

"Oh, God, no. That's not true." She placed a hand on his knee. "Don't ever think that."

"I don't know what to think. You're paralyzed even after Cameron lined up all the evidence against him. Is he guilty? I don't know and neither do you. I think you still hope he isn't." He gazed at her with his lopsided smile. "And for your sake I hope so too."

"There are still so many details that don't make sense." She chewed a few raisins before continuing. "For instance, the old man who paid the boy to use the poison on the cats, the same poison that killed Wedgeworth. Who was he?"

Joe shook his head. "Let's just say Alex is innocent. Then who killed your sister?"

"Alex said he heard a motor just before we found her."

"Did you?"

"No."

"I hate to leave you when you're feeling so low, but I don't know what I can do." He stretched out, leaned back on one elbow and squinted in the sun. "I rented a two bedroom house with a large yard up in Bellingham. I signed a year's lease. Plenty of room for you and Lydia."

"I'm going out to Beastly for a week. Try and get my head around all that's happened." She smiled as she said, "When I return, if you still want me, I'll join you."

"You will?" His face lit up and he pulled her to him.

She smiled. "I love you." She placed her palm on his cheek, then brushed her lips against his. "I can't let some other woman grab you. And I want a future ...with you."

By the time the light had faded, they were back in his truck headed home.

* * *

The day after Joe left town, she boarded the *Bertie Blue*. In the wheelhouse, she sat next to Lydia and draped her arm across her dog's shoulders as the trawler's bow slapped against heavy waves, rocking them back and forth. There was little discussion between captain and passenger. The engine chugged through the whitecaps crashing against the hull. Despite the din, she wished Clarence would recite one of the tales she'd heard many times before.

After a larger wave hit the bow, Clarence glanced at her. "Storm's building. This old boat can take a pounding, but are you sure you still want to cross? We're about midway."

"Keep going." The island was her refuge, the place she knew she had to be to make the final decision to bury the past. Jennifer laid her cheek on her dog's furry head and sighed so heavily that Clarence turned and looked at her. Rising from her kneeling position, she grabbed a handrail and stood next to him. "You've been super about taking me across. You'll be okay getting back, won't you?"

"It'll be rough, but nothing I haven't seen before. Besides this old boat has a hull like a tank. Walt Whitman called the sea a 'fierce old Mother.'" He glanced at her. "Do you want to put on your wetsuit? The water'll be rough even in the cove."

"I'll only be in the open for a short time. My rain jacket will suffice."

They stared out the wheelhouse window into the gray world that surrounded them. Rain mixed with seawater splattered the window and the the ill-tempered sea washed over the bow. Jennifer flexed her knees, riding the rhythm of the boat. Lydia lay sprawled out with her head pillowed on her large paws, her eyes glued to her mistress. Jennifer wondered if her Newfie might be a wee bit seasick.

"Bertie and I have known you since you were a teenager," Clarence said. "We liked Alex. It just seems odd that he'd kill Carla even in a fit of anger. That wasn't like him. Maybe you don't want to hear my opinion, but Carla flirted with everyone, a real tease."

She swallowed hard. "I know you mean well and I appreciate the friendship you and Bertie have always shown me."

"Hell, girl, you're like family. Bertie packed some goodies for you." He took one hand off the wheel and pointed to a plastic box in the corner. "It probably looks like more than it is, but you know how Bertie packs everything in enough paper to start a newsstand."

Jennifer remembered all the times Bertie had stuck in something homemade whenever she headed to her island. Today it felt like a talisman of good luck. Now more than ever, Jennifer appreciated the woman's gift. "Give her a hug from me."

Jennifer's cell phone beeped. She dragged it out of her pocket and held onto the rail with her one hand as she held it up to her ear. It was Cynthia. "You're fading in and out," Jennifer said. "Talk louder. I can't hear you over the crash of waves. I'm in the middle of a storm at sea."

"… about Ken Sullivan. Detective Cameron was here. Warren told him that Ken was a frequent visitor. News to me. I found Ken's name in a letter to Cliff about clown makeup. I know Alex is wanted by the police, but this information even gave Cameron pause, so I thought you might want to know."

"I knew Ken was into clowns. Thanks."

"You be careful," Cynthia said. "I don't think this business is over. Bye."

"Bye." Jennifer jammed the cell phone into her windbreaker and had to agree with Cynthia. There were too many dangling strings. But she had to let it go or she would ruin her chances at a future with Joe.

Clarence smiled. "You young folks and your cell phones. You all walk around looking like aliens with those things. Half the people I meet on the street don't even say hello anymore, cuz they got some gizmo plugged into their ears. Drives me nuts."

"They can be a nuisance to others, but a great help out on my island."

Clarence nodded. "Hold the wheel a moment, will you?"

Jennifer took his place at the helm and felt the boat buck and yaw as she struggled to hold the bow steady into the oncoming swells.

Clarence grabbed his yellow slicker off a peg and donned it over his waterproof bib overalls. "Okay." He took back the helm and like a horse obeying its master, the boat quieted to a throbbing steady course.

Twenty minutes later, Clarence nudged his trawler into Beastly Island's cove, dropping anchor next to the buoy that marked the beginning of the shallows. The boat shuddered to a halt and bobbed on top of waves muted by the arc of the land. The granite rock cliff to the south gleamed from the sea water crashing against it. The brown speck of the cabin's roof peeked out above the pines on the hill. Lydia's head perked up. As soon as Jennifer opened the wheelhouse door, Lydia scampered out on deck her nose held high, sniffing the air and quivering with excitement.

Clarence and Jennifer worked in unison, putting the kayak over the side, lashing its painter to the back of Clarence's skiff, where they stowed her supplies. As Jennifer slid onto the small craft next to Clarence, Lydia leapt into the sea and swam toward shore.

Clarence's craggy face crackled into a broad smile as he watched Lydia from his place at the tiller. "Newfies sure are water rats, God love 'em." He laughed. "God love Newfies that is, not rats."

After Clarence ran the skiff onto the shore, Jennifer got out and hauled the kayak onto the beach. In the meantime, Clarence unloaded her supplies kept in plastic containers and waterproof bags. He never offered to carry them up to Beastly Manor, and Jennifer never asked. It was an understanding between them. If Jennifer could live on her island alone, she could tote her own gear.

After he'd unloaded the last box, he stood and arched his back. "Back's been giving me trouble lately." He shrugged. "Age is a damn nuisance." He picked up the skiff's line and toyed with it as though he hesitated to leave her. "Call when you need supplies or want to return. If I don't hear from you in a week, I'll come over and check on you."

She felt the urge to cry on his shoulder as if he were the grandfather she'd lost long ago. Their eyes met and held. He gave her a warm smile and patted her shoulder. She threw her arms around him, and he held her against his broad chest. "You're the best," she said. "Give my love to Bertie." With a lump in her throat, she waved to him as he motored back to his boat.

Lydia paddled ashore with what appeared to be a grin on her face and shook, sending showers of water through the air. "Okay, girl," Jennifer said, "it's time to help me haul this stuff to the cabin."

Jennifer's Teva sandals crunched on the coarse sand as she hurried to the straggly pines near the shore where she kept her homemade sled. After pulling the sled to the beach, she put her gear on it and attached a harness to the dog's broad shoulders and attached one sling, the other she slipped around her own shoulders. Together they hauled the sled up to the gate leading to Beastly Manor.

"Thanks, girl." She removed the harness and sling and scratched behind the dog's ears. Jennifer detached the gate's cowbell and checked the cord under the sand. It hadn't been disturbed, assuring her that no one had been up to the cabin during her absence. She began the process of carrying gear up the stairs. While she worked, her hood fell back and the cold rain spattered her face and head. It felt good and clean.

By the time she returned to the shore to get her kayak, white-capped waves churned toward the shoreline, slapping harshly against the beach. The pines lashed by the wind looked like wild men waving their arms. The storm seemed to reflect her own chaotic feelings. After hauling the kayak to the clearing, she covered it with a heavy tarp, lashing it in place. Lydia dabbled at the edge of the watery foam until Jennifer whistled for her. Jennifer hooked the gate closed behind them with the cowbell in place.

Inside the cabin's loft, she dried her hair and brushed it to frame her face. After putting on jeans and a soft plaid flannel shirt and wool mukluks, she went downstairs and lit the wood burning stove. She had stored plenty of wood inside the cabin and kept the fireplace primed for a quick start. Soon a fire warmed the damp cabin. She pulled a rug over the boot scraper grate on the floor by the front door, sealing off the flow of cool air from outside. Lydia immediately tugged the rug off and plopped on top of the grate. Jennifer stood with her hands on her hips, then smiled. "Okay, you win."

She put aside Bertie's box of surprise goodies for the following day. Having treats to look forward to would be fun. After stowing her supplies, she cleaned the cabin. Inspecting the outside sidings and roof would have to wait till a sunny day. After feeding Lydia, she sat on the couch and enjoyed Emma Mae's gift of hardy homemade stew.

She thought of Joe and fiddled with her cell. Finally she called him, but all she got was his answering machine. She left a long message about what Cynthia had said and asked if he would check with Cameron. Before hanging up, she added, "I love you."

That night she avoided the loft where good and bad memories sang to her. Jennifer snuggled into her sleeping bag on the couch by the fire. It was a restless night. The wind howled across the island; pine cones bounced on the roof sounding like footsteps; branches scraped against the cabin. Rain pelted the roof and cascaded down the front steps. Rain always had a plus side, providing plenty of fresh water in the barrels and the water tower.

Toward dawn the wind died, and the rain slackened. After letting Lydia out, she watched the once angry sea prance like a horse, now all show and no danger. She closed her eyes and inhaled the pure breath of forest and sea. Clouds still hulked on the mountains of the mainland, while above the island the sun poked through drifts of milky puffs. She wondered, as she often did after a storm, how the animals and birds survived such tempests. When she was twelve, she'd gone out early in the morning after a terrible storm and found a doe with her fawn huddled under the water tower. Instead of running to tell the family, she stayed to watch the fawn nurse, a magical experience.

After toast and coffee, she grabbed a fleece lined jacket from the front closet where old coats had been stored for anyone's use. Lacing up her boots, she took a stroll along the beach. Lydia romped in the water, then ran for the trees in search of interesting smells and scurrying wildlife. Soon her tongue lolled out the side of her mouth.

Jennifer hiked all the way to the northernmost point of the island. Standing on the rocky outcrop, she surveyed the tiny inlet as she had done hundreds of times before and wondered about the accessibility of a small craft mooring here. At low tide, rocks jutted their knobby heads above the shifting sea, but at high tide the narrow opening was navigable, although dangerous. She shook her head. It was no use. Her idea that someone had landed here two years ago and perpetrated the murder was a fabrication. It was an ending she wanted, not the one that now seemed a reality.

In a subdued mood she walked back to the cabin. On the porch she sat on the bench under the eaves to remove her sand laden boots. As she un-zipped her jacket, the sides fell away and clunked against the wall. Curious, she felt the seam of the back of the jacket. A hard object was lodged near the bottom hem. She probed the side pocket and found a large hole in the lining. Fishing through the fabric, she pulled out a small digital camera. She frowned, then realized the jacket had belonged to Carla. She opened the card slot and saw that it was still in place, but the batteries were dead.

In the kitchen she rummaged in the junk drawer and found a package of AAs. After inserting them, she turned on the camera and began looking at the pictures on the card. Some were of her and Carla making faces; one of Alex flexing his biceps. She laughed and scanned through shots of the island and then stopped at a picture of a man's profile in the distance. Ken! Carla knew Ken. She went through the rest of the pictures and found two others of Ken, all taken on the island at a distance. Apparently, he was unaware of the photographer.

God! Carla had been with him. Ken knew all about the island, all about the family. So why had he pretended otherwise? This added a whole new wrinkle to the mystery and she realized this was evidence Detective Cameron needed to have.

She paced around the room, clutching her cell phone. She put in a call to Clarence. "Bertie?" she asked over crackling interference. "This is Jennifer. Is Clarence there? I need a boat back to the mainland right away."

"Clarence wrenched his back. Are you okay?"

"Yes, but I've found evidence that might help solve Carla's murder."

"I thought Alex did it."

"Not so sure about that. Please, can you help me get back?"

"I'll check with other captains and see who I can get to come for you. Be patient. I'll call you back as soon as I have someone."

Frustrated, Jennifer called Joe, but once again he didn't answer and she had to leave a message explaining what she'd learned.

She tried calling Cameron, but static disrupted the reception. "Damn!" She'd wait awhile to see if the interference lessened. In the meantime, perhaps Bertie would call back. To keep herself occupied, she opened Bertie's container. As Clarence had warned, five jars of homemade pickle relish, jam and chutney were buried in reams of newspaper. The family had often joked that it wasn't necessary to bring reading material to the island if Bertie presented them with a package of homemade goodies before they left the mainland.

After placing the jars in a cupboard, Jennifer smoothed out the week old newspapers. Later she'd put them in a bin to use for different chores, cleaning windows, starting fires, or stuffing paper in leaky windows. With her elbows on the counter, her chin in her palms, she impatiently scanned old articles. She turned the page and a headline caught her eye. *O'Hare Food Workers on Strike.* All airport restaurants had been closed. After checking the date on the paper, her body stilled—the day of Ken's flight through O'Hare. Her mouth went dry.

She circled the article with a pencil. Ken had said he'd eaten dinner at O'Hare. But he couldn't have. Had he lied about going east or had he just been making conversation? But what if he hadn't talked to the curator? "Oh God," she muttered. If this were true, then what else was true and what was false about him? Everything?

While she stood in the kitchen, she thought about Ken's ties to the murders. Cynthia had asked Jennifer to do the book appraisal. When Clifford found out, he'd hired Ken to check out Jennifer. The first time she'd told Ken that Wedgeworth had hired her to appraise his new collections, he had acted surprised and upset. At the time she didn't think too much of it. Had Ken sold Wedgeworth *The Big Sleep?* The pages had been ripped out of Wedgeworth's ledger and there was no way to prove the prior owner. Now she'd learned Ken knew Carla and had been on the island. Alex claimed to have heard the noise of a motor just as they found the body. Carla had the book with her when she left the cabin, but it was gone when they found her. The money Ken received from the sale of Einstein's paper could have allowed him to refurbish his sloop. It all fit.

Ken murdered Carla.

"Emma Mae, you hired him," she said out loud and shook her head. "Talk about putting the fox in the hen house."

All the pieces fell into place. If Ken hadn't gone to Chicago, he could also have killed Bjorn. Ruth said her brother had talked about Carla's murder at his favorite waterfront bar. Ken spent time around the harbor and wouldn't appreciate questions that might lead to his unmasking. And there was the fact that Ken had paid Bjorn in cash for retrofitting his boat, cash he got from selling the Einstein document.

Jennifer gritted her teeth so hard she ached. The timeline of Ken remodeling *The High Life* so soon after Carla's death should have set off alarms. Even Jennifer's theory that Wedgeworth had been killed to prevent anyone from learning the provenance of the book made sense.

She picked up her cell phone, her lifeline to the mainland. Bertie would get back to her, but when? She gazed out the window as a peregrine falcon swooped across the sky and darted into the forest. She smiled at the predator's freedom. As she refocused on the view of the sea, she gripped the sink, her knuckles whitening.

"Jesus!"

The black hull of *The High Life* entered the cove.

Chapter 32

She gulped down her fear and rifled through the drawer where she kept a booklet with emergency numbers. Fumbling for her cell phone to call the Coast Guard, she stared at it in disbelief. Dead. "Damn it." She slammed the phone on the counter. Joe had warned her to get a more trustworthy phone, but she'd procrastinated.

Jennifer glanced around the cabin. So little time. What should she do? Act normal. What if she was wrong about him? But she wasn't. Her mind skidded from one idea to the next. The only plausible reason for Ken to come to the island was to ensure that she would no longer be a threat.

With Lydia's help, she might be able to fight him off physically, but the outcome could be disastrous. Running into the woods made no sense. All he had to do was wait her out. She could paddle to the mainland, but his boat could overtake her in the open sea.

As she stood thinking what to do, Ken anchored, lowered the sails and put the dinghy over the side. Her plan might not be the best, but she had to give herself a chance. She grabbed her wetsuit from the porch rail and ducked back inside the cabin. After stripping off her jeans, she pulled on the stiff neoprene suit and booties. She glanced at the knife she wore when kayaking. Grabbing it off the table, she stuck it inside the bootie. Not comfortable, but secure and not too noticeable. Lydia circled her. The wetsuit meant water, and water meant fun. As Jennifer stuffed a water bottle and two energy bars into a small waterproof bag, the gate cowbell clanged.

Lydia barked, ran to the window and slobbered on the glass.

Jennifer's heart raced. She took a few deep breaths. If all else failed, the police needed to know the truth about Ken. Her fingers fumbled as she shoved in a fresh cassette into her tape recorder. Please, oh please let the battery last, she prayed.

Lydia's barking grew sharper.

Jennifer stuck the tape deck behind the table lamp and pushed: *Record.*

Ken knocked on the door and without waiting for a response, opened it. "Hi," he said, sauntering in and closing the door behind him. "Would you welcome a stranger to your island?"

Lydia confronted him with a growl, but stopped when he held out a large rawhide bone. She smelled it, but refused the tempting bait. Instead, she turned her head toward her mistress, who refused to give the dog a signal to accept the offer.

Ken reached out to tousled the dog's fur. Lydia backed away.. He continued moving forward, offering her the bone. "Go on. It's for you." He glanced at Jennifer. "Why won't she take it?"

"I've trained her not to take food from strangers unless I give the okay."

"I'm not a stranger."

"Of course not." Her lips trembled. *No, you're a killer.*

He shrugged, walked over to the kitchen and placed the bone on the counter. "Maybe you can give it to her."

"Sure. Outside, later." Jennifer forced a smile.

He leaned against the counter and studied her. "You coming or going?" He tugged at the zipper on his windbreaker, sliding it down part way. His gray eyes, like a shark's were unreadable, his face passive.

"Going." She rubbed her palms along her thighs. "You surprised me."

"Surprised you? With Lydia barking and the bell clanging?" He folded his arms across his chest. "You seem nervous."

Jennifer managed a weak smile. "Lydia and I were going kayaking. Why don't you make yourself at home and when we get back, we can have dinner together. Any fresh salmon on your boat?"

His laugh sounded hollow. "Not this time." He turned and looked out the window. "Storm certainly was a hellion. I'm surprised you came over during it. I saw some of the trees along the shoreline went down." The heel of his palm rested on the counter near her cell phone and the newspaper. He looked at the paper and frowned, then inspected her cell phone. "Battery's gone. Too bad." He grinned like a hyena anticipating a meal. "You can use the phone on my boat." He glanced down at the newspaper and tapped his finger on the article Jennifer had circled.

"Make yourself at home. Lydia and I are off to kayak." She edged toward the door.

"You don't want to do that." He blocked her progress. "I thought you'd be glad to see me. You're alone now. Alex is wanted for murder and that cop, Joe, you were interested in left town."

"You seem to know the latest news. Why the interest?"

"You've been in my thoughts for some time."

"How did you know I was here?"

"Emma Mae, of course, although I surmised as much. Where does Jennifer Frost go when she's feeling blue?"

"We can sit on the porch for a while before I paddle off. The falcons are back. We could go see their nesting spot."

He smirked, before he said, "No. You should go kayaking. I'll help you with your kayak."

"Hauling it to the shore is a one person job."

"Hey, can't a guy be a gentleman?" He walked to the front door, reached for the doorknob and stood for a moment facing the door, then turned around slowly and faced her. "I heard you visited Bjorn's sister. Why?"

"I liked Bjorn, and Ruth wanted to talk about his murder." She heard the squeak of the tape turning and hoped he hadn't heard it.

"Murder?" His gray eyes narrowed. "Who told you that? The story in the paper mentioned arson not murder. Old Bjorn most likely fell. You seem to enjoy the role of detective. That's how you get into trouble. I'd think by now, you'd realize it's not safe to mess with investigations."

The cat and mouse game was over. She needed him to confess in case she didn't escape. "I've found out a great deal more than the police."

"Oh?" He raised an eyebrow. "What exactly?"

She swallowed and felt a flush creep over her. "You knew all the parties involved, Wedgeworth, my sister, Bjorn."

"Jennifer, are you accusing me?" He glanced toward the newspaper on the counter. "From the first time I met you, I realized you were smart." He drew a handgun out of his waistband. "But a terrible liar."

Lydia growled and moved toward Ken.

He pointed the gun at the dog.

"No!" Jennifer shouted.

"I'll shoot her if she attacks."

"Stay," she commanded Lydia and grabbed her collar.

"Better. Now, you said you wanted to go kayaking. So that's what you'll do …with a slight alteration. Put a leash on your dog and keep her under control."

She grabbed the leash off the hook by the front door and clipped it to Lydia's collar. Getting him angry and out of his comfort zone was the only way to make him talk while still in the cabin. "You don't like women, do you?"

"What?" He seemed flustered for the first time since he'd entered the cabin.

"You heard me. On your first visit here, you said your mother stood by while your father beat you. You've harbored a grievance against women ever since."

His laugh was cold, raw. "Who the hell do you think you are spouting such nonsense?"

"It's not nonsense, is it?"

"Fuck you."

She nodded. "Hard to accept that I know the truth about you, isn't it?"

"You know nothing about me."

"Oh, yes, I do. Only a man with a phobia would kill over a book. And you killed Carla for no other reason." She was amazed at how calm she now felt. "You took the book from Carla, and sold the Einstein letter. It wasn't necessary to kill her, but you did."

"It was an accident."

"If it was an accident, why not stay and explain?" She watched as he shifted from one foot to the next. "It was foggy that night, but you had chartered a boat from Bjorn and put in at the north side of the island. A difficult task."

"I'm a good sailor."

"But a very disturbed man." Her grip on the leash tightened.

"No. I'm brilliant. The police will charge Alex for the crimes." He waved the gun up and down as if it were his finger. "But you've become a problem." His eyes glazed with a hate he must have held in check for all the times he'd been with her.

"If you turn yourself in, the courts might be lenient."

"Don't make me laugh."

"Carla never meant you any harm."

"Harm? Hell, I'd be saddled with her. Your bitchy sister had it all planned, and I went along with her. She was going to inherit a lot of money in two years. Two years! I had debts and a chance to buy a great boat. Carla thought we'd go away together to some Shangri-La that night. Fat chance.

She brought the book and the letter with her. The letter was worth a lot more than her meager inheritance or the book. If she'd just given me the letter, nothing would have happened."

"You're sick."

"Stop saying that." It was more of a yell than an order. "Enough of your jabbering." He motioned with his gun. "Let's go. Don't try anything or your dog gets the first bullet."

Jennifer didn't budge. "Even if Carla's death was an accident what about all the others? You were the old waiter who offered the poisoned crackers to Wedgeworth."

"The art of being a clown is more than makeup—it's the art of deceiving your audience into believing whatever you want them to see. Kind of like a magician."

"You killed Wedgeworth to prevent him from telling me the provenance of Carla's book."

"Cliff's wife caused his death by hiring you. If it weren't for her, I'd be sailing off the shores of South America today and she wouldn't be a widow."

"And Bjorn?"

"He asked too many questions. You learned something from him that could implicate me. I had no intention of hurting him, but he caught me rifling his files." He shrugged. "He was an old man anyway." He motioned Jennifer to go out the door in front of him. "Go, or I end it here."

She took a firm hold of Lydia's leash and walked down the steps ahead of Ken. In the clearing, Ken ordered her to stop. Lydia growled, and Jennifer had difficulty controlling her.

"It's time to take her out of the picture." Ken pointed his pistol at Lydia.

"No!" Jennifer planted herself between Ken and her dog. "It makes no sense to shoot her."

"She's your soft spot. You know it, and I know it."

Jennifer was desperate. "You're right. You want me to go with you. Okay. I'll do what you want, just leave Lydia alone. I don't know how you plan to get rid of me, but you obviously want it to look like an accident."

He bit his lower lip as if trying to make a decision. "You're smart. That's been the problem from the beginning. Getting involved with smart women is not a good idea. I kept telling myself that, but you were a challenge, an obstacle. You've been quite an opponent, but I always win." His voice trailed off and his eyes shifted away. "Of course, it'll be an accident." He paused. "Or suicide. You lost it when you learned your ex, your partner in the murders, was humping your sister." He sneered.

Bile rose in her throat. "Bastard."

He threw his head back and laughed. "That hit home, didn't it?"

She swallowed hard, trying to remain calm and rational.

"Move away from your dog. Wouldn't want to shoot you instead."

Jennifer tried to remain between Lydia and Ken, but her dog kept pushing forward, making her an easy target. "If you shoot Lydia, the police will know my death was suspicious. What if I tie her up? She won't get free until someone comes to rescue her. I'll go with you willingly, won't struggle or cause trouble."

"You're a patsy for that dog, aren't you?" He hesitated, then said, "Okay. Tie her to a stake or something."

Jennifer breathed easier. Could she trust Ken not to shoot Lydia after she tethered her? "You don't consider yourself a killer, then prove it by letting Lydia live."

He thought about her argument, nodded and lowered the gun slightly. Jennifer pulled on the leash and ordered an unwilling Lydia to follow. She tied Lydia to the Beastly Manor sign. Her grandfather had buried the sign's stakes in concrete and it had remained solid through the years. Jennifer looped the end of the leash over the top of it. She prayed Joe had gotten her messages and would come and free her.

Ken walked over to Jennifer's kayak and pulled out a rope. "I don't trust that leash," he said, tossing the rope to her. "Tie this around her neck and then to the sign." He jeered, "How fitting. Lydia, the guardian of Beastly Manor."

"The leash will hold her. She's not going anywhere."

"Do it. She's too powerful."

Not wanting to tempt his patience further, she knelt next to Lydia and did as he asked. She put her head against Lydia's. "Bye girl. You're the best." She gulped and stood.

Ken jammed a paddle into the kayak's cockpit. "Can't have you going off without a paddle, can we?" He motioned Jennifer to carry the bow. He picked up the stern with one hand and kept his gun in the other one.

As they headed to the shore, Lydia lunged against her tether and barked frantically. Jennifer's heart broke for her dog's predicament, driving out thoughts of her own fate. At the water's edge they lowered the kayak. She waited, wondering what Ken had in mind.

"Tie the painter to the dinghy," he ordered.

She tied it securely, wondering what chance she had against him. "What now?"

"I'll give you credit. You are one cool bitch. Not like your flighty sister." He motioned with his gun. "Get in and row us out to the sloop. I have a surprise guest aboard."

After stepping into the boat and sitting with the oars on either side of her, she asked, "What did you hit Carla with?" His glance at the oars gave her the answer. She trembled as she gripped the paddles. Could she knock him over the side with one of the oars? That would be proper retribution. But he was too alert, sitting in the stern with his gun trained on her. The drag of the kayak, as its painter tensed and released with each pull of the oars, made rowing slow.

She had a vague idea of what he planned. He'd go out to sea, bash in the sides of the kayak and toss her overboard. That's what she'd do if their roles were reversed. Somehow, she had to get into the water before they were too far out to sea. Her chances of surviving in the cold water, even wearing a wetsuit, were slim unless she was close to land. She'd heard stories of seaman who'd died within three minutes of being in the cold waters of Rosario Strait. Hypothermia grabbed at your core. But whether she lived or died, the tape would convict Ken.

The dinghy bumped against the sloop's hull. He lashed the boat to the rail, grasped the ladder with one hand and held the gun on her with the other. Agile as a cat, he stepped up the ladder, never taking his eyes off Jennifer. From above, he motioned for her to clamber up next to him. Standing on the deck of *The High Life,* she looked back on her island and heard Lydia's frantic barking.

He stuck the gun into his waistband. "Hold out your arms." He tied her wrists together, then lashed the rope to the railing. Despite the slack tether, she wasn't going anywhere. He tugged the rope downward, forcing her to sit with her legs dangling over the side of the boat. "I think it's time to introduce my guest." He disappeared into the cabin.

She wondered if she'd have enough time to extract the knife from her bootie. As she bent her leg upward, he returned pushing someone in front of him.

"Alex!" Jennifer exclaimed.

His hands were bound behind him, his face bruised, his clothes rumpled. Caked blood plastered his temple and beard.

"Jennifer. Oh, God, you too. I am so sorry," Alex said.

Ken shoved him to the deck a few feet from Jennifer. He fashioned a noose and dropped it over Alex's head and tightened it around his neck, then looped the end around the boat's rail. "Don't get any ideas or you'll hang yourself." Ken smiled. "Alex decided to come along, didn't you?"

"Bastard!" Alex said.

Ken tightened the noose. "Is that all you can say? My, my, here I thought you were a learned collector of books." Ken stood over them gloating. "You both are so pathetic."

"You're insane," Jennifer said.

"Shut up." Ken slapped her across the face.

She tasted blood and shook with anger mixed with fear. "You won't get away with this. They'll catch you and you'll rot in jail."

"Don't be so sure of that." He moved away, hoisted up the dinghy and lashed it to the deck, then walked to the stern with the kayak's painter and tied it so the kayak would lie well off from the rudder. When he came back to them, he said, "Actually, Jennifer, it's your fault Wedgeworth and Bjorn died. If I'd known from the beginning that Cynthia had hired you to appraise her husband's books, I'd have finished you off when I first came to the island. You've caused me a lot of trouble."

"He tore the page out of Wedgeworth's ledger," Alex said.

Ken shrugged. "A trusting man is easy to fool." He left them and prepared to put to sea.

Jennifer turned to Alex "Where have you been? How did Ken get you?"

"Ken hadn't gone east after all. I traced the curator to London and found the agent Ken used to sell the Einstein paper he'd stolen. I didn't think Cameron would listen to me, so I confronted Ken. Stupidly, I thought I could handle him."

Ken returned to stand next to them. "Getting reacquainted? How nice." He laughed. "It's off to sea for the three of us, only I'm afraid you'll find it cold."

A horn split the air. Jennifer knew its discordant sound. The *Bertie Blue.*

Ken's jaw went slack, his attention shifted. He started the engine and hurried to the bow to hoist the anchor.

Pulling on the slack rope, she half stood and peered over the top of the cabin roof. Clarence was at full throttle bearing down on them. The sloop's engine throbbed as Ken turned her into the oncoming sea swells.

Jennifer bent her leg and reached inside her bootie to retrieve her knife from its rubber sheath. She clenched the hilt in her teeth and sawed at the rope that looped from her wrists to the rail. Although her hands were still tied, she scooted over to Alex and removed the noose from around his neck. Taking the knife out of her mouth, she grasped it in her hands and cut at the ropes holding Alex's wrists.

When Alex's bounds dropped to the deck, he took the knife and freed her. They crouched on the deck out of Ken's sight and looked across the hull to starboard. The nose of the sloop lifted as it turned into the ocean swells.

"It's our chance to get away," she whispered and motioned to the water.

Alex shook his head. "He'll outrun the trawler." As he stood, the sloop veered and Alex lost his footing. Stumbling, he grabbed a stanchion.

His movements caught Ken's attention. Dropping his hold on the wheel, he took his gun out of his waist band and fired. As Alex pitched forward. His head hit the deck with a thud. Jennifer grabbed his legs and pulled him behind the cabin as bullets smacked into the wood around them. She crouched lower. Silence. Alex bled onto the deck. The sloop veered sharply and tilted. She grabbed for a handhold, preventing herself and Alex from sliding into the sea.

When the boat righted, she edged around the corner of the cabin to see what was happening. Ken was at the helm, but the sloop had lost momentum. The *Bertie Blue* was closing the gap. Someone stood on the trawler's bow. Joe. Ken fired wildly at him and tried to steer away from the *Bertie Blue* at the same time.

The trawler grew closer. Jennifer stood to signal Joe.

Joe yelled. "Jen," His voice drifted away, garbled with the onrush of the boat's motor.

Ken put up his hands as if he could ward off the inevitable.

The trawler's blunt bow shattered the side of *The High Life*. Timber shredded into giant splinters, stays, wires and ropes whipped through the air. The crash knocked Jennifer against the cabin, stunning her. Then she was hurled headfirst into the choppy sea.

Chapter 33

The cold water snatched her breath away. She sank fast and deep. Recovering her wits, she kicked toward the surface. A wave smacked her in the face and she gulped water. Coughing, she treaded in place. Alex's body remained sprawled on the slanted deck.

Before the *Bertie Blue's* engine reversed, Joe jumped onto the sloop. Jennifer lost sight of the action as she drifted down into the bottom of a swell. When she floated to its crest, she saw Joe and Ken grappling with one another. The glint of the sun reflected off Ken's gun in his hand. Ropes and wires lay like tangled snakes. Debris littered the deck. Both men fell, narrowly missing the splintered wood sticking up like pikes.

The sloop slipped deeper into the water. Waves pushed it back toward the cove. When the sloop's keel hit the shallow shelf, it rolled like a whale onto its side. Alex slipped into the sea and went under.

Jennifer screamed. "Joe, get off. It's going under."

Joe glanced up, momentarily staring at the scene around him, then leaped over Ken, and dove into the sea.

Ken clawed his way across the deck, trying to avoid the wires and ropes. He writhed as a flapping wire lashed his back. Ensnared in the ropes and wires, he wiggled like a worm and freed himself. He stood to jump into the water, but a wave shifted the wreck. He stumbled backward and smashed into a giant wood splinter. An inhuman scream pierced the air. Blood flowed from his impaled body; his head lolled to one side; his arms flapped like a rag doll. The sloop sank sliding down from the shelf to the deeper part of the ocean and took Ken with it.

Jennifer couldn't look away. It was horrible. It was surreal. It was justice.

Thrusting aside debris floating around her, she swam to where Alex and Joe had disappeared. Joe surfaced, holding Alex with his arm across his chest. He nodded to Jennifer and they swam toward shore.

She stroked next to Joe. Cold seeped into her; her senses dulled; her stroke weakened. She gauged the distance to the beach. It seemed a continent away.

The water roiled around her. Lydia's large black head emerged next to her. As she reached out for her dog, something hard slammed into her side. Wood, large and wide. Startled, she recoiled, then realized it was part of the Beastly Manor sign. Lydia had broken free, carrying the posts and sign with her.

Jennifer pointed to the broad plank and she and Joe hoisted Alex onto it. Alex groaned and spit up water.

"Good girl. Go," Jennifer gasped. Lydia swam toward shore, hauling the sign with Alex on top. Nearer the beach, Jennifer felt gravel underfoot and her flagging spirit soared. Land. Safety. Floundering, she tumbled sideways and Joe put an arm around her as they staggered onto the beach. Lydia pulled the sign onto the sand. Alex's eyes blinked open. Joe took off his t-shirt and pressed it against Alex's head wound.

"You'll make it," Joe said. "Helps on the way."

Jennifer's knees buckled and she sank to the sand. Lydia licked her mistress's face and plopped down next to her. With icy fingers, Jennifer freed Lydia from her collar and the rope and sat, staring out to sea.

Joe sat next to Jennifer, and they remained holding each other as the *Bertie Blue* chugged into the cove and dropped anchor.

CPSIA information can be obtained at www.ICGtesting.com
Printed in the USA
LVOW070643140113

315520LV00031BA/2404/P